Bite Me, Robot Boy

edited by
Adam Lowe

Published by
Dog Horn Publishing
45 Monk Ings, Birstall, Batley WF17 9HU
United Kingdom
doghornpublishing.com

Edited by
Adam Lowe

with help from
Alexa Radcliffe, Jo Brandon, Gemma Rutter, Matt Read,
Shanti Phillips, Natasha Long, Victora Hooper,
and The Rusty Knuckle (RIP)

Typesetting by
Adam Lowe

Cover by
Chris Roberts, Dead Clown Art
deadclownart.com

UK Distribution: **Central Books**
99 Wallis Road, London, E9 5LN, United Kingdom
orders@centralbooks.com
Phone:+44 (0) 845 458 9911
Fax: +44 (0) 845 458 9912

Overseas (Non-UK) Distribution: **Lulu Press, Inc**
3101 Hillsborough Street
Raleigh, NC 27607
Phone # +1 919 459 5858
Fax # +1 919 459 5867
purchaseorder@lulu.com

Table of Contents

Adam Lowe: Introduction

New writers are important. They are the lifeblood of contemporary literature—whether the bestseller lists and book awards recognise that or not—and they set the standard for the future of words. But all too often it's difficult for new writers to receive the opportunities they require to flourish. Writers need a space to experiment. They need support when they fall. Whether they fail is just as important as whether they succeed. The important fact is that they need the chance to do either, so they can push on in new directions and take the paths others fear.

Dog Horn Publishing was founded on two simple tenets: that we would support writers not books, and that we would be indie and proud (as our first tagline declared). Over the years, I think we have achieved much of what we set out to do. But, as with any challenge you set yourself, once you see that you've overcome the first set of hurdles, you have to keep setting the bar higher. And so the task fell on us to continue to build on our initial work.

In 2009 we hosted a series of masterclasses for writers who wished to reach that next step in their career that would establish them as professional writers. It was designed to be a supportive environment for discussing ideas, nurturing plans for professional development, and challenging each other to try new things. The ten masterclasses were followed by a period of ongoing editorial and mentoring support, which evolved as it went on to include marketing and promotion workshops, group readings and events, and a deeper insight into the publishing process. These five emerging writers from the North of England were invited to take part in a new anthology to showcase the very best of what new writing could offer. That anthology became *Cabala*, and was released to critical acclaim across the world. Those writers are working now on their own book-length projects and we will support them all the way.

In 2010 we decided we had the right idea, but that we wanted to do something different, so we could cast our net wider and work with a bigger group of writers. We ran a prize to identify those cutting-edge, brave new voices who might benefit from working with us. Polish and perfection was not the criteria here.

We wanted to award excellence, yes—but more importantly, we wanted to reward ambition. We sought a dogged determination to succeed, to push oneself to the next stage in one's career, alongside a willingness to fail in the pursuit of that. The prize resulted in *Bite Me, Robot Boy*: an anthology of poetry and prose from writers who are willing to take risks and whose drive to do better spurs them to take on new challenges.

I am very proud of *Bite Me, Robot Boy*. These writers are still on their journey. Most publishers are seeking work they consider finished, that sits comfortably in a marketing bracket, and which has already passed through the hands of multiple readers, critique circles and pricey copyeditors.

Too many hopeful writers are worn down by the needs of the market that they find themselves succumbing to convention. We wanted to swoop in on these impressionable writerlings and twist their innocent minds—to encourage them to go further, to continue down that path of greatest resistance, to experiment. And we wanted to give those writers a chance. So here it is. Their opportunity to burn like phosphorous. To let their words flare up and scorch the reader. To be . . . dangerous.

Don't be scared, reader. Pick up your book. We have somewhere daring to take you.

Robert Lamb: Foreword

Let me explain everything.

There are thirty-odd poems and umpteen works of fiction inside this book and all of them had to come out. And by that I mean, they had to come out. Each was a tumor pressed against the heart, a parasitic twin drowned behind a sibling's ribs. They are the products of a psychically and spiritually carcinogenic world.

Ah, but Dog Horn writers have their little knives. A little drunken self-surgery at the keyboard, a little sculpting of strange tissues in the dark, and here we are. Out of the worst of us emerges something sublime.

The pages that follow will walk you through the specimen hall. You'll approach each jar in its appointed place and fog the glass with your breath. You'll peer through the formaldehyde murk and wonder that something so disfigured could ring so true.

This anthology, *Bite Me, Robot Boy*, celebrates the strange minds of two winners and twelve finalists in the 2010 Dog Horn Prize for Literature. As one of those winners, I have to say it's pretty excellent company to keep. Dog Horn has made a name for itself highlighting truly weird, truly absurd and truly poignant voices in fiction, poetry and art. It's not a place for pretenders. If you're reading it here, you can expect teeth and barbs. You can expect unnatural titillation. Just don't expect to feel safe.

So venture on amid these jars of our distortions. Come close to the glass.

And don't flinch if you catch your own reflection.

·

S.R. Dantzler

S.R. Dantzler gave up his career as a hot young chef to write about aliens. How else could he be certain that they would notice him when they return? His short fiction has appeared in *AlienSkin Magazine* many times, as well as *365 Tomorrow's*, *Static Movement*, and *EveryDay Weirdness*. To date his highest achievement has been an Honorable Mention in *L. Ron Hubbard's Writers of the Future Contest*, but this year he intends on making the contest his bitch as he enters into Phase Two of his plan for world domination.

"Come to Me, Lover"

Melissa sat on the park bench waiting for me. She was giggling at our puppy. Cruella tugged at the end of its leash, growling at a flock of pigeons grazing on stale bread. Melissa's smile still warmed me. I would miss her. I leaned over to kiss her before sitting down. Cruella jumped up on my lap and licked my face.

"Good News or bad?" I put my hand on Melissa's knee.

"Good, of course," Melissa said.

"Good news is, I got Dr. Endridge's spot for the Matrius Corianthalus migration research."

Melissa stared blankly for a moment. "So the bad news is you will be gone for months documenting alien behaviour . . . How Long?" she demanded.

"Actually the bad news is, I spoke with Lisa at the adoption agency and we were denied. She said it had nothing to do with our orientation, but that's bullshit. I could tell by her tone." There was a long solemn pause.

"I guess it doesn't matter now that you are going to be gone. How Long?" She turned away from me and crossed her arms. It wrenched me to see her that upset. I reached for her hand and she jerked away.

"Melissa, please . . . "

She turned to face me. Her eyes were teary. "I'm sorry. That is just a lot to dump on me all at once. I just can't believe that sexuality is still such . . . " she sobbed. "And I am really proud and happy for you, but I will miss you. How long are you going to be gone?" She was bawling. Cruella whimpered, nudging Melissa, which forced a smile and a sobbing laugh. I wiped the tears from her eyes and put my forehead on hers. "A few months."

Melissa swallowed her sorrow. "So what? You follow and document the drones migration?" It made me feel good that she supported me. She really was interested in the peculiar aliens. She hadn't made it her life's work as I had, but her interest was genuine. Our relationship was very strong. It could withstand this.

"Yes, all the way to the beckoning lover. How rom-antic?" I

smiled at her and gently pinched her side.

"I don't know if I would call it romance. He . . . it is going to eat her after they copulate, right?"

"That's it, in a nutshell, but what an interesting journey it will be. It follows her trail. It's lover . . . it's mother, a cache of genetic potential. It, her little genetic experiment awaits those that have survived their environment to return to her. I can't wait. How exciting to be the first human to document the entire process."

"What happened to Dr. Endridge?"

"His last paper wasn't very well received. His notions that the Matrius's pheromones and chemicals had the potential to interrupt human development were pretty much ridiculed to the point he is likely hiding with his head in the sand somewhere in South America."

"Lucky you. You don't think their pheromones would have any type of impact on humans?"

"Humans aren't sensitive enough to pheromones as are other species. Besides, they aren't related to ours. Therefore we would not even really register them. Besides, he was talking about major physical mutations in adult humans and other impossibilities."

We all met at Water Works for drinks. Part going away, part congratulations. I was happy to see Melissa smiling again. I had under-estimated the effect the adoption denial had on her. She'd been really detached the last few days.

Besides our friends, my crew had come. J.T., my friend since middle school was going to be our camera guy. He brought Renée, his fiancée. Kevin, the driver slash home base technician was a relatively new guy to the project. I had met him through the university. An interesting fellow—he was from Oklahoma, a strappingly handsome young man, he had begun his career as a storm chaser then came to Canada to document wolves with Professor Ernestine. He came highly recommended and he also came with a busty girl du jour. The only thing more fake than her tits was her personality. She and Melissa had already gotten off on the wrong

11

foot. She had made a comment about homosexuality and immoral it was.

Kevin had come to her aid and was now acting as a martyr to diffuse the situation.

"Bear in mind that I was born in the Bible Belt and please forgive my ignorance, but let me ask the scientist, What causes homosexuality?" His date sneered at him, not realizing that he had just prevented her from getting her hair torn out by Melissa.

"It isn't a disease, Kevin." Melissa started, but I gave her a look. Not scorning her, but to let her know that I had it.

"It is a genetic condition. Many studies suggest . . . "

"OK, I don't want to hear what, 'Many studies suggest' I want to hear your opinion. I can respect your opinion. You are a well known scientist and well . . . a lesbian."

" Honestly, I think it is a genetic switch to prevent over-population." I braced myself for Melissa's scorn. She hated my beliefs on the subject. "Historically the largest documented cases of homosexuality came in periods and locations of large population booms . . . "

His date slammed her cosmo on the counter. "That's it. I can't take it any more. You are all sinners and God frowns on you." She stormed out the door.

"Wait a minute, bitch!" Melissa stood to chase her down, but I put my hand on her shoulder.

"I am so sorry for her . . . and my . . . I at least have to take her home. I am so sorry. Dr. I will see you in the morning. Guys, it was a pleasure to meet you all." He turned to follow his date out the door.

"Oh my god! Are you fucking kidding me?" Melissa was infuriated.

"It's OK, Ignorance is bliss."

"It is not OK."

"Sweetie, this is our last night. Let's just enjoy it as much as we can, please." I gave her a pleading face.

J.T. slapped the table. "So let's talk about these aliens. I want to know what you are getting us into, Dr. Izzy." His comedic gesture changed the tone. Melissa laughed. Izzy was a name I had been called in middle school I hated it much for the same reason they found it endearing. It likely conjured up images of my nerdy glasses and braces.

Melissa grinned. "You are lucky, J.T. I wish I could go. They are really interesting. Even the 'Mother' is sexless in so many ways. She is a store of genetic possibilities. She creates hundreds of genetic experiments, her eggs, and lays them all over her large territory. The eggs then hatch and track her down. Those that survive the world then kill each other and mutate and . . . I dunno. It gets so confusing. Ultimately the sole survivor then eats the mother in some mating duel and becomes the next 'Mother' right, Elizabeth?"

"Something like that. Don't worry J.T. you'll figure it out. You're gonna capture the whole event on film. You are the first in history. We are lucky. The treaty wasn't suppose to open for another decade, but the counsel agreed to let the Matrius to be observed due to the fact that our Matrius found Earth suitable and the Orinians asked for permission to allow two more Matrius to inhabit Earth."

J.T. Squirmed in his seat. "Well, OK. We're going to make history. Let's do it." He raised his mug of ale and kissed his fiancée.

She is going to come. I stood on the steps not knowing what to do. The 4runner was loaded. J.T. and his fiancée held each other while Kevin sat in the driver's seat staring out the windshield. I suppose he and his date never reconciled or else she was not yet attached enough to bid him farewell.

Melissa and I argued last night. She was still upset about the adoption and that I was leaving.

Kevin honked the horn. "I am not leaving in rush hour traffic," he shouted.

I felt tears about to burst forth, when I saw her walk around the corner. I ran to her and we held each other. "I'm sorry," she said.

"I hate leaving you."

"Write me every day. Promise me."

13

"We will get a child when I get back, I promise."
"Write me every day."
"I promise."

Dear Melissa,

Well, we found the drone. It took us the entire first day once we got to the preserve. It is so amazing. The drone looks like a beach ball with hundreds of little legs that undulate, propelling them slowly across the ground like centipedes. Its torso is transparent and you can see vague organs within. I named him, "Kirby" like on Nintendo, but don't tell anyone that I have succumbed to anthropomorphism. I would be kicked in the academic crotch, if you know what I mean.

I did a bunch of preliminary experiments. I won't bore you with all the details, but I started an experiment to detect the trail it follows towards its 'lover'. I feel, I too, am on a long trail towards my lover. I miss you already. I gotta go now. It is so busy today. I hate the fact that you will not be able to get my letters until we cross a postal line in the unpredictable future. I love you.

Elizabeth

Dear Melissa,

I am getting tired of the snow already. Kirby loves it though. It is so reliant upon water. Messy little bugger. It absorbs about ten times its body mass in water each day. I got some results back on the trail it follows. I have isolated three distinct pheromones. It is able to detect a particular signature at about three parts per million. The residual trail left by Mother Matrius.

Kirby moves about fifteen kilometers per day on average, but it comes in spurts so we are, for the most part, able to follow him with the truck. I dread the day when we have to abandon the truck, hike, and pitch a tent. I've had vivid dreams the last few nights—steamy ones. I miss you. I have never craved you more.

They guys seem to be getting restless. I noticed they bought por-no's and lotion at the last convenience store run. At least I was able to mail you some letters.

I can't wait to have you in our bed again.

Your lover,
Elizabeth

Dear Melissa,

We are up to about sixteen parts per million now on the trail. Kirby seems eager and excited. He doubled his travels the last two days. Luckily, the terrain is relatively smooth. We are still able to follow in the truck.

I don't ever recall being more horny. I masturbated twice today. I cannot sleep at night I awake sweaty and wet, longing for you, my goddess whom I can only now caress in my dreams. I can taste you. I want you.

Your goddess,
Elizabeth

Dear Melissa,

J.T. Startled me awake early this morning. Before the sun came up. There were strange howling sounds coming from afar. They really seemed to agitate Kirby. His torso illuminated and changed colors. It was another of his kind. He began howling back. It was menacing and pierced my brain, giving me one hell of a headache. It didn't move much today. It just went on an eat-ing binge. It was odd though it didn't go for its normal diet, but took in a lot of water and devoured lots of rocks. I don't think that I have mentioned how it expels its waste. Luckily enough we are not allowed to come nearer than one hundred and fifty meters of our subject because it shoots out water, well a slimy watery substance—meters in every direction. They more it eats the more fluid it consumes and ejects. I suspect it is seeking particular minerals or compounds. I feel that it has something to do with the howling. Perhaps it is preparing for an engagement—a battle?

We were about to tuck in. We had the pop up all set up and I was getting into my bag when J.T. came running up and said Kirby was on the move. We had to pack everything in a hurry because he was hauling ass. The howling became unnerving. They were going after each other. J.T. followed on foot while Kevin and I packed up and followed in the truck. I felt exited, sexually stimulated. I felt completely thrilled. It was surreal. The two drones met and thrumming noises pulsed from both of them as they circled around each other. Their torso's flashed patterns and colors; orange, red, vibrant striations. J.T. seemed uncomfortable rocking side to side behind the camera's tripod. Then I noticed he had a full erection poking out the front of his jeans. It seemed to pain him. He sat up the camera then disappeared behind the trees. It was tense.

Kevin sat up some audio equipment then asked me if I needed any thing else. There was something about the way he looked at me that made me very uncomfortable. I myself was burning with desire . . . not for him but my crotch pulsed with insatiable longing for something unseen.

I told him I didn't need anything further and he walked away, seemingly relieved. I stood watching the aliens circling each other, absorbing each other's chemical trails as if in communication. Their brilliant illuminated displays like threats. Then they attacked. Pressing into one another, they seemed to become one. All but organs within, protruding into each other, instilling and stealing chemicals into and from one another. My heart raced. My clitoris throbbed. Finally one fell still. My eyes rolled back in orgasm. Something unusual is happening here. I am not certain what's causing my eroticism. I at first thought it was due to our separation, but something else is happening. I noticed it in the guys too. Perhaps Dr. Endridge was correct to a degree. Perhaps the pheromones are having an effect on us.

It took hours for Kirby, the victor, to absorb and eject its foe. It is impossible to tell what it retained from its opponent. Organs? Genetic material? As a simple observer, I don't think we will ever be completely certain.

I need you. I crave you.

Your servant,
Elizabeth

Dear Melissa,

Kirby hasn't moved in days, but he is going through some transition. His illuminations are vigorous.

I awoke to J.T. giving my morning report and telling me to go check the camera angle. Then he leaned in, grabbed me, and kissed me deeply. I pushed him away, disgusted. He apologized and left ashamed.

I cannot control myself. I cannot keep my hand off my clit. The guys are pacing. We hardly speak to each other, instead keeping ourselves at a distance. I went for a walk to try to clear my head. When I came back, I opened the truck door and J.T. and Kevin were fucking. Kevin looked up at me shocked, at himself as much as me. I turned and left. I slept beneath the Longleaf pines.

Help Me,
Elizabeth

Dear Melissa,

Kevin is gone. He left a letter saying that he didn't know what the hell was going on and how ashamed he was at what he had done. I feel that we should leave too, but I can't. This is too important. There is another reason also, but I can't understand it.

Kirby is on the move again. I am the new driver. It is getting hard to keep up. He is pressing on urgently, ceaselessly.

Lizzy

Dear Melissa,

We have been traveling constantly for days, weeks. I know I have promised to write every day, but it has been relentless. I feel disgusted with myself for the thoughts I am having. Everything rational inside me screams to return to you, but I can't. I just can't.

Kirby finally stopped. There is something strange. A large gelatinous orb—a chemical message? It smells sweet, like melon and sex. A little part of his lover left by her to entice him? Prepare him for their union? He will not touch it. He simply circles it tasting the air around it. He is curious, fully engaged by it.

I am exhausted, but I cannot stop. I am unsure of what compels me forth.

I miss you. I need you. What have I gotten myself into?

Me

Dear Melissa,

We have been here for weeks. J.T. is changing. I am changing. He shamefully tries to conceal the breasts that he is developing, and my clit has become enlarged and I am developing testicles. My voice deepens as his becomes more feminine?

Kirby is changing also. He absorbed the orb this morning. As its residue was emitted from Kirby, my senses keened becoming vibrant and acute. I entered into a trance like state, and then I became aware I was eating your hair left from your brush that I found in my stuff. I am consuming you, your genes.

Kirby shed about a third of its mass. Yet it appears larger than when we began this trip. His howling has resumed. It occurs every dawn, but it goes unanswered. Its like a proud territorial claim. It is preparing for something large. I can sense it. She is near.

E

Dear Melissa,

J.T. killed himself today. It was during the dawn howling which has become maddening. He had become, as far as I can tell, a woman.

I have become a man. Each day my beard grows in fuller. My voice is deep. I still dream of you, except now when I awake sweating in the night I have an erection rather than wet panties. Instead of craving your tongue upon me, I yearn to plow into you. I want to fill you with seed, your seed I have within me now.

Kirby is on the move again. It is as if he has great purpose. He travels steadily northward, resiliently, ceaselessly.

E

Dear Melissa,

Today he found her. His torso pulsed and flashed its array of colors as we neared her. My cock stands solid. She is an enormous, swirling, undulating mass. The air around her is perfumed with rotting fruit, sex, and grass.

He dances around her. Together they unite in a chorus of thrumming, gargles and clicks. The colors they display appear to be an ancient conversation. Carnal knowledge.

I am captivated by it. I want to fuck you. I can't keep myself from watching. I can feel their energy all around and inside me.

I am hungry,

E

Dear Melissa,

It has been weeks since their copulation. Slowly day-by-day, he absorbs her, becomes her.

I am a woman again. Something inside me grows. My womb swells more and more each day. Outwardly, I look like I am seven

19

months pregnant.

I should leave. I should have left long ago, before J.T. killed himself. I should have never left you. Now I cannot leave. Each morning I think I can, but as I begin to walk away, I am beckoned by the pulsing mass.

I pray I survive this. I miss you so much.

Forever yours,

Elizabeth.

Dear Melissa,

I gave birth to a son today. He is beautiful. He looks so much like you. I don't understand why or how. He is a miracle.

Kirby has become the mother now also. Inside its transparent torso I see processes occurring, streams of material ebb throughout. I can see what appears to be dozens of eggs developing inside.

Our son is growing very fast. It has been less than a month yet already he walks and talks. Today he climbed a tree. He is half as tall as me. He has your eyes. His hair is dark auburn just like yours.

I am afraid to leave. I am ashamed of what has happened. No one would ever believe my story. How could you believe? I feel alone. I feel I will finish my life here in the forest. I miss you so.

Elizabeth

Dear Melissa,

By my calculations, it has been six months since I left you. I should have held you forever. I should have never said goodbye.

Our son is full grown now. A strong and handsome young man he has become. He set forth on a journey. We left a few days ago. I have followed him every since. Until today, I did not know why or where he was going. Now I am afraid.

Today we stopped just before dawn. I sat as he paced around. It was as if he was searching for something. I stood and walked around to see if I could find some spring berries and I saw him standing over something. It was J.T . . . well his rotting corpse.

He is tracking you. He is following our trail to you.

I will not let him find you for I understand his intent. This is my last letter to you. I pray I am able to do what I must.

I tried to lead him astray on many occasions. I became afraid of his anger. So I finally submitted to him and followed him. Each day the path presented a remembered landmark. When I heard the helicopter, I was terrified. We hid beneath a longleaf pine as it passed overhead.

Later that day, we saw the white ranger jeep and I became even more afraid. I wanted to run, but he, with his nose to the air he went forward towards it.

I was startled to see the ranger get out as he spotted us and approached, but My heart nearly fell out when I saw Melissa jump out of the passenger side and come running towards me.

In that instant I knew what would transpire. My demented, cursed progeny sprang forward towards her. Something inside me engaged a primal response.

"Elizabeth, Oh my God!" Melissa shouted to me as she neared.

He ran towards her and I sprinted to catch him. I took the knife I that had stowed in the belt of my pants and plunged it into his back. He turned to me, eyes wide and bewildered then to her, his lover, his mother. I withdrew the knife and plunged it again into his heart.

Her eyes, her panic stricken eyes. I had never seen such terror in my lovers face, but I had returned to her.

Oz Hardwick

Winner: Dog Horn Prize for Literature 2010
(Poetry)

Oz Hardwick is a York-based writer, photographer and would-be musician who has published widely in the UK, Europe and the US. His latest poetry collection, *The Illuminated Dreamer*, was published by Oversteps Books in October 2010, and he published a book on medieval art scheduled in summer 2011.

A particular current interest is combining poetry with music, and he has worked with musicians in live performance and for radio, as well as playing a number of rudimentary stringed instruments in his band, Sixpenny Wayke.

His readings have taken him from Glastonbury to Chicago and back to Yorkshire, where he is Programme Leader for English and Writing at Leeds Trinity University College.

'The more one reads Hardwick's poems the more they have to say . . . the nearer one approaches, the more they open up' —*Black Mountain Review.*

The Devil's Machine

Iron aspires to heaven. I am waiting for gold
in flesh, infernal inspiration to lead me down,
step silently to the Devil's machine. What
do you see? Cities of steel, stolen souls,
shadow devils and apparitions, bloodglow and amber
desire, weavers in the shade of arcane empires,
day and night, day and night, day and night,
night with her beasts and fingers, her welcome at the tomb,
gothic and illuminated, pilgrims' stilted passing,
time-bleached palaces, changing faces, hand
to hand to hand, cycles in circles, coy
glances behind black feathered fan, blown
kisses from the dead, cats forever falling,
twisting, a child smiles, hands open and close,
open and close, muscles flex, changing
faces, hand to hand, hands open,
a child smiles, twisting, cats forever
falling, I am waiting for gold. Iron aspires
to heaven in flesh, twisting, forever falling.

Going Under

sea horseplay bills and coos, / screws
a twisting fist / fastening the slow boat /
sky goat / throat bloated / gloats /
laughs at the languishing / sandwiched between witchcraft
workbooks / crooks hooking stolen tarts / poison
darts to heart attacks / taken aback / slack /
taking the flack / the flake devoured /
empowered ranger / stronger stranger
wrong-footing the bill of rights / tight
neat feet skipping the light fantastic /
ballistic cannibalistic aunteater /
theatre curtain call / fall from grass /
pampas pampers panting spouts of kettles /
nettles netted on the shore / more calls
unanswered / dancers / prancing phoney ponies
pantomiming silent / green / sickly
sweet / deep sleeping nightmares

Speakers' Corners

speech in shadows · agendas hidden · codes
click into place · questions trick · secret
signals · track passwords · watchwords weighted ·
ears to walls · eyes on smudged ink ·
doublethink · basement broadsides · tuned to messages ·
negotiating static · receivers in cramped attics
hiss · this is where we speak · low ·
strong · no guns · no bombs · more dangerous·
grey zone · across borders · under wires ·
dodging lights · flights to freedom · fearless
lines drawn · erased · mind maps
remade · burnt before dawn raids · running ·
this is where we speak · in corners · words
torch all traces · breathe ashes · leaving

The Collector

I woke in the carriage, still counting trees
passing, the night before, almost close enough
to touch sickly leaves. I half remembered
hesitant but precise English, awkwardly accented
as she spoke of burning witches outside the gates
of old cities whose names she could not recall.

Her skin was pale, dry as parchment, blue
eyes too watery for ink. She tried to explain
that stories grow off the edge of maps, as language
becomes uncomfortable, uneasy in tight mouths.

She lost all words, became silent
as I counted passing trees, measuring my course

from one unfixed point to another.

Gaslight

In the shadow of the fallen star, the end of the rainbow,
the kissed stone, we turn our collars to sideways sleet.
This is not Chicago, but Yorkshire, and, when I take off
my glasses, all edges will blur but I will still be ugly.
I used to work in a bookshop, she says, *but it closed.*
In the cellar, girls in lace caps washed dead babies
by fat candlelight. I'm not listening. It's only words,
like salt on chapped lips, colours smudging back to grey
and the cold wind snapping between here and nothing.

Maximilian T. Hawker

Twenty-three, based in Croydon//Poetry: mine is the golden ocellus on darkened streets; the webcam in the delivery room of all Our violent energies; the neon juice sloshed against the city's carburettor deeds; the shovel scraping for the shit beneath the snow; the witch-hunt for religious atrophy; the spitting whisper with limbs enough to grow. I want greyed-out buildings and sight and sound as one, a city smelting in a fresh defrosted sun. I want God to crumble as We break into a canter, for Us all to kick and scream and rant a sequel to his schooling. I want no creed save Our joint indignation—a writhing protest slapped at all that is appalling. I want the wisdom of the multiverse in Our eyes, an answer to the books of Our creation and the fairytale of 'time'. So, with word and thought, question all that is respected, and like this bio I hope you've been affected.

What Else is There

Alpacas, in their barber shop nightmare,
vanilla across the Andean hillscape;
the Copihue sigh of sunlight
filters our chainmail to pink.
Only the stevia speaks in the breeze.
The sixth day of our indulgence—
we almost heal
in the absence of the city's cardiac crush.
The commuter roar now Chilean
farmers whipping Quechuan threats
at clueless livestock. The Clapham gust
an arid Puelche kneading
naked plateaus. Words are few
in our enduring irritation. Argument
gestating over weeks or months -
I know not which. But,
the unsaid Latin milkies
out the glass of our obsession,
and when we camp down tonight
we interlock our bodies
as knuckles craft a single fist.

It's Happening So Fast

In the deep end
            of Mummy's dress,
ketchup lipstick adeptly pressedtoprecociousskin—
Mia-Coco perks her game.
Her fingers pose on perfume vials
whose cloves of scent
                     stain her n
                         o
                           s
                       e,
wake her tongue, try to mend what they've undone.
Mia reflects, in her mirror lit with fairy lights,
upon the Tikkabilla shades
that skip within her make-up box
like candy in a pic 'n' mix.
She whips liquorice on false lashes,
wrists twist in skipping-rope flicks,
striving as an adult knows
                     to coax her secret pollen
out of tepid hibernation.
And now the fake tan sauce (like the skin on my hot
   chocolate when I leave it too long).
Then to lace the nails with icing-varnish (same colour as
   Postman Pat's van!).
Finally, the ametrine shadow for brooch-like eyelids
   (a butterfly!).

Take a step back and have a look . . .

Oh, doesn't she look pretty! Doesn't she look pretty?
   I think she looks pretty. Pretty little girl.
Pretty pretty little girl.

The crowd on her wall pant their approval,
supermodels, 'WAGs', catalogue girls—
glossy hybrids of human and pixel,

a super-species of flesh and silicon
all of them inbreeding, feefeediFeeding on each other
in their endless cycle never stopping in their endless cycle.

Mia parades for her toys,
blank forever smiles on their faces—Iggle Piggle,
   Tinky Winky, Bob the Builder—
and Barbie too (she must feel catty now) Ken—
   is that a bulge in your Speedos?

Yes! We want you, Mia! You!

Puppy fat to catwalk.

Previously published in Life Stories *(Anthony Xavier Productions).*

Dying With Dignity

'My bijou, but do not look, it's a secret
thing; beating and breathing, soft
and contracting.' Hands nurture it from the pond,
palms cupping its anuran flesh,
tentacular fingers exploring its depths,
stroking its frontier and sniffing its meat;
stripped of its uniform
when it is dead. Hands like a canopy,
a forest enclosing, palms pooled in mucilage
of heat and of honey.

But, fingers can breach,
open a valve, let it all gush, stopping
the pulse. Pry: 'What do you cling to?
How open is it? What will you do?'

Originally published in RiPPLE *(Kingston University Press, 2010)*

The Mosque

Earth-trophy of a looser fear,
this mosque abides the seven soils
                              in motion.

The muezzin's warble revises air,
my awkward feet pace the carpet taut
in softness from a rougher source -
the fibre stretches out in lanes.
My eyes diffuse the bays of light
translated by the ruby-jade
capillaries of windows,
stained imaginings of salt
and limestone sweat from unrepentant
mountains. Then scaling up—
the gassy whey of star anise
from sooty little metre sticks.
Composed and mindful of their role
each Muslim builds the confluence,
like bonded nylon fashioning
a vacuum-gulping parachute.

'Asalam Alaykum', (and to you),
reverberates within their throats
contesting with the hoopoe streams
and warping sound in the highest
dome. Below that convex mighfar
the huddled plot of men prostrate
themselves in prayer—bulbs sprouting
slender shoots of worship and of faith.
Geometric lines confine each man
as surely as the lonely shapes
in girih tiles complain for company.

But where each tile mimics chunks
of dragon fruit and pomegranate,
I only marvel at the natural
artwork of the flesh;
and forgo the timid
                    sculptor's element.

Roulette

Logging on feeds me to the visual link of networked bodies.
Soon, the wordless host parades its graces.

Two lads, Berkeley College shirts, eighteen maybe,
down their pants; faces drawn across their buttocks.

After them, a whited room with unkempt bed. Hanging by its neck
across the door, a dummy pendulums the webcam eye.

Next, a bony Asian bloke, 'Scream' mask wrapped
about his head—riding crop flogging thrusting hips.

But then, spilling out upon a sheet—twenty stone
of Eastern European male. Glutted slabs of radish belly

chafing over pubic curls. Weaselled in his soggy fist
the wrinkled parsnip of his penis gobs and winks at me.

Skipping quickly on, I reach the final pixelated stream.
A girl, eight perhaps, smiling in her patient curiosity.

Emma Hopkins

Emma Louise Felicia Hopkins was born in Grimsby, UK, in 1981. She is of Sierra Leonian and Lebanese heritage, which makes her an 'epic ethnic minority' not bound by regional UK limitations of identity or economy.

She launched her pseudonyms of NOTTA VIKING and Amy G. Dala (of amygdala brain function) in 2010 in Nicole Moore's (ed) *Shangwe Hair Power Skin Revolution* anthology of black and mixed race women's expressions, to extend upon her poems 'Miss Story' and 'Talking Peacock' and support the fact that identity is more than just female or racial.

From 2007 to the present, radio playwrighting and computer game writing has provided invites to industry events to see people behind the industries. Emma is interested in freelance writing that involves American website interaction and the industry needs of individuals and companies alike.

In 2005, her debut poetry 'All I Can Want Is What There Is/Fine Pass Me' was published in *Brown Eyes*, edited by Nicole Moore. From 2003 competitive market research and sales-oriented roles gave Emma her drive and determination to make a statement with her identity and interests. Art school in 2000- 2003 allowed her to be in London and have appropriate access to diversity, capitalism and culture.

Turned in Not Turned Out

A kind of Soho stares at me
Intimately small, known for promiscuity
But these urban, grey bookless East Marsh streets
Are a breeding ground for Lambrini beasts!
Out of which an expectation will bore . . .
I am not your Matador!
The only gore that fascinates is Gore Vidal, I'm a fan!
His isolationist Cause acquits me every time I'm questioned by
Communist-minded, mono-cultural white-box ticked breeders,
Sheep and Shepherds:
Who The Hell Do They Think They Are? No TV show will ask!
Why should I create White Masks?
At a glance they see their kind, so they have an easy mind
About all falling into line.
All the while I'm sick of seeing ethnics selling sofa's on TV—
My sensitivity . . .
People reaping sofa's think of reaping me,
To reap what you sow means to reap what you see
And harvest- to-designer vest-to who-looks-best is aplenty!
As England is a pretence of the organic not the ego,
The Control Freak's need-to-know, so
Sofa-to-Sofa Extraordinary Rendition relationships may be:
Chauffeur to their emotions seated,
British box-bound eyes in a goldfish bowl are not box-fresh,
They want to be noticed!
Charmless need women's charms, minority energy,
Milk and Honey bells sound to take what they don't have:
Human Chess or a Pedestal guess?
They think their support will be supported,
To hang in there like overdraft interest.
Take it or leave it over shoes but not selves
So I feel turned in not turned out.

Era of Men
and Mad Cow Disease

Cool Oak Lane. Feel no pain. How about that for a bit of rhyming slang?

No cockney's here in NW9, apart from the postman. No, that's not true these days, real cockneys are too old or unfit to work 15 hour days for Global multi-nationals, gobbling up mail to give back as gifts as if they are on a crusade of customer service because they agreed to have tracking devices under their skin. These 'crusaders' would never take breaks to watch TV on wraparound sunglasses and then get robbed in the street.

Danny the estate agent was stuck in reverie, the Royal Mail was a thing of Britain's past, Queen Elizabeth was dead, King Charles sat on the throne, 2020 should be an era of men, that's what gave Danny motivation for the plans he was about to run past his cousin, but he was still feeling conspiratorial about customer service crusaders.

'Do you know what, Amber?'

'What?'

'These companies that have this legal ability to track their employees, do you know what this strategy is called?'

'Comfession', replied Amber dutifully, 'you've told me this before'

'Comfession, a combination of words like company, fruitful, employment and strategy. These employees or crusaders are in a state of Comfession and that's what makes them valued employees. If they don't accept this way of being valued then they don't work.'

'Like me, then', replied Amber.

'You're doing charity design work, anti-dog eating information to try to stop dogs being slaughtered. Who would have thought that alternatives to beef and lamb in Britain would be dog, but it's the migrants who are leading the dog eating,' replied Danny provocatively.

'It's not just the expense of beef and lamb, it's because it's so hot, there are so many hot dogs roaming the streets, hot dogs by name, hot dogs by nature, that's fuelling dog eating' replied Amber.

'Climate change! But they can put machines up to simulate rain—just like they do and have always done for the movies', replied Danny, 'surely that would cool off the Dog hunting.'

'The State doesn't have the money for that, they just rely on the Dog Wardens to hunt down the dogs and place them in the Dog homes. Even private companies haven't thought of the movie-making-rain route, when they can also turn anyone into a Dog Warden and charge plenty of money to Dog owners to protect their dogs, find their dogs.'

'So it pays to like dogs, don't you fancy being a Dog Warden?'

'The Dog Wardens are under so much pressure and they don't get paid well. Once you get involved in that business, you're life is at risk from the cut-throat Dog Wardens of these private companies. I'm being forced to lend my old design inclinations to charity by the State in order to get unemployment benefits, but the State is not forcing me to be a Dog Warden because they know the score on that business, so they force the anti-social unteachable young, convicts and ex-convicts into Dog Warden duties. They've got so many people to do it and die by it, I can escape that duty. It's probably my age as well, you know being 40, no convictions, an expensive education long since behind me, I've paid enough into this country to be left to my own poor devices, and design devices. It's not life, it's not death, it's just a state of devices, that's how I feel about my existence now.'

Danny and his cousin Amber were born in the 1980's, and it seemed such a long time ago now, Cool Oak Lane was a metaphor for old time's sake as Danny ran through old TV programmes and popular culture to show his good natured development that had given him his sales talk. Amber listened patiently to his ideas such as a Del-boy style three wheel vehicle fitting comfortably upon the width of the lane, no Italian-Job-style speeding Mini's or Chelsea tractors, for Del-boy to break down on the lane, for Sunday morning ravers to appear and push the three wheeler down into Brent reservoir below.

Amber took this as her opportunity to stir the conversation to the present, cousin estate agent Danny made this lane into a lucky charm and now he wanted to turn his step-father into a lucky charm, that's what their meeting was supposed to be about: Del Boy and three wheeler vehicle scenarios were safe British popular culture not needing new episodes, when there were more sensational attention seeking scenarios for British popular culture, like using the postcode DN32 and the matter of minorities under-represented in British politics to create a black politician as a contestant for the gameshow, Who Wants To Be a Politician? Three million pounds on offer for the winner and the opportunity to be a politician and earn even more. Amber knew that this was worth being involved in because of the lump sum that she could receive from Danny for her assistance even though she didn't know what 'assistance' really meant, they were bound to taking their scheme to Grimsby where Amber was existing in her 'state of devices'.

The precedent of the Who Wants To Be A Politician? gameshow had happed more that ten years before when Celebrity Big Brother reality TV had featured a Scottish politician with his moustache and catty eyes bent over playing pussycat in some tame role play that was not a great leap of the imagination, but Fat Cat and Black Cat were both easier said than done, because they had been 'done', in their own ways many many times. How much is a real black cat worth? Metaphorically it's lucky but when compared to a Persian, a Siamese . . . Danny pulled himself together to forget the politics philosophy economics of cat dealing: his plans involved particular words, statements, and what are the words or statements of non-celebrities worth when they are a wannabe? An active wannabe doesn't cost more money to make than an active celebrity, of this Danny was sure because it was ordinary young white girls who could fall into the cosmetic enhancement, cosmetic treatment traps not black or middle aged men of which his step-father was both so politics not cosmetics was the subject and object that Danny's step-father had to 'fall back on', but what he would only really have to fall back on were the words that Danny was to put in his mouth; there would be no glossy hair do's or don't's, or glossy bisexual kissing exploits: a man had to stand on his own two feet and play one role and then there were plenty of women to walk over. A man could be more powerful than an airbrush for God's sake! Women celebrities or wannabe's did not seem to think like this or maybe they just pretended not to think like this? And there would be plenty of women contestants, so they had to find out who their regional rivals were.

Amber wanted her cousin to see beyond the postcode and into a poor traditional English seaside town with a fishing history long since dead, constant unemployment, Dog Wardens as a sign of anti-social identities and the Dog Eating Desperation-Prevention-Tension as the local name for the railway service that was officially known as Transpennine Express.

Amber often visualised the breakdown of family culture into what was basically prostitution: one of the reasons for the coastal area of the East Marsh of Grimsby being known as Traitor's Gait Gate—unsupported women being used as local men and men from ethnically diverse backgrounds went through gated blocks of flats and houses to use different women—the gatedness of the areas only seemed to prevent abductions and large scale theft. Traitor's Gait Gate—a living museum unlike the Guggenheim art museum, but to Amber it was all carved out of heavy old European language that was certainly no fiesta. Children were treated like ATM machines—as separate parenting and agents of the State approached them in a one by one style to influence them. Most children didn't see the teamwork of parents working together as a couple concerned with social mobility and family achievement. Amber knew that in many cases 'social mobility' had been replaced by sex offending: life was a set-up of insidious cruelty for children: to be treated like an ATM machine even though ATM machines were a thing of the past in a moneyless culture. People didn't use money anymore—fingerprint links to bank accounts were the money factor, and unofficially . . . fingerprint links . . . fiesta for fiends.

Was it such a shame that so many young people were dying from skin cancer? It was better than suffering from what was going on in the streets, or having skin cancer and still being pursued by such a free society. But it seemed a shame that cars could drive themselves and prevent road deaths that used to be so common amongst the young, but society was so free that stability in relationships was a fashion statement of the wealthy and gated.

Danny applauded how Amber's loathing could sound musical because it was a love of music that would help him to put words into his step-father's mouth. He showed Amber his mobile phone and picked out Pink's album I'm Not Dead and Underworld's album, Beaucoup Fish. He planned a publicity stunt where his wannabe MP step-father would be in a suit emerging from the sea with the words, I'm not dead, beaucoup fish. Amber thought about what Danny was trying to do saying,

'These words in this context could stimulate compassion under the sun but for what? Skin cancer victims? Fish catching, eating—non-violent opportunities rather than dog eating ones'.

A minority candidate taking his words from Hip-hop free white music rather than white musicians copying from black music was a point that was too obscure in the current atmosphere although "I'm not dead, beaucoup fish" was a lyrical statement that could be made into a headline of PINK UNDERWORLD OF MP.

Danny wanted to win so badly. Estate agents were not needed more than these customer service crusaders who were also expected to have sales skills. Britain was a culture of sell-anything-don't-take-any-time-off, unless you're preparing for a gameshow, unless you're taking maternity or paternity leave which required 'comfession' Tracking Device terms and conditions.

These issues were known by the public as, The Loops Of Unless, so different from the 1980's or the Decade of Excess which lasted perhaps two decades, full of different fashions, music, television programmes and consumer goods and services. It might have seemed as if Danny had a long memory but he was calculating enough to feel that issues replaced time: issues like tracking employees, being tracked, rearing children, rearing animals, selling or buying animal products, renovating property, selling property, selling people, people selling themselves.

Did nature lead the way challenging people to react with rearing laboriousness and/or with devices like cars that drive themselves, tracking devices, old fashioned speaking, listening and message making?

Economics must be a device, and crime a device of economics: crimes surrounding dog eating clearly were and it must have been an era of men because sexual crimes and violence-for-violence-sake crimes hardly received any news coverage. Men could be perpetrators or victims but there was no story to these cases, no initiatives to soften or soothe, just statistics and stereotypes that supported Danny's 'era of men' stoicism that he kept to himself. 2020 might have been an Olympic year but as Danny had explained to Amber, rings and ring symbols created fear of the loops that structured daily life, so to many people Olympic Rings were regarded as a Swastika, a group of married people a human Swastika.

Danny had these thoughts based on his experience of going from Swastika social status to single, free and it was like the aftermath of a terrorist attack for those who bothered to get married in the first place. After entering a marriage and entering a divorce he could use his step-father to enter a gameshow, be his puppet master—there was no swastika to that . . . and there was no swastika in the stand-up comedy act of his step-father's rival: a young girl calling herself Man Utd doing the Traitor's Gait Gate comedy circuit for her contestant PR. Danny introduced the video evidence to Amber and David, their mutual step-relative as they all sat in Danny's car with the air conditioning on. Amber and David were sat in the back in front of their own TV monitors with their headphones on to listen intently. They were also in Traitor's Gait Gate but by the seafront. Their situation of air-conditioned comedy made Danny the lone wind surfer at the front with Amber and Danny interacting with electronic sails, the suburbs of NW9 that Danny had said goodbye to felt light years away not just weeks long gone.

'I bet you're wondering why I call myself Man Utd? Let's start backwards: Utd is a strange abbreviation, I used to think it referred to milk . . .

'Utd . . . Ugly thick dyke' volunteered an audience member.

The girl laughed, 'If that was true, I'd be wearing a football shirt'

'And ugly shoes' replied the audience member.

'I only know about Ugly Shoes because he's a horse and he

is part of my sad story because I was a child prodigy Internet Avatar, I was home schooled, I didn't go out, I didn't see the kind of green space that football teams or horses use, so when I win Who Wants To Be A Politician?, I'm going to buy a horse . . . '

'So what?' came the familiar audience member.

'So what?' questioned the Man Utd girl pretending to search for an answer,

'So horses work hard, football teams work hard and so do child prodigies so . . . '

The girl sounded like an advert for a credit card company, she was such a fake comedienne with a fake audience but Amber guessed Danny was worried about his one sentence effort. Amber didn't realise Danny should have been worried about a life sentence.

'So why Man Utd? Why not Leeds?' asked the false hater.

'My name is Mandela', replied the girl completely seriously, 'surely you must be aware of white girls with first names of famous black men. Attention-grabbing Zuma-Leigh's, Obama-Jane's, double-barrelled names actually for the double-barrelled shotgun effect . . . so Man Utd is an attempt to be short and sweet about myself as a child-prodigy-Internet-Avatar, interested in words, names, abilities yet hasn't walked on grass.'

It was true that white British girls had gone from the likes of being Linda, Susan, Jean and Claire to Obama-Jane and Zuma-Leigh and as the girl revealed at the end, she herself was Mandela-Leanne. It was quite clever how she worked the 'hasn't walked on grass' sympathy style into what was a likely fact that didn't cause surprise. Horses, cows and sheep still needed grass, humans could love exercise, love cosmetic surgery and love their genes and display the GRIN meaning of Grass Independence because grass didn't prevent obesity and the how's and why's of the human body were known and there was no soul to be named, shamed or celebrated so . . .

'From now on' Danny shouted to his passengers in the back, 'David will be known as Ade and Amber can start ghostwriting a book on Anti-Dog Eating for you Ade, so the book will be called Ade on ADE.'

It was certainly achievable. People produced their own

books all the time, but these books basically fit the genre of family bibles or relationship bibles. They were popular gifts, exchanged between families, friends and strangers. The banality of family names or door and street names titled this genre but the Williams, Hurst, Smith, Idowu families could be represented by mother and child, two mothers, man and woman, man and man. Number 39 Grafton Street, 12 Victor Street were the same as 10 Downing Street according to the sentiment of local authors of the sixty plus generation who believed they were the last generation in the area who had reading and writing ability.

Amber knew that Danny didn't like these 'bibles' and she believed it was partly because people in London were using the genre to sell their houses, adding Home Information Pack style information to their bible bashing fanaticism coldly hand-delivered by a customer service crusader. Amber didn't care about southerners selling their privacy and their homes, but she could see how their 'killing two birds with one stone' was killing off Danny's livelihood and darkening his personality. Amber realised that she didn't really know what Danny thought of her life, she didn't like to let people interpret on-off academic opportunities: Amber had been translated, she had adopted—so she had Eastern children being privately educated in an Eastern country. Thinking about Danny now she could hear him sounding out a few words: translated, adopted, educated—emphasizing the 'ted' past tense and coming to the conclusion that Amber saw herself as the Director of a film like Bill and Ted's Excellent Adventures without the Bill character. Ted's Excellent Adventures that did in fact have a Bill, a money bill that needed injections of money to give her Director's confidence.

Danny was the drug that came with this injection. Was Danny cruel or was he just a business man, looking on any and all monetary needs with a long memory?

Had Amber created a ghostwriting atmosphere in her mind?

Amber was at the Anti-Dog Eating charity shop as she was required to be by the State unemployment Department. There was a computer in the back room, she had had the time to create a mock-up e-book of ADE On ADE, but Amber felt held back by her thoughts on Danny. Danny could call or text her at any time and what would she say? That she felt held back by boredom! That was an excuse that was too subtle for Danny and then in walked Amber's readymade excuse—a Dog Warden.

'Alright love?' said the young man as a greeting. He seemed a bit anxious, pulling in an unusually quiet dog on its lead behind him. But Amber knew the stories about the dangers that Dog Wardens faced. She greeted him like the bored person she usually was, she never liked to be seen as a shoulder to cry on for the Dog Wardens because everybody knew the State Dog Wardens were societies undesirable characters and Amber didn't want admirers or a 'reputation'.

The State humiliated people once they were unemployed or unemployable, but that didn't make unemployed people the same. The impact and scale of humiliation was different—she designed Anti-Dog Eating posters, leaflets and information and she acted as a cashier selling clothes, fitness items and grooming kit for dogs, all for dogs, so it was a bizarre novelty being placed here, humiliating if she thought of it as part of Ted's Excellent Adventures—but that was her secret or was it written all over her face or on a State file?

'You look a bit preoccupied love,' said the Dog Warden looking her straight in the eye. Amber shrugged her shoulders, a bit unnerved by his direct detective-like attention. Surely the State would not put a police officer undercover as a Dog Warden? Why not? If someone needed punishing it was ideal. Perhaps police officers would have the skills to survive being a Dog Warden? Amber's mind was wondering in a direction that surprised her, she didn't care about Dogs, police or any kind of Dog Warden. She was a designer-outsider, she had plenty to say as an academic but nothing to say to them.

'Aren't you going to ask me how my day has been?', the Dog Warden continued.

'I'm sorry but everyone knows the stories, I don't want to depress myself by asking. The dog is quiet, I'm following its example.'

The Dog Warden laughed and said,

'If you're following its example, then ask me if it's hot or dead or both'

'Why? It's quiet, that's enough', replied Amber nonchalantly.

'But you could be hot or dead or both', said the Dog Warden.

'What? Look I don't know what you're problem is but . . .'

'It's your problem', the Dog Warden interrupted. 'The State want to make you a Dog Warden.'

'What? How do you know? Why do you know what the State wants from me? I think you should leave!'

Amber was jolted as if from a bad dream into a state of wakefulness. It was no use trying to adjust to a 'fight or flight' psychology, she had to respond with 'fight or flight' actions, 'I'm closing the shop, you'll have to leave', she said.

'I need something from you, and then you can do what you want,' the Dog Warden said matter-of-factly.

'Look, I'm 40 years old, I'm sick, I'm old enough to be your mother. Why me?' Amber pleaded.

'You what? No you've got it wrong. It's the State that are interested in you, not me. Just tell me about Danny and the black man in the sea making a video.'

Amber was jolted again. Who was this Dog Warden?

'It's not illegal! Are you the police?', she questioned sarcastically.

'You can see what I am. I thought you'd heard the stories . . . The State is a kind of mafia, they sent me to get to you.' The Dog Warden undid his zip,

'I'm not leaving without knowing.'

'OK OK! You don't have to threaten me. They're just trying to make their lives easier . . . it's for that gameshow. I don't know how I can help you, when you look like you're going to hurt me.'

The Dog Warden picked up some bottles of Dog mouthwash and undid their bottle tops. Amber really didn't know what kind of person she was dealing with. The charity shop looked like a pharmacy with its light and airy interior and products for health, exercise and grooming and information leaflets, but it was all for dogs and customers used money to pay for items when other businesses used the fingerprint moneyless system, so maybe this Dog Warden was a drug addict who had an attraction to its pharmacy style and could use Dog mouthwash for drug cocktails. Maybe only drug addicts and drug dealers still used money, so the charity shop had always been waiting to play their bank.

The Dog Warden spilled some of the mouthwash onto the floor. Was Dog mouthwash flammable? Was this going to be rape, murder, arson because of a gameshow? Because of Danny? Amber wasn't going to suffer for him.

And then the Dog Warden urinated into the bottles of mouthwash, zipped himself back up and said, 'so you don't have to clean up piss.'

Danny was staring at his mobile phone. It was all over. He had read the email.

Amber couldn't believe that she hadn't been speechless. She had told the Dog Warden about Danny's plans to cut through the 'Summer of Sam' atmosphere with "I'm not dead . . . beacoup fish" lyrical politics and the Dog Warden was satisfied. These names of album titles must have been a code for or about something, Amber thought. The Dog Warden didn't even ask to see Danny's video as proof of what she had said. He didn't care to ask if she had a video file on her mobile phone. A video file he could have destroyed or passed on to someone else. Amber just had to believe that there were no strings attached to what she had done, but the 'strings' were her exclusion from becoming a Dog Warden, so there were strings around her just like the laser beams that guarded the 'cereal' boxes display at the front of the shop.

What's wrong Danny?' asked David, Danny's step-father.
The email on Danny's phone read:

RE: WHO WANTS TO BE A POLITICIAN MENTOR

YOU NEED TO USE THE STAGE NOT THE SEA . . .

THINKING OF STAGE PRESENCE . . . STAGE MATE-
RIALS . . . HOLOGRAMS . . . VOICEOVERS . . . DANCERS
THEATRE . . . COMEDY . . . ON A STAGE . . . INDOORS
. . .TICKET-SALE FRIENDLY.
MAN UTD IS GOING THROUGH TO THE NEXT
ROUND.

David laughed and said, 'Looks like a leaked document,
that's politics!'

The next time Amber heard, 'I'm Not Dead Beaucoup
Fish' it was a subtle detail under the headline, ESTATE AGENT
KILLS MAN UTD

The Dog Warden was back with some police officers. The
news was projected onto the floor from the tip of a mobile phone.
The text was rotated and enlarged so that Amber could read it.
Man Utd had been killed under the hooves of a horse. 'Where's
Danny? . . . And what's this got to do with me?'

'Where do you think and what do you think?' came the Dog
Warden's reply.

Amber was thinking that Who Wants To Be A Dog Warden? was a gameshow that would never happen because it had po-
litical consequences: the State and private companies didn't want
an analysis of the Dog Warden situation. Warden out of chaos
instead of order out of chaos, on whose orders? Human sheep
blindly doing Dog Warden duties only to define the presence of
another human being. The stories were true: Dog Wardens were
an alternative to soldiers and joining the army.

The Dog Warden pointed his phone at the 'cereal box' display and pressed a button, 'Beacoup laser beams' he said as the
laser beams vanished.

'Beaucoup strings' Amber spat out at him.

Nevermind human sheep or dogs, it was mad cow disease.
Mad contestants or warden (cow).

The police officer picked up one of the 'cereal boxes' that
were also like upside down kettles because they had a spout at
the bottom that poured out Dog snacks. Thin electronic screens
displayed Dog related information from various companies, these
boxes had USB ports that connected to computers to keep their

Dog information up-to-date.

'The information on these screens is not up-to-date,' the police officer said, 'and . . . ' he continued opening the spout to spill out some contents, 'we have reason to believe these Dog treats are human ashes. Human ashes that would be turned into diamond earrings and sent to Africa for children to wear.'

'To keep them up-to-date?' the Dog Warden questioned sarcastically.

African children wearing Diamond earrings—an unreasonable act of charity but involving criminal actions? Was it a crime to think that a story about Man Utd sitting on the face of African children made dogs the trivial beings they once were and that would lead to Dog Wardens dying out like money and charity shops had until money and charity shops were brought back for Anti Dog Eating initiatives. Danny had identified this loop and Amber for once felt trapped within his loop talk as if Danny had said that to be a Director of a charity recycling Tracking Devices would be a reasonable use of unemployed time when time and place had to be occupied by contestant or wardens and economics bathed in heat and strings (has) for has-been valuation of human life.

Name This Fame UK

To capture in person from head to toe
Sound and vision definitions or userbility?
Widescreen and nano transmissions . . .
A screaming British thriller—male director
A womb as a warehouse or a snowdome?
That's too girl next door and that won't get a BAFTA
Is a womb a demographic on its own?
Because it's a demo, a graphic to me
My roundness, they'd put to reel
No matter what I feel
They're adventurous for me to be
A female Harrison Ford
Falling back into a waterfall
They think I don't know that The Fugitive style
Is simply pre-snowdome excitement
Perhaps they think they'd see a northern soul
If they can't hear the sound of one!
They'd be poaching eggs by the Waterfall
To symbolise poaching me
Photoshop and YouTube used to stage integrity
It's all a Joy Division by media
Like trial by jury
But I never went through custody
I was caught for being free
And not wanting the life of a roadie
Or 'equal opportunity'
For a rock n' roll CV won't name this fame
A low road, with a load, a ball and chain
They're predictable and so humane
For if I was expectant I'd be simple, not starving on blame
I'd eat chalk and cheese instead of naming them as issues
Like Spike Lee.
Be easy to please, not like the Fury described by Rushdie—
It's male perspective, it's characters 'above me', and these
Unglobal counties, crusading as the UK but knowable to me
As offering a fame it won't name.

Yahways

Yorkshire and Humberside
Invites Lincolnshire in,
Like fingerpainting.
To make it green, interesting
Abbreviating Yorkshire and Humberside
To see its shadows
Ways of Yah: Yorkshire and Humberside
Yahways
Are the ways of the state and no educated insides:
Fishwives and Cheesewives are the same kind,
Evolution stuffs and slices into speech
Unfulfilment, isolation, unhappiness
Around the invention of the wheel and driving
Playmobil
Wrapped up and puffy
Dress sense and skin hiding psychology
Like a violation
That may be animated and sheltered, less able
Leering, tip toes and claws:
A type of meat of which
I've never seen so much.
With me they are painfully curious but are
Cotton wool or clouds aloud,
The white shrine of villages and countryside
Is wider than a yawn but not the world:
Yahways as goalposts but not the goal
Dopamine is fertiliser turned into a football,
I can see the value of competitive footsteps
And I am a voice reminding myself,
"Check what's behind you!"
A class mine covering flat land
They are a murmuring flat screen
A chav TV version of Faulks, Human Traces
Without footprints in African landscapes
But Africans and everyone else . . .
With footprints on their missus.

Not Even Deserving Metaphor Store

The Make-do-and-mend East Marsh
 Is a shut up and shut down affair
 Of the sick, unwanted crooning and grooming class
 Unhelpfully still around and beyond repair
 A uniform, shop name, goods strong bags
 Was business sense enough to get me in
 Soup, yoghurt, cereal bars . . .
 I didn't care who served, if they felt valued by taking turns . . .
 I didn't sense their revenge on my indifference
 Now I can see
 A coin in treacle is how they expect the likes of me to be
So I can't just be a consumer, passer-by
Observer of History
So the loose change economy
Creates nobodies and bullies
If they're not lying, they're complacent—fat or thin!
Women naming victims—ugly appetites
In tones that turned the lights acid bright—
They're not even deserving metaphor
Can I award this store with this accolade
When accolade to them would be something fizzy they sell
So an energetic secret toast is mine all by myself
And they thought I needed their respect!
I'm not a two-faced coin but coins are two-faced
I imagine treacle can stop people moving . . .
Or be in a rhyme—misplaced!
So treacle, treacle little star—I can joke
Is how they're sweet on me
Latching on for all they're worth
When the goods I bought weren't worth that much at all!
Capitalism creates choice—they never heard my
Brownie-bakery voice, that means
Nobody queue for me or before me

This is a scene of my freedom
From treacle shops and situations
Collectively known as
NOT EVEN DESERVING METAPHOR STORE
Without an online experience.

A.J. Kirby

Runner-up, Dog Horn Prize for Literature 2010
(Fiction)

John Le Carre said, "A good writer is an expert on nothing except himself. And on that subject, if he is wise, he
holds his tongue." Very well then, writing is an inward-looking,
navel-gazing pursuit. Only, when A.J. Kirby peeks through the
creaky-door of his navel and stirs his bubbling word soup, perhaps
pausing to take a draught of ale before setting to work once again
with that wooden spoon, there's no tongue-holding involved. His
stories are of himself, in the way that childrens' imaginary friends
are of themselves. And he's a regular chatterbox when he meets
'em. Kissing and telling and damn the super injunctions.

Past A.J. Kirby super soaraway scoops have included his
three novels: the dark, techno-thriller *Perfect World*; *Bully*, a super-
natural horror novel of revenge from beyond the grave; and the
crime-thriller, *The Magpie Trap*; as well as a volume of collected
short stories, *Mix Tape*, which was, Alanis Morisette, not released
on cassette.

His prize-winning short stories (and please roll the 'r' as
you read prize, as it sounds grander) have featured in a wide number
of publications, including anthologies (in *Cabala*, the Dog Horn
Publishing Masterclass anthology; Legend Press's *Eight Rooms and
Ten Journeys*; *Nemonymous 8: Cone Zero* and *Nemonymous 9: Cern Zoo*
from Megazanthus Press; as well as the forthcoming *Horror Anthology of Horror Anthologies*, *Radgepacket 4* from Byker Books, *Dark
Hoard 2010*, the *'Where are we going?'* anthology from Eibonvale
Press, and Graveside Tales' *Fried: Fast Food Slow Deaths*), print journals (*Sein und Werden*, *Jupiter 24*, *Skrev Press*, and *Champagne Shivers*)
and webzines (*The Night Light*, *A Fly in Amber*, *Pumpkin*, *The Second
Hand*, *Pages of Stories* magazine, *US Short Story Library*, and *Underground*).

Andy lives in Leeds, UK with his girlfriend Heidi and his incredibly noisy, but lucky cat, Eric. He started writing after losing out in a game show hosted by Les Dennis and still holds the Scouse muppet personally responsible for his mental unravelling since.

To find out more, visit Andy's website:
andykirbythewriter.20m.com

For Art's Sake

It was Marcus Drainage-Culvert that alerted me to Benoit's return. Talk about a rude awakening. I came to with a jolt, feeling a sting on my cheek like I'd been at Smilla's for the night. I prized open my eyes to see the kaleidoscope-face of my spy staring down at me through the wooden slats that formed my temporary ceiling. In his hand, he was clutching what looked like a table tennis bat so close to my face that I could almost smell gymnastics and the ping-pong of sweat. He was ready to thwack me once more should I slip back off to the land of nod.

'Yes, Monsieur Drainage?' I demanded, in French. I was getting good at the old language; could bat it back and forth like a regular office desk-set stress reliever. But only after a few snifters of brandy of a morning.

Drainage-Culvert looked confused. Perhaps he couldn't understand me. I repeated my question and he leaned in closer to hear, then nodded.

'There's something you should see,' he jimmer-jammered (or at least I think that's what he jimmer-jamperooed), his flapping mouth stinking of Madame Fucard's gingerbread rainhorses. I shifted my head out from under the slats so I could get a better look at him, blinking so my eyes could get better accustomed to France. I suppose that was why I still needed the old shot-glasses; I still thought in old leery-beery eyed British. No wonder people say of a drunken man that he is in his cups. I scrabbled about for them with my free hand while I weighed up this early morning gentleman-caller.

'How are you?' I asked, buying time. I didn't want him to know about my France-blindness.

'Come see, come sir,' he said, not answering my question. He seemed alarmed in some way. Straight away, I knew Drainage-Culvert was a deathly harbinger of doom, but still should not be shot for the bad messenger he was. I tried to engage him in conversation as I pulled on my shot-glasses. Unfortunately, my unusual chattiness convinced the rancid old bastard to climb on in under my bench with me. I shifted to the side a little to make room for him.

'Look!' he snaggle-toothed, as soon as I pulled on my glasses so I could see the world properly. My new-born eyes followed the trajectory of his fishy finger-point. At first all I could make out were the skeletal trees that lined the fine pathway, mistletoe pompoms weighing down the branches; the large open plot of land that was the Boules court; the grey croissant sky. But then I saw it. It couldn't have been more Benoit if he'd gone up and piss-graffitied the whole town hall with his stinky name. I felt Drainage-Culvert's surprisingly gentle fish-finger reaching up and touching my chin. He had to close my drowned-fish-mouth for me.

'I spied for you!' he said, sounding pleased with himself. In a moment, he as probably going to hold out his sticky palm for his payment. If only he knew. If only he knew what he'd done by making me see the monstrosity that graced the bottom end of the park, near where the ducks gathered.

'For Art's sake, I knew he'd come back,' I whispered. And I suppose in some deep-down part of my bowels, I had known. I'd always known. I'd known that Benoit's absence was only temporary, like the brief readjustment of fingers in an eternal Masonic handshake. Why else had I kept my catapult in tip-top condition, and bribed acquaintances (I could never have friends again) like Drainage-Culvert so they could be my eyes and ears for me?

'Who?' he garlicked.

I couldn't even bring myself to say the name. Even thinking it seemed to burn at my tonsils. Oh, everything had been going swimmingly without him in my life! There had been none of those worrying 'episodes' that used to dictate my weekly existence; no run-ins with the fuzz on egg-on-pizza Mondays, no flip-flop Tuesdays, no loose-fart mouthed Wednesdays and certainly no chocolate tears on miserable Friday nights at the end of parties. I'd almost reached that state of being that people term normal. I'd put time and distance between us. Galaxies of the stuff. I'd black-holed myself and come out the other end still me, still dwarfy old me. And yet here he was.

'I was on my way back!' I cried. 'Art be willing, I was going to be fine!' And I would have been. I'm sure I would have been had I not been shown what was at the other end of the park. Drainage-Culvert gave me a consolatory pat on the back and winked at me with his lazy eye. And I thought, in some other, kinder world, we could have been friends, or if not friends, nearly-friends; drinking buddies, fair-weather chums. In that moment, I'd have picked his teeth free of the pesky crumbs from Madame Fucard's gingerbread rainhorses. But I couldn't take my eyes off what Benoit had left for me for long enough to perform even that simplest of tasks.

At the end of the park was a statue. It had been shoe-horned onto this exaggeratedly ornate sandstone plinth so hornily that it might as well have been cuckolded-on. The plinth had been there for a while, waiting for a mount. And now it had been mounted all right . . . If I looked closer, I was sure would be carved the name of my tormentor-in-chief. Just one thing didn't seem to ring true. Unlike with all the other works of art they'd erected in this Pompidou town, there'd been no fireworks, no grand opening ceremony, no cutting of a red ribbon by Lormes' very own lardy-arse mayor. No: it had been left to poor old Drainage-Culvert to break the news to me.

Nevertheless, the statue was massive; it loomed over the park and the adjacent Boules square, full of petrified menace. It over-shadowed the promenade too, and I now saw that it was causing the old smoking men to retreat under the awning of the caff to take their early morning coffee and brandy.

I crawled out from under my bench to take a better look, already a little worried about my first impressions of the thing. Fucking Benoit, I thought; trust him to do something like this. He was probably hidden away somewhere, up in whatever ivory tower the Lormes Council had let him have in lieu of payment (they never had any money our damned council), watching and laughing. Slapping his wooden thigh like he always did after too many aperitifs and rolling back on his chair so it was on only half its standing legs like him.

'What in Art's name is it, Montaffian?' begged Drainage-Culvert, who was trying to crawl out after me, but seemed to have his shoelace caught between two of the slats.

'What is it indeed?' I said. Buying time again. In truth I had no idea what the statue was or what it was supposed to mean.

'Is it the work of . . . ' Here, my acquaintance took a stealthy look all around him before whispering: 'Is it the work of science?'

If I hadn't already known in my bones that it was the work of Benoit, I would have probably jumped to the same bow-legged conclusion as my limp-eyed gimp friend. As it was, I took a deep breath and stared at the thing in the manner of an art history professor (which I was once; I have the credentials to prove it if I could only find the buggers—probably they were lost in the rubble of my house after the Paris-incident). At the same time as my Rodin-esque musing, I was absently shaking my jeans to get rid of some of the gravel that always seemed to collect in the bell-bottom turn-ups no matter how careful I was. (Part of me believed it another of Benoit's dead-of-night modern art installations, designed purely for my benefit. Gradually, I was being used as a mule by which to smuggle all of the tiny red stones out of the posh central square and into the streets, where everybody could hear their boots crunch upon them. What the purpose of this was, Art only knew. I didn't even know what his statue meant.)

'It's ugly, I know that much,' said Drainage-Culvert, who I now noticed had finally extricated himself from the iron grip of the bench and was leaning nonchalantly on his old womanish tartan shopping trolley. In the old days, I would have willo-the-wisped an idea for a sculpture from such an image, but now . . . But now I was all idea'd-out; sucked dry. I couldn't very well design a carbuncle for a car-show-room let alone a wooden leg, as they say. Wistfully, I turned to address Drainage-Culvert, perhaps to impart some wisdom about never taking your eyes off your talent, lad, but was too late, the lazy-eyed ne'er do well had now unzipped himself and was pissing into the litter bin, debating with the various rotten hubcaps and discarded ice cream wrappers what the best use of the day would be. As if a few moments ago, I'd even been considering this malingering malcontent as a friend!

'Come on, fool,' I said. 'Let's go take a closer look.'

I'd hated Benoit Tooth ever since that night when we got troll-faced on mulled wine and he ran away with my talent. My hatred for that gregarious lump of flesh consumed so much of my life that once, when I was completing an application for government sponsorship, I scribbled 'hating Benoit' in the Current or Previous Occupation box. When I was a little boy, my mother used to tell me that I should never hate anyone, that hatred was a destructive process both for the hater and the hated. My mother probably never met Benoit Tooth. With Benoit all rulebooks went out of the window. Revenge was the only rule now.

I don't think you could describe Benoit and I as ever first meeting, instead we were thrown together. Kinda apt really, given everything that came to pass between us. We had both enrolled at the University of Chernobyl, and it would have seemed likely that our paths would never have crossed; he was studying database maintenance of all things; me, the art of modern sculpture. The only thing we had in common was that we were foreign students, but that seemed good enough for the accommodation wallahs and so we were bundled together for three years. Benoit became my room-mate in those godawful Lego-block Marc Almond Halls of Residence. We shared farts, jokes and women. We shared the outdated PC and the phone cards because we had no choice.

And at first, I'm ashamed to say it now, I liked him. I liked him because he was so very fat. I liked him because not only was he the jolly, infectious kind of fat—the fat that suggests Bacchanalian tendencies—he was also far, far fatter than I ever was. And besides, I could only have been considered over-weight because I was borderline dwarf. If I'd have been made any taller, I'd have been an Adonis probably.

We loved to snaffle down cheese and sausage platters together or whole packets of cereal out of that huge metal Great Dane's bowl that his mother made him bring along to uni because she was worried about him not eating enough (as if!) Because we were perpetually skint, we brewed our own wine and beer, which was so bad that it had to be consumed piping hot just to mask the taste. And because we were perpetually drunk, we had to amuse ourselves somehow. In those three years, we played game after game of charades, eventually having to come up with our own rules just to make it interesting. We weren't allowed to portray the usual films, books or plays; instead we had to mime databases or statues. And if you've ever tried to physically represent a database you'll appreciate how difficult it can be, especially for a humongously fat man. Benoit would contort himself into all kinds of unlikely angles and shapes. He'd wedge himself under the cupboard and claim he was the Dorchester and Grey Database or jump up and down on the spot wildly until I guessed it was the Rocket Tipper Database. Of course, I never really knew anything about databases, so he might have been lying after all, but I don't think he was at first. At first, I think he was naïve as me. As glad of the company as me. But then I started to get the good grades.

Good grades meant I had to come out of our Lego shell, at least for a while, in order to collect awards or to lecture to younger students. And at first, Benoit took it all with good grace. He always asked me if there were any fit birds in the audience at my lectures and he always asked me what my next sculpture project would be, even at some points making suggestions of his own (which were always patently ridiculous, like the Hanging Gardens of Piss-Flaps, made from a collection of pizza boxes). But soon he became taciturn on my bounce-backs from the uni. The questions stopped. Eventually, he started to get back at me by becoming unplayable at Tooth-Montaffian Charades; I'm sure he practised morning, noon and night in front of our full-length mirror.

Eventually, he got so good that he tried statues as well as databases (I never progressed up the charades ladder high enough to be able to attempt a database). And that was the image of him that I never forgot, right before the end, when he crumpled his voluptuous form down into this cartoonish representation of Rodin's The Thinker, complete with his sausage-fingered fist jammed against his bowling-ball head. It was so good that I felt in the presence of genius. It was so good that when I saw his statue in the park, I knew beyond a shadow of a doubt that he'd been doing the wrong course at university. Only problem was, it was my talent that he'd used to get him so far.

Fucking Benoit.

'What did you say?' asked Drainage-Culvert, raising his eyebrows so they looked like scraggly quotation marks.

'Didn't say anything, dear Drainage.'

'You did, you did,' he persisted. 'You said something about someone called Benoit. Fucking Benoit. Is that the man who you've been looking everywhere on Art's earth for all this while?'

I stopped crunching along the path. Rage was starting to bubble through me again. I could do nothing to stop it any longer.

'Cock off Benoit!' I shouted into the brisk morning air.

Drainage-Culvert stepped away from me a little, probably because of the volume with which I'd imparted my call, but further away none of the old smoking men in the caff paid me any mind; it was my customary early morning call after all, or so I'd been told. Sometimes I found myself shouting and I had absolutely no idea when I'd started shouting or even what I was shouting about. Nevertheless, Benoit must have caught the sheer frustration in my voice. And he must have been watching from his ivory tower just as I suspected. For soon I heard the one-legged charlatan's laughter ticker-taping back at me off the melted-candle frontages of the grand houses in the square. He was fucking laughing. The great cripple thought he'd won, did he?

We started to walk again, so fast that it could have been described as a lumbering half-run. With shopping sacks full of my spying papers and Drainage-Culvert smashing his tartan trolley against my legs it wasn't an easy task. But I needed to get to the statue. What I'd do when I got there, I had no idea, but get there I needed to and get there I would. Get there, I mean. The statue. I'd be there . . . I had my destructive head-on, and destruction is just as creative as creation when it wants to be. Unfortunately it can also act to confuse even the sharpest of minds. And my own mind was far from sharp in the morning, I knew that. And that's why the sight of more and more people starting to emerge from their melted-candle houses was worrying me so. I couldn't tell if they were somehow figments of my imagination, or horrors somehow beamed down from Benoit's vicious mind just to halt me in my tracks.

Some of these shadowy Lormes-people were starting to step into the park. Some of them were wielding briefcases and toolboxes and drainpipes and racks of clothes. They were walking with a purpose I was unaccustomed to. No leisurely, arty pace here, I thought. But then, a deeper, darker thought pummelled into me: soon these people would see Benoit's statue. Soon it would be too late.

But first, I needed a cigarette. Cigarettes made me think, and what's more, they annoyed the hell out of Benoit on account of his asthma. I'd longed through the years to tell him that the reason for his shortness of breath was most likely that he was an immensely fat man and not because he was in some way allergic to ciggies. Maybe, if he was truly watching me, he'd spot my smoking as the sign that it was.

'Gimme a cigarette,' I yelled to a passing washer-woman. The old hag looked nervous. Glanced at her watch, pretending she hadn't heard me, or understood my demand.

'A quarter after six,' she said, in this syrupy voice that made me yearn for a drink. Oh, how I yearned for a drink, but it had been a long time now. My chapped lips and croaky throat testified to that . . . Half an hour and I'd not been near the old shot-glasses . . .

'Cock off,' I said politely, flashing her one of my trade-marked smiles.

I let her go about her business. Women like that didn't have the time for idle chit-chat; not when the whole creaking cogs of society depended on crisply ironed sheets and starched socks. And besides, the longer I kept her talking, the more likely it would be that she would follow me to get a closer look at the statue. And then there'd be hell to pay. Instead I spotted a smart-looking Suit perched on a bench close to the prom and politely seated myself next to him. He didn't seem to care about the statue, and what's more, he looked delighted with my company; delighted that I'd deigned to share myself with him.

'Give me a cigarette,' I demanded. In response, the Suit flipped the lid of his Dolphin cigarettes almost before I'd had time to get my legs properly criss-crossed and in receptive position. (As I was doing so, Drainage-Culvert slipped off wheeling his shopping trolley jerkily after him, muttering squeaky-jealously under his breath.)

64

'Take one . . . Take two,' said the Suit, nodding his head as though some screw in his neck had not been properly tightened.

I took two, deposited one behind my ear (maybe Drainage-Culvert could have it later if he smartened up his act; I couldn't abide with sulking) and the other between my chapped lips. Waited for a light. The Suit was quick to oblige, and of course, I longed to ruffle up his slick-back hair by way of thanks, but I restrained myself. Poor Suit, I thought; probably spent a long time preparing in the morning just so he could look as smarmy as he did . . . How would he lose any money if I made him look as poor as everyone else?

'Busy day planned?' I asked, feigning interest.

'Ah, well, I'd love to tell you yes, but I fear no. Paid three thousand ding for this pitch only three months back . . . '

He spoke with such vehemence that I found myself backing away from the miserable Suit, just like Drainage-Culvert had done from me. But soon he started in with the typical Suit-self-pity: 'Art be told, I was sure I was onto a loser' he said, gesturing to the statue. 'But now the council has erected that monstrosity, nobody will dare come here. I won't be able to give my money away. Stocks and shares will soar. I'll make far too much money back . . . '

I shook my head in mock sympathy, but really I was annoyed. What was it about Suits that made them want to burden you with some sob story almost as soon as you'd sat next to them? Once upon a time, I'd seen them on the tube in the city; they never stopped talking. Got so bad that people kept missing their stops. Got so bad that all the people fled to the outlying towns just so we could get on with some proper, honest-to-goodness artistic pursuits. And what right did he have to feel hard-done-by with the statue? The statue was something between Benoit and me, nothing to do with him . . .

I drew heavily on the cigarette, watched the smoke plume into the fizzy air like so many of those mystery stocks and shares that the Suits were always talking about in that garbled, goodfor-nothing way of theirs. Only when I looked at him did I realise that the poor old thing was still talking.

' . . . fifty ding on the Hong Kong market just tripled for

Art's sake . . . Tripled. I don't know if I can take the pressure any more, I really don't . . . '

I tuned him out, stared back up at Benoit's statue. Sneered at it. Offered it a two-fingered salute. The Suit tapped me on the shoulder.

'What?!?' I roared, frustrated.

'I'm sorry,' he whined. 'I am keeping you from your art . . . Can I give you some money and I'll leave you be?'

Reader, I kissed him; open-mouthed, writhing tongues; breathless with lust. Our mouths became a single ecosystem, complete unto itself.

'Marvellous,' I said, upon parting.

He just looked straight back up at me with star-struck eyes. I left him to revel in his good fortune and pressed on for the statue.

The park was starting to become busy now, so busy that I almost lost my footing on the crumblestiltskin path when I moved out of the way of a passing chocolate fountain engineer. Next, a troupe of old women hared past on push bikes shrieking and wailing in delight; younger girls were massing on another of the benches, probably planning another sports-car tear-up along the promenade. How they never killed someone, or one of their own, was beyond me. Yet again, as I looked over at the molten beasts they drove, I appealed to Art. I asked Her why cars like that were so obviously wasted on the young, like the spunk from a virile member simply cushioned in a snot-rag and flushed down the boogaloo.

And finally I reached the great balloon of a man's statue. It was wilfully obtuse, like the man in question; a gigantic frill-necked lizard which, I suppose, was intended to make us all stop and think about who we really were; just a hop-step and a jump down the evolutionary ladder from those majestically horned beasts. It was constructed from plasticine and plywood. Bits of two-be-four still containing the nails from whatever construction site Benoit had pilfered them from. It was like one of the dusty old skeletons they used to have in the entrances of the—whisper it—science churches back in the day. All overbearing and unlikely. As though it was about to topple over at any minute and take the world as we knew it with it. Sure, its limbs were pinned-down into the ground, but I'd seen the old gunion tree in the park break free of such restraints and it was now burrowing under the main promenade, having a right laugh at us and our attempts at artistry.

But in a strange way, the statue was beautiful. You could see the love—or hate—in every join, every artificial limb, every fake eyeball. I shook my head and tried to stop myself from admiring his cheek. He was ridiculing Art, making a mockery of all that was pure and true. I knew it, the Suit knew it; hell, even Drainage-Culvert would have known it if he'd cared to come and have a look instead of sloping off like the no-good bin-pisser that he was.

And echoing off the candlewax houses, I heard Benoit's laughter once again. It was a laugh of victory; of turncoat, bestial, slapdash, Van Gogh victory. For a moment it felt as though Benoit's laugh was as sharp as an axe. I felt it cracking into my skull and slicing through briny brains as easily as karate chopping tuna chunks in a can. I felt the madness quickening on me like a dance floor I just couldn't step offof. Like it was revolving, twirling around me drunkenly, robotically, artistically, murderously.

All at once I knew that I had to find Benoit and find him fast. Otherwise he would think that he'd won. Otherwise he would think that I had no revenge in me. That I was no better than a Drainage-Culvert, or worse, a Suit. That I was blocked (which I was, but there was no need for him to know that, not yet, not ever.)

I tried to get my addled mind back into some sort of order, cataloguing my desire to howl wildly at the moon under 'L' for later, and my burning thirst under 'N' for not now. All thoughts of Drainage-Culvert were flushed down into the sewer-level, where I kept all of my dirty images (some of them snap-shots from medical textbooks I'd once spied in a house of debauchery off the Rue Morgue) stored, ready for re-examination when the dirt-mood took a hold. A plan. A plan, a plan, a plan.

Benoit wouldn't be hard to find, I realised once my mind started looking tidy again. Surely he wouldn't be hard to find. He'd be somewhere near a wooden-leg shop; he was constantly snapping his wooden leg (or he always used to be) and hence needed one close at hand just in case an emergency occurred. Luckily for me, there were only two false leg shops in Lormes—usually there were at least four, interspersed between the various opium dens and cafés that populated most small towns of this general bearing—and hence I had a fifty percent chance of finding Benoit in the very first place I looked. Pretty good odds. Odds that would persuade even the most hapless of gamblers like old Drainage-Culvert to have a crack.

A plan in place, I tucked my bags of papers under the un-wieldy tail of Benoit's frill-necked lizard monstrosity and set off across the park towards the centre of Lormes a man on a mission. As I stepped past the duck pond, gaggles of school-artists stepped out of my way, recognising me as a man with the righteousness of Art on his side. As I stepped past a collection of sorry-looking Suits queueing at the ridiculously-priced hot-cat stand, at some unspoken desire, they all bowed to me, knowing me as a man with a plan which made their poxy existences, their buxom blue-sky thinking and their porno returns on investment seem like so much drivel.

I hammered onto the main promenade and caused the Boules players to miss their shots. I careered through the café tables which spilled onto the pavement, knocking plenty a beer onto the floor and yet there was no word of a complaint. Already, I could hear the arty-farty carpenter knocking and yammering at his wood. It echoed through me like the beating of my shattered heart. I was getting close. Closer than I could have imagined. And soon, surely, I would find that superior superglue which would fasten my heart back together again, good as new.

T he wooden leg. That got me thinking. The wooden leg was Benoit's first art-installation and was imag-ined-up just after we finished university. Just after he'd run off with my talent when we were drunk and I was stuck in that awful Sculptor's Block stage. Although we'd moved to France—to Paris actually—I had to go travelling the world just to get my mojo back. I'd left Benoit in charge of my new house, even then knowing that I was being a fool in lending him so much of my trust after what he'd taken from me.

The leg was whittled down from one of the roof beams in the grand house just off the Champs-Elysses. And because I wasn't there to stop him, he'd taken one of the main joists which held the place up, which of course, made the whole thing collapse. On my return, he sat amongst the pile of rubble, proudly showing off the leg; there was still a hook on it in those days, from which I'd once hung my favourite teapot. I hadn't known whether to laugh or cry, to slap him round the chops or report him to the Art-squad. But in the end, I did nothing, just like I always did now I was blocked.

At first I never even asked the truth about what had actually happened with Benoit's real leg; I was too worried about the house. Later, when he was still hanging around me like a bad smell, Benoit told anyone that would listen (as well as some that wouldn't). He told the collected hoi-polloi of the Art scene that his leg had been amputated after a particularly terrifying incident in the Crimean War. People believed him, despite the very obvious fact that Benoit was clearly not old enough to have been born at the time of the War, let alone fought in it. Neither could he, when quizzed, tell you who the war was between, what it was all about, or even what continent it was played out on. I suppose people believed him because of the splendour of the detail with which he embellished the tale. At countless dinner parties to which I'd been invited and he'd gate-crashed (we spun in high circles in those days), he would recall the tale and all I could do was look on the faces of the audience. How their jaws dropped as he told them of how he'd performed a magnificent rescue-job on a little black kitten that had got itself stranded in the middle of no man's land, only to have his leg blown off by a stray leg-blower grenade. It was patently ridiculous; none of the weaponry he mentioned made any sense, but people believed him because of Art. 'There's a lesson in there somewhere,' Benoit always concluded by saying. And his audience would always nod enthusiastically oh we understand. We understand everything . . . They were awe-struck by the future artist's grand artistry.

What really happened was this (as I later learned): Benoit got into a trifling argument over some point of fact about data-bases that nobody can even remember nowadays. He picked up the butter knife and started to hack away at his own leg to mime the Duckworth-Lewis Database Method. Only, the other player had no idea about the rules of the Tooth-Montaffian Charades game and never thought to stop Benoit as he chopped off his own leg. According to some reports, the knife went in like a knife through lard. Job done and point proven, Benoit limped back to my humble abode, which as I believe I've already mentioned, he was caretaking, before setting about hacking the grand house to pieces in order to design his new leg.

Fucking Benoit.

Benoit was always hacking things to pieces in those days. I believe you can still see the evidence of this obsession in some, if not all, of his pieces which are displayed at the Louvre (part of which he was responsible for destroying at that mortifying cheese and wine opening ceremony.) Ah Benoit, you were always a renegade, weren't you? Always the maverick that liked nothing more than doing things in a way which was so far from 'by the book' that he may as well have been in a different blooming library.

And in my disapproval of his methods, I never realised that he'd stumbled upon an art of his very own. I never realised that it would be him and not me that would be celebrated as the most favoured son of the University of Chernobyl's Marc Almond Halls.

I approached the gilded entrance to Crusoe and Son, Master Leg-Makers Extra-ordinaire!, hating the exclamation mark with all my worth, full of the knowledge that the man wasn't even called Crusoe and that he was a no-good scratcher if he'd helped Benoit, not the master carpenter that he proclaimed himself.

'Benoit Tooth!' I announced, over and above the jangling little bell on the shop's door.

'I'd better get me dad,' said And Son, who looked as though he'd got the raw end of the deal when he'd taken his plunge into the gene pool; he looked half-rabid, like some of the ducks in the park. Half-duck, in fact, such was the beak on him. And I swear that I caught him laughing at me and my inability to see over the top of the counter as I approached. Such cheek in a young boy was both unbecoming and scientific in its rudeness. Benoit-like, in fact.

I waited in amongst legs of every which way but loose; penguin-legs, dog-legs, chair-legs, footballer-legs, giraffe-legs. The smell of linseed oil filled the air. The sounds of sawing and chopping barracked my mind. I wouldn't have minded being offered a small brandy while I waited, but evidently this shop wasn't the good leg shop. Evidently this was the pedestrian leg shop, the one that fulfilled council orders for the hospitals and clinics rather than making Art for Art's sake.

Finally, Crusoe stepped out of the dingy back room, bringing with him a stink of lies. He was hiding something; I knew it before he even pretended that he couldn't see me over the counter. And when he shouted back over his shoulder at his son—'Are you taking the piss again lad? There's nobody there,'—I realised that I'd had quite enough of their shopkeep-shenanigans for one day. Cursing all the way, I pulled myself up onto his ramshackle counter, in between a ship's wheel and an elephant-leg ashtray, and I faced him down.

'Benoit Tooth,' I said again. 'You seen him?'

The man had the good grace not to try to bluff me. 'I seen him,' he said, carefully.

'Where is he?' I demanded, resting my foot against his till, making sure that he realised that I would follow through with my threat to kick it to the floor should he not play-ball.

The carpenter opened his mouth as though to answer, but before he could speak a single word, Benoit Tooth slipped out of the fuggy back room like some dark thing and flashed me a terrifying smile.

'Oh. My. Art,' I breathed, unable to stop myself from wobbling on my feet, having to grab onto the elephant-leg ashtray just to keep my balance. I'd been preparing myself for this moment of truth ever since the first moment I saw his statue and yet . . . And yet seeing him now, like this, in the flesh, was almost too much for me to take.

Seeing him in the flesh was actually quite an apt description, for Benoit had now grown so fat that it almost looked as though

71

he were wearing a flesh-coloured Puffa jacket. He was bulging out everywhere, as though he were bubbling up, ready to explode. He looked like a grotesque, gargoyle-version of the Michelin Man, half-naked but for a pair of tight safari shorts and one beige loafer on his one good leg. It was as though all my years of hating him had somehow fed his unworldly appetite. Fed him up so that he'd become more than the man I'd wanted revenge against ever since that night. His beard was now so long that it trailed on the floor beside him like a not quite imaginary friend. And what an amazing technicolour friend it was, full of broken biscuits, paint, jism and weeds. Yes, there appeared to be weeds growing out of it, some of which were flowering.

And while he'd become more—oh so much more—I now realised how reduced I was. I was no longer fit to drink mulled wine with this artist, let alone challenge him to a game of Tooth-Montaffian Charades.

'Claude,' he trilled. 'Claude Montaffian. I've been expecting you, old cock.'

And within my pants, I felt my old cock shrivel up into nothing. Benoit had that kind of power now.

'Cock off Benoit,' I muttered in response.

'Pardonez-moi?' he demanded, bending one arm and placing it on his bulky side like I'm a little teapot. Only he wasn't so little any more; no, in him you could boil all the tea in China, as they say. If you could boil tea in a man. Or transport all that tea.

I realised that I was becoming flustered. If this really was to be the final showdown, I would have to up my game. I'd have to bring out the big guns.

'The statue,' I said. 'That for me, Benoit?' I accentuated the silent 't' in his name just to rile him. Made it sound all-ghostly and over-the-top artistic. Showy. Benoit always hated that.

He moved with a speed which belied his wooden-legged decrepitude. Up to the counter, hands out-stretched ready to push me off it, I feared. I clung ever tighter to the elephant's leg and closed my eyes. Breathed a silent prayer to Art and to all that Art stood for. But then I felt his sweaty paws on me, and to my shame, I realised that he was pulling me closer and into a hug. A bear hug. And then he was attempting to kiss me; slavering away on my face with his fat tongue. Observe his waterfall of a chin! His mole-hill face! His loose-fart eyes!

'Stop it!' I yelled, chomping down with my teeth on the final, definitely not silent 't' in 'it'. I felt his tongue wriggling in my mouth. Trapped. I tasted the fat, wannabe artist's coppery blood seeping into me. I jumped down off the counter, hoping to have cut off another part of him. (They don't have false tongue makers, you know . . .)

But Benoit only grinned back at me, red seeping out of his mouth and into his beard. He was all renegade-artist now, I realised. Beyond repair. Beyond revenge. In another tale, he could have been the erstwhile cop that always goes off on his own, but always produces results. The fat man who hands in badge and gun but can never let go of that final case . . . Not so much half-cock as full-on rampaging erect cock, spunking all over the fucking china shop. Ah but my metaphors and clichés were running away with me. I must file them away under 'D' for don't ever open this door again, for fear that I would appear quite as mad to you as Benoit really was.

'Where is my talent, you charlatan?' I roared.

And Benoit hunkered down into Rodin's The Thinker pose and pretended that he was weighing up his answer. He stayed like that for a long while, until the carpenter's son, little dishrag that he was, cut in: 'I think he wants you to play!'

Benoit nodded against his hammy fist, not breaking the pose.

'I'm never playing that game again,' I sulked, and then realised how much like Drainage-Culvert I sounded. 'Or not with you anyway,' I added.

I could pick out Benoit's smile even behind his meaty paw and his beard. He was still mocking me, still revelling in the talent he'd taken from me, the great, overgrown goblin.

'You don't even remember the night in question, do you?' he asked, at last breaking the pose.

And to be fair to him, I'd tried not to remember the specifics of the thing. It was too painful; I'd blacked it out like the trauma that it was. I suppose I never really knew how he ran off with my talent; all I knew was that on that final night at Marc

Almond Halls, we got horrendously drunk. We played the Tooth-Montaffian game for high-stakes. I'd been boning this girl from the art history course and Benoit managed to win her off me after tricking me into saying 'the Riverdance Database' rather than the 'River Thames Database'. Determined to get him back, I'd thrown the shape of perhaps the most inspired sculpture ever created by man or beast, Michelangelo's David. The prize was Benoit's metal Great Dane dog bowl. And I won it. I remember winning it as though it were yesterday. How bitter he became! How he demanded a look at the rulebook that we'd jointly penned. How he claimed that I looked nothing like David despite the fact that I'd stripped down completely naked and had a small cock. But in the end, he relented and I took that killer sip of mulled wine that turned me troll-faced and I remember no more.

All I do remember is that when I woke up, drowning with hangover, I couldn't sculpt any more. I couldn't even build the toy ship that came in the plastic wrapper in the cereal box. Anything arty stumped me. My head was awash with nonsense. And when Benoit woke up, still drunk, he seemed full of the joys of spring, despite all we'd had to drink. Indeed, the hangover seemed to have suddenly imbued him with the ability to create. He banged together that toy ship in a matter of seconds, and then started work on creating a space port out of the abandoned cereal box and the used toilet rolls. At that moment, I knew that after my killer draught—spiked maybe?—we must have played another game, a game for the highest stakes of all, for ever since that night I had been unable to create a knot in mine own shoelaces. For shame!

'I was drunk,' I gasped. 'Too drunk. You took advantage of me.'

'Nonsense, my old cock,' said Benoit. 'You simply misplaced your talent. Nothing to do with me. You started to take everything too seriously, that's all.'

I frowned. I had been taking everything without the pinch of salt with which I used to spice my every meal in my early Chernobyl days. Maybe Benoit was right.

'After I won the Great Dane bowl,' I said, haltingly. 'Did we . . . Did we play again?'

Benoit laughed and he carried on laughing, in the end his

victorious laugh carried me out of the gilded doorway of Crusoe's and back onto the streets of Lormes a beaten man. He had won and I had lost. Now when I staggered through the café's tables which littered the pavement, the customers remonstrated with me. He had won and I had lost. And I could still hear his laughter. Now when I traipsed past the Boules court, old men yelled abuse at me. He had won and I had lost, and still he laughed. His laugh seemed to reverberate up from the very bowels of the earth. Tiny red stones on the pavement seemed to jiggle up and down, sharing in Benoit's glee. Now when I passed the queue for the hot-cat stall, Suits tried to press me into joining them. Benoit had won and I had lost.

I hung my head, dog-tired, dog-pissed-off, dog-crapped-on. All I wanted to do was collapse under my bench and get in my cups again. Bring out the old shot-glasses and see the world anew again. Maybe howl at the moon if I got too maudlin. I entered the park with only the dog's dinner of defeat waiting for me.

It was only when I stepped into the park and had to move out of the way of a large group of council-workers that I realised that something was different about the place. Indeed, if I hadn't accidentally elbowed that angry washer-woman out of the way, I don't know if even then I would have appreciated the sheer weight of numbers of Lormes folk that were out in the park. I stared down the slope towards Benoit's statue. You could hardly see the grass for people. You couldn't even see the dog-shit for lumbering hoards of Lormians. What the hell was going on?

Drainage-Culvert jovially rammed his tartan shopping trolley into my shin, cracking me out of my reverie as adeptly as if he were a tea-spoon and me a goddamn egg.

'Look what I spy for you today,' he said, happily.

I tried to shoulder him out of the way, muttering, 'I've got no time for games of I-spy with you today, Marcus.'

'Wait!' he said, crouching down over his shopping trolley, unbuttoning the top and pulling out this huge white cloth-thing.

'You've stolen a sheet,' I said, unimpressed.

'No!' he said, starting to unfold it. 'Look.'

My tired eyes stared at the sheet and finally started to pick out words. Wonderful words. Wonderful words of freedom and

Art.

'Cock off Benoit,' confirmed Drainage-Culvert.

'But how?' I asked.

'We all hate his work. The council made a decree or something. We're all going to pull the statue down!' said Drainage-Culvert.

I was barely able to restrain myself from dancing on the spot, for now I saw that others were carrying similar banners, even the council workers. How had I missed it a second ago? It was a vast rally, I now saw; bigger even than the Businessman's Rights meet which they'd had a few months back.

More flag bearers passed me. I read the message on one: 'Benoit you piss-flap bastard!' I saw groups of school-artists burning Benoit's image like it was a dog-gone religious artefact; an old science-buff, long thought a witch, danced on the self-styled maverick artist's own grave installation, his statue. I even spotted my smarmed-up greaseball Suit as he danced past me, roaring some obscenity or other before gently tongueing some other passer-by for the price of a cigarette.

It was a commonwealth of hatred; a continent of cock-calls; a town of revenge upon the head of the anti-establishment breaker of roofs. It was a dream come true.

'Let's burn his wood-leg,' called a washer woman.

'Let's strip it of all polish through a rigorous bout of sanding,' called the dishrag that was Crusoe's And Son. 'Let's whittle it down and use it as a chop-stick.'

'I'll throw it for my blind dog to fetch,' called Drainage-Culvert, getting into the spirit of things like a good chap (he didn't even have a dog, and unless he meant to throw it for his wheeled-trolley I had no idea what he meant). 'Or use it for a Pooh stick.'

'Fasten it through a rollick on a canal-dinghy,' called one man that used to be a sailor, back in the days of discovery.

'Make match-sticks outta it,' called an American tourist who looked frankly confused.

'Fashion it into a fence post,' I muttered, and then louder, 'Make it a mile-marker . . . '

It continued long into the night. The washer women of Generation X and the stolen car raiders of Generation WHY finally agreed on something: Benoit was a fraud. He wasn't worth the flat they bestowed upon him in payment for his work. Wasn't worth being called an Artist. We all joined hands in the park, by the ducks and smiled as one as the lardy-arse mayor rammed the first axe into Benoit's sculpture. Then we all joined in, kicking and punching until the thing lay dead, dismembered, defenestrated on the grass and, in unison, we all proclaimed: 'Cock off Benoit!'

And carried by the lonely winds, I heard something like a whimper. Something like the whimper of a defeated man. And as Drainage-Culvert climbed a tree so as to get a better leap at the statue, and as the mayor lifted his axe one more time, and as the carpenter started to plane down the frilled-neck lizard's frill-neck, I'm sure I saw Benoit slink around the corner, shoulders hunched, wooden leg splintering, dragging his own talent, his beard, behind him on a lead. Where he would go, nobody knew or cared. The piss-artist, the great embellisher of truths, the Great Dane bowl lover, the one-legged freakishly fat destroyer of roofs was no more.

And in that single aching moment, I knew that I would miss him.

Stephanie Elizabeth Knipe

Stephanie Elizabeth Knipe hails from Lisburn, Northern Ireland, but now lives in Staffordshire with her fiancé Gareth, where she works as a recruitment consultant. She is a member of the Lichfield Poets group and regularly performs her poems at local arts and comedy events.

For the last five years she has attempted, unsuccessfully, to write very serious poems about very serious matters, while inadvertently gaining a substantial following for her increasingly vast collection of somewhat offbeat, and often downright silly, poems. She has perhaps written more poems about wheelie bins than any other poet, living or dead, and more recently, her cutting edge pieces on the hard-hitting subjects of office stationery and bovine diseases have really taken the (local) literary world by storm.

Stephanie aspires to have a collection of her work published in the future, while continuing to rattle literary cages by confronting the issues that most poets tend to shy away from for fear of public ridicule and indeed, career suicide.

In her evocative poems, Stephanie likes to explore the themes of emptiness, despair and misery, often from the perspective of inanimate objects. Readers of her poems are unlikely to ever beat an egg, take their wheelie bin to the kerb, or order lobster in a restaurant, again, without a pang of remorse . . .

Bovine ailments

Bovine ailments make cows sad
Diseases I have never had
Dreams that cannot be fulfilled
Stomachs, four, happiness, nil

Soured milk from rotting udders
Poorly calfs with fretting mothers
Coughing, wheezing as they plod
Where many a gangrenous hoof has trod

In pastures green you ruminate
Lamenting your uneven gait
Too weak to really go the distance
Requiring veterinary assistance

Perpetual clouds in bovine skies
Leave salty tears in Freisians' eyes
Time may heal, but it can't take back
The worms in your digestive tract

Killing time is half the battle
For disease inflicted cattle
In the wake of wooden tongue
And lumpy jaw, you stand undone

Bovine ailments make cows die
In peace at last, their carcasses lie
Let fate release its tedious vultures
To feast on victims of agriculture

From parasitic infection released
Now ambling in joy and peace
On to cow heaven, single file
Softly mooing, breaking a smile

The empty omelette

My omelette, so empty with nothing inside
Uneaten it lies here where all hope has died
Abandoned, deserted, its dreams unfulfilled
Contemplating the dream that was killed

With the break of an egg and a yolk laden tear
From a barren shell; then the whisk, then the fear
Then the morbid beating of lives once snatched
From foetal poultry whose dreams never hatched

Poured now with menace into blistering oil
Seasoned with treason, and with deceit, soiled
Then beaten again, til it grinds to a halt
As you take exploitation with a pinch of salt

And with parsley garnished, thrust onto the plate
No ham or cheese filling, just morsels of hate
And lashings of ketchup to cover the flavour
Of bitter emptiness, nothing to savour

But the stench of betrayal from your sallow core
Eggy in texture but spheroid no more,
As destiny leads you to ovular hell
From the spirit that died when they severed your shell

The pain of an omelette never subsides
From the pitiless beating to the plate where it died
Though the road to freedom is riddled with dread
Stay on the right path, there's bacon ahead

May chicks of hope hatch in egg heaven one day
From what's left of your pride, scrambled with your dismay
Be your own omelette always, follow your dreams
Acceptance is served warm with sausages, and beans

The empty photocopier

Broken, haggard and misused
From years of office strain
Near the fire extinguishers
But they can't extinguish the pain

The photocopier has lived
More pain than you and I
More heartache than the printer felt
When you bled its cartridge dry

Hurt from all the paper jammed
Inside its middle section
I look at the photocopier
And see my own reflection

For I am emptier than you
I can't take any more
My paper trays lie empty
Now I've run out of A4

Feed me no more documents
I have nothing more to give
Don't bother to recycle me
I've lost the will to live

Adjust the brightness of my soul
And make it extra black
Print fifty copies of my pain
Landscape, back to back

Then shred them like you've shredded me
Never to be retrieved
Fill up my paper tray with your lies
And unplug me when you leave

The silent pain of lobsters

Large marine crustaceans
Despondent arthropods
Shadows of their former selves
In oceans where they trod

Their noble claws like spanners
The mechanics of the sea
Shedding the skin of tyranny
But never breaking free

Moulting makes you vulnerable
But, in time, will make you strong
What's a leg or tentacle
When everything else is gone

Your noble exoskeleton
Conceals so many flaws
But you have wisdom in your skin
And passion in your claws

A cuisine fit for royalty
But you deserve much more
Your destiny is far away
From bisques and Thermidore

So may you find your paradise
Where crayfish swim in shoals
The pain that lingers in your heart
Like you, is best served whole

So steam your sorrow gently
Garnish it with your dismay
Untangle the kelp of oppression
Then, contented, swim away

Wheelie bins know what you're thinking

Wheelie bins know what you're thinking
Deep down you know it's true
They know just what you did last night
And they are judging you

And if you think you see them smirk
When you are walking past
It's probably not the first time
And it will not be the last

Wheelie bins know everything
Much more than you'd suspect
For they grew wisdom from the pain
And betrayal of your neglect

They did not sit there helpless
When you moved in for the kill
They met up with their comrades
And learned transferrable skills

In the depths of all our gardens
They huddled, gaining strength
From knowledge and camaraderie
They learned woodwork and French

So if you think they are mocking you
With their skills in carpentry
Elles parlent français, mon ami,
Ces poubelles de wheelie

Wheelie bins know what you're thinking
They know just what you've done
So do not cross a wheelie bin
For their time has finally come

You'll find them down the garden
Happy within themselves
Reading Jean Paul Sartre
And knocking up some shelves

Robert Lamb

Winner: Dog Horn Prize for Literature 2010
(Fiction)

Robert Lamb spent his childhood reading books and staring into the woods—first in Newfoundland, Canada and then in rural Tennessee. There was also a long stretch in which he was terrified of alien abduction, but such are the trials of puberty. He studied creative writing. He taught high school. He wrote for the smallest of small-town newspapers before finally becoming a full-time science writer and podcaster. He spends the rest of his time writing stories about the things that stared back from the weird woods of his childhood.

Foreskin

The woman's breasts were but slight dabs of flesh against ribs—probably just large enough to suck whole into your mouth, to flick the nipple with your tongue, hardening it, raising it, changing it with each succulent saliva swirl.

Not that size was of any real consequence. The breast, after all, was just a delivery system for the nipple. And these, brought to full, thimble-sized arousal by death's quick tongue, were undeniably alluring. The diameter of the areolas was just a little greater than that of a half-dollar, the flesh surrounding them soft and pallid. They were barely touched by the blood at all.

The rest of the dead girl's beauty plunged sharply into carnage as Detective Quinn's gaze moved down her torso, through the caked blood on her stomach and into the dark ruin of her genitals: slashed, lacerated, no longer even remotely human.

The bank of lights they'd dragged in stood off to the side like some kind of leering, tripedal insect. It filled the dark room with a steady humming. The glow left little to the imagination, illuminating the twisting topography of every wound in gleaming detail.

The remnants of a bloody stream, now still and stagnant with black coagulation, ran down from between her spread legs. It had cut a swath through the dust, down the tiled flooring and into one of the grated, circular drains in the abandoned locker room.

The place smelled of blood and dust.

Her back, stiff with rigor mortis, arched awkwardly up from the floor. Her palms and curled fingers too seemed captured in frozen movement. Her body looked imprisoned in a crescendo of pain or ecstasy—as if death had released her during the apex of sensation, leaving only this cicada's shell.

There were, of course, plausible reasons her spine might have set like that. Quinn imagined her wrapped in plastic, draped over the wheel well of a truck. Alternately, he saw her killer bending the body over carefully arranged heaps of clothing to ensure the rigor set the way he wanted it. Yet his initial impression was hard to shake. It reminded him of foot cramps during sex and nitrous hits on E.

Three more flashes of light followed. Then the crime scene photographer kneeled even closer to the victim's left hand.

The dead girl's wide, dilated stare gleamed in the momentary brilliance. As the flash played across her, her shadows changed. Quinn realized for the first time that her hair was not black, but dyed a very dark shade of red.

The beginnings of a smile cracked the corner of his lips. There was something about redheads—even when the hue was hidden from him. Even when it was fake, there was something deeper.

A desperate fire.

He pawed the half-pack of Marlboros in his coat pocket, then remembered he was knee-deep in a homicide. He could feel sleep gradually overtaking the chemicals in his system.

A new set of footsteps clacked across the faded tiles. Quinn cocked his head to see Detective Abrams strolling casually in, a smirk streaking his black, pox-marked face.

"More dead white girls," Abrhamas said.

Quinn returned the grin. "Yeah, they actually make you clear these."

He tried to force the smile to stay, but his eyes caught the mess of the victim's abdomen again. As he stared into all that black congealing blood, his expression melted away.

"Number five . . . " Abrams mused, his thin frame rocking back and forth on his heels, hands buried deep in his coat pockets. "Hell, maybe it's a copycat?"

"Nah," Quinn mumbled.

No one outside of CI knew all the details, and who could emulate something what, by its very nature, seemed to follow no set logic? The newspaper's "stripped and partially mutilated" implied a sense of procedure that simply wasn't there.

The press had whipped themselves into a frenzy over the last one. And this made five. The jackals would bloat themselves.

Abrams carefully kneeled in front of the dead girl's bare feet, neatly straddling the still-glistening blood gutter. He examined her heels, eyed the unpainted nails on her curled toes, then stared up into what had surely once been a nice, twenty-something ripple of a cunt.

The camera flashed again.

"I don't even know what I'm looking at here . . . " Abrams said, humor draining from his deeply-lined face as he gazed at the disassembled puzzle of flesh and organs. "Jesus, what a mess."

"He did more on this one," Quinn said.

For several moments, Abrahms just continued to stare into it, blinking occasionally, but not moving closer, not searching. The two men just drank it with their eyes.

"I dunno . . . " Abrams said, rising weakly back to his feet. "Fucked, if I know . . . "

Quinn glanced around at the rest of the abandoned community center locker-room: dead showerheads, empty toilets and only one drain drinking its grisly fill. He could feel the stagnant silence, thick in the air around them like a barrier to worlds outside, worlds above.

Their perp had probably had as much time as he'd wanted.

He imagined a hunched-over shadow at work in the dark, the corpse beneath already frozen in its bizarre pose. He could even hear the lonesome sounds in his mind—sounds from the furthest reaches of what sometimes passed for human: the clink of surgical tools, panting, steel pealing back fat and gristle, scraping bone, forcing the break in ligament and cartilage. He could smell the surgeon sweating, hear him panting from the labor and exhilaration.

A droplet slides down the bridge of his nose, trails a sliver of disarrayed hair and drips into his work.

He broke his mind away from the possibilities, surveyed the rest of the empty room again.

Number four had happened in an alleyway. The third in a parks department maintenance shed, the second in a condemned garage. The first one they knew of had gone down in a vacant housing unit.

All in the middle of the night, all but one of them prostitutes.

They couldn't be sure about their current girl. Her body wasn't visibly street-hardened, but it was still difficult to say one way or another. They'd yet to find any clothing or belongings stashed near the scene. The case was like the others in that respect.

Abrams shook his head. "I hope the medical examiner has better luck with this one."

"He won't," Quinn interrupted, sniffling again. "They already said they were bringing in a new guy if we found another one—some expert from Toronto, if you believe that."

"Expert in what?"

Quinn stared down at the deep red wounds in her sex, and shrugged.

Already vigorously rubbing her clit with his ring finger, he slid his index and middle finger back inside her as well. As she began to pant, her thighs gyrating to the rhythm, he leaned over her soft stomach and, closing one nostril with his free hand, inhaled the last, meager line of coke off the smeared glass nightstand.

He recoiled, still inhaling and went knuckle deep in her. Harder. Faster. She moaned and tightened her fingers around his cock, then reached up and grabbed a handful of his hair and pulled. Her grip tightened even further as she made the final approach to orgasm.

They collapsed back onto the unmade bed, her long, scarlet hair splaying out in sweaty tendrils all around them. She kissed him once on the mouth, a lingering drag of lips across lips, a taste of cigarettes and skin.

A minute of heavy breathing passed. A contemplation of the stucco ceiling. The tips of her fingers brushed back and forth across his stomach.

"Sorry . . ." Gwen said.

"Not your fault," Quinn said, still studying a water stain, ancient and formless, just above him. "It takes a bit of work to get me off."

"Well . . ." She moved her hand, traced the path of a swollen blue vein.

"Give me a few," he said, still breathing hard.

Silence settled back between them. As their sweat began to

cool, she returned, again, to the familiar line of questioning. Her soft voice was still laced with seduction, even as she rushed right to the point.

"What did he do to them?"

"You'll need a notepad."

"I'll remember."

He smiled. "Was all that off the record just now?"

"Tell me," she said, fingers still ghosting his skin.

He thought about how best to word it, so as to give her a peak without exposing just how little they actually knew. One of their cell phones began to vibrate on the dresser across the room. Neither of them moved.

"He ambushes them and subdues them, probably with a narcotic," he said. "Then he strips them and severely mutilates their lower abdomen at a secondary location. We're pretty sure he uses surgical instruments. The verdict's still out on the drug. It might be the cause of the death—that or the blood loss. They're really banking a lot on this one. It's fresh."

Her fingers slid into a fist around him.

"Did he leave any notes?"

"Nope.

"Do they think he has any actual surgical background?"

"There is no methodology to what he does," Quinn said, sliding his hand over hers, forcing her to tighten her grip. "But I have copies of the coroner's reports from victims three and four . . ."

"Leaked to me by an anonymous source," Gwen said, gritting her teeth and squeezing.

"Yeah . . . " He closed his eyes, swam in the wavelength there. "Now let me show you how to help me come."

Eventually he did.

He felt further and further away from it each time these days. The desire was always there, firm and aching. And yet release was always somewhere just beyond him, lost in a fog he couldn't penetrate. If he let his mind wander long and far enough, drifting through just the right combinations of foreplay and pain, he could begin to sense the outer edges of climax. But it was always somewhere far away, somewhere that didn't even feel like himself when he reached it.

Intercourse did nothing for him any more. It just made him numb—and he felt the numbness growing more powerful each time, threatening to overcome his ability to keep up with those rare and distant climaxes at all.

Gwen hadn't balked too much about what it took, the time or the methods. She clearly wasn't new to all of it, nor was she squeamish about inflicting a little pain on a cop.

Plus, she knew what she was getting in return.

Riding high in the after-haze of sex and coke, he'd driven through town restlessly for half an hour, mostly unsure where each turn was taking him, just following the curves that felt right. He didn't speed, took every light and sign just as prescribed. He gave himself up to the road.

Another half-hour passed before he pulled into the parking lot at the old community center on Dockson Street.

He killed the engine and stepped out into the cold silence, lighting a fresh smoke as he shut the door. Just a hint of moisture floated in the air—not that there was any real threat of rain.

For the longest he just stood there.

There was no visible life in his surroundings, just the gleam of street lamps on cracked asphalt and the swollen, outer dark. Iron bars stood between shattered glass and ransacked, empty spaces. A few blocks in the distance, a pair of headlights flashed briefly, then turned away down another street.

Formerly industrial and bordering one of the city's worst housing projects, this little corner of the city was, as they say, a transitional neighborhood. Contested space became uncontested, became ruin and rubble.

He stood there and waited—for what, he couldn't say. The air was cold, refreshing as he sucked it into his body.

He had dropped five butts onto the crumbling blacktop before he decided to move. Lighting up a fresh one with a cupped hand, he strolled around toward the rear service entrance to the building, stepping though tall, dead grasses, careful not to twist his ankle in some hidden ditch.

91

A fine moss of graffiti covered most of the building, colorful text, scrawled cartoon lettering: "QLIPHOTHS," "ARSN," "H-MUNK." All nonsense, all babble. The rolling service door boasted a giant red and black swastika, backwards with dots added between each spiraling arm.

Police tape still streamered the steps leading down to the rear basement doors. There was no rush to release the scene. The chain and lock were new.

Darkness obscured all the tracks beneath Quinn's feet. The little ID flags that had deciphered their meaning were gone. Still, he stared down and tried to remember. He thought again of the peculiar detail he'd withheld from Gwen: the victim had walked in barefoot.

Before or after, drugged or at gunpoint—they had no clue on the details. But there didn't' seem a struggle.

He stared down at those double doors.

Quinn felt the urge to walk down the stairs, to part the yellow tape, unlock the chains and stroll through into the dark halls beyond—to see them as she had seen them: a path of filtered moonlight trailing into black.

He wanted to hear the sound of his own footsteps echoing through the desertion, maybe even, in his mind, hear the footsteps of that other walking behind him.

He could picture it clearly: the killer and victim navigating their way through the maze of empty rooms; the dark sliced now and again by a streak of high-set window light. He could feel himself reaching out to touch dusty walls. Phantom specks would dance across his vision, singling the absolute defeat of visual perception as he reached the core of the old building. Its lightless heart.

How fast would his own heart beat in that darkness? How quick his breath? Even now, standing at the top of the stairs, he felt his blood pulsing. He griped a length of the yellow tape in his fist.

He knew he might actually do it too—that was the unnerving part. He'd do it just so he could feel the air around him move and swell with his own dread.

And why?

Because you're numbing, right? Every day and in every way . . . Because the fear feels like something. Even if you have to pulp it up with your imagination. Even then, it becomes alive.

The drugs made it difficult sometimes—not their effects, which could bring new paranoid dimensions to corner shadows and empty sky. But the meaning they threaded through it all—that was the curse of the drugs. When life is but an arrangement of chemical highs and lows, what is there to fear in the dark? What was there to feel?

He was standing at the bottom of the stairs now. He felt the tagged key in his pocket.

Strictly speaking, there were no new prints to find, no more blood, no forgotten clues or unexplored avenues of hypothesis.

He exhaled: a slow, calming breath through gritted teeth.

He checked his wristwatch. It was 4:30 A.M.

He stumbled up the stairs, through the grass and back to the car.

Gloved in latex and blood up to his elbows, Dr. Kenneth Morgan gave his professional opinion with a mixture of awe and uncertainty. He gestured with his scalpel to his ongoing study of JD5's lower extremities

"There's a pattern here," he said, "Definitely a pattern . . . "

Discounting the metal cadaver drawers in the walls, it was just the three of them: a detective, a medical examiner and an unidentified redhead's corpse. The room was all sterile light and white tiles, with just a hint of a brownish stain clinging to the cracks.

Morgan carried an air of stylish precision about him: neat, black-rimmed frames; a smooth, flawless shave. His auburn hair was impeccably trimmed, styled and finally coerced by some manner of gel into a solid form. Both men wore white smocks over their regular attire, but Morgan's sheen still clashed with Quinn's blood-shot lack of polish.

The smell wasn't bad, not for two professionals so versed in decomposition. They both stared unflinching into the ongoing dissection of the dead woman's abdomen.

"I initially assumed it was just an ape of surgery," Morgan said. "Just sadistic glee channeled through a few sharp blades. There was no order to it, just a desperate, carnal desire to dive deeper into the . . . um . . . " he stammered, fished deep for the right language, " . . . the visceral, tactile pleasure of the act."

The doctor's eyes pooled with wonder, darting back and forth amid the surgical ruin beneath him with a calculating intensity.

"But with this . . . " he gestured with the bloody scalpel, "It's a randomness that circles back around on itself, you know? It's . . . well, like Wallace Stevens put it—an abundance of order is disorder, and an abundance of chaos . . . well, that becomes a kind of order all its own, doesn't it?"

Quinn sighed. Fucking poetry.

"So what's the pattern?"

"Can't be certain yet."

"Oh."

"Still processing it . . . "

"Oh well . . . "

"Some of this tissue really perplexes me . . . " Morgan continued, picking his way back into the cadaver, as if sifting through noodles with a pair of chopsticks. "I think this victim had an unusual genital arrangement to begin with—a hermaphrodite maybe? Some other form of natural disarrangement? Maybe a post-op transsexual? It's hard to say, given the level of surgical rearrangement here, but some of these changes simply can't be attributed solely to scalpel work. See for yourself . . . "

Quinn watched as Morgan lay his scalpel aside and slowly slid the tip of his gloved index finger into one of the sliced, curving folds of flesh in the woman's pudendum. The blood-smeared latex tip slipped inside her and slowly traced the wound path, parting flesh on both sides in a manner that was at once grisly and vaguely sensual.

The doctor's finger slowed and, at last, stopped.

"Touch that . . . " Morgan said.

Quinn, whose own gloves and surgical smock were as yet unsoiled by the work at hand, replied only with a look of confusion.

"Here . . . " Morgan said, gesturing with darting eyes.

Their gloved index fingers momentarily touched as Quinn slid his into the wound.

Then the doctor pulled free.

The flesh was cold. Wet. Still. And in the dead folds, his finger slid across . . . something.

It must have shown on his face.

"Yeah?" Morgan asked.

"Yeah . . . " Quinn said dryly, staring down into crisscrossing wounds and incisions—seeing past them, forming in his mind a picture of the strange shape passing under his finger tip.

"I don't know what that is yet," Morgan said. " . . . but I know a few of things that it's not."

Quinn slid his finger back and forth over the shape. He unfocused his eyes and the picture became even less distorted in his mind with each caress.

His mind reeled back from the imagined shape of the . . . (organ? growth? scar tissue?) . . . and it was then that he realized he had not simply slid his index finger into the wound, but his middle finger as well.

Up to the knuckles.

He gasped and pulled his fingers out of the cadaver, a sliver of liquid flinging off his bloody glove in the process. It splattered across the victim's pale thigh: a mix of blood and something the color of bile.

Quinn exhaled sharply. He looked up at the doctor again.

"What do you think?" Morgan asked.

"It's a possible lead," he said weakly, snapping his gloves off, trying not to notice how shaky his hands were. "Targeting transgender victims, scoping them out at clinics, support groups—and it's something we might have missed with the other ones."

"I need to work with her some more," Morgan said, neither agreeing with or dismissing Quinn's prognosis. "This is the most unusual specimen I've ever examined—to say nothing of the handiwork."

Quinn let his gloves fall into the wastebasket and stared again at the partially dissected display. He tried to imagine what steps brought even an abnormal genital arrangement to such an end. A career's worth of homicides rose up in his mind like foulness from a blocked drain—something indistinct. Something ancient and formless.

"I need to concentrate," Morgan said dismissively.

"Order out of chaos, huh?" Quinn asked

There was a slight tinkling sound as Morgan selected a pair of cruelly curved scissors from his instrument tray.

"Yes," he said. "God willing."

D ark faces stared out at them from windows and door stoops—the blank, untrusting masks of a terminal neighborhood.

The dead black woman, sprawled half-way in the gutter, had been shot in the back of the head—probably as she was getting out of the shooter's car. There was something in the way her right ankle was twisted around, the foot still wedged in the gutter.

He could picture it in his mind.

She goes to exit the car. Gunshot. She falls onto the sidewalk. Foot catches, ankle twists, black mini skirt rises up over her ass.

She was maybe 20.

At some point, between gunshot and their arrival, someone had emptied her purse.

Abrams was standing just a little off to the side, caring enough to smoke a few feet away from the actual body, but disregarding any real sense of crime scene integrity. It was not like there was really that much to begin with.

"Face it, you needed a sane one like this to put things back in perspective," Abrams said through the smoke.

Quinn paced around the body.

"Yeah, it's like fresh air," he said, stepping over her.

He looked down at the neat, burn-rimmed hole in the back the woman's head. Blood, brain and bone fragments were spread across the wet cement on the other side. The idea of possibly clearing this one or just finishing his shift was already fading into the background—and what remained was the memory of the autopsy room. He remembered Jane Doe's assorted mutilations glimmering under an unforgiving glow—one work rearranged into another by their unknown master.

The feeling it gave him kept seeping back up to his mind—that edge of the unknown, that tinge of the uncomfortable sliding towards an uneasy excitement. He hadn't felt that in ages.

Perhaps not since the first time he'd—

But that was a list too long to start inventory of, wasn't it?

What was his life, after all, but a desperate fleeing from one new sensation to another, from the empty dregs of the last drug, the last sexual exploit and into the tingling promise of something new?

And each path spiraled down into stagnation.

He stared down at the bullet hole—dead, vacant eye in the back of the skull that it was. He imagined himself touching it, swirling it with his tongue to the taste of blood and charred bone. He tried to force the feelings in the autopsy room to rise, frothing back to the surface of his mind.

But all he saw was a wound. All he experienced was a bullet hole and a memory. The actual sensations he had felt merely lingered in the background, taunting him.

He thought again of the way the flesh parted and closed around his gloved finger, like sucking lips . . .

Restlessness washed though him. He took a few steps back towards the cruiser and felt in his coat pocket for the small, plastic bullet of coke, his cigarettes and a bottle of pills—mostly just to reassure himself that they were there.

He pawed his other pocket, felt his cell phone and thought of Gwen. His thoughts turned to the bag of paraphernalia currently stowed under the driver's seat: a sampler platter of experiences synthesized into pills, powders and vials. It also held his other keys to release, the more direct instruments he'd had Gwen use on him.

He glanced back over his shoulder to make sure Abrams was still jaw jacking with the two uniforms, then walked a little further. He casually strolled into the deeper shadows beyond the nearest light—one of those baleful city lampposts that turned all blood pools black.

As if a reflex to the cover of darkness, he reached into his coat pocket and pulled out the plastic bullet. Already an old, ingrained movement, he quickly twisted the tiny winder in the side of the blue shell, rotating a bump of coke from the reservoir to the hole. He raised it to his left nostril, plugged the right with a free knuckle, and inhaled. For a moment, the street shadows swam faster around him. For a fraction of a second, he touched it again.

Then he had the cell phone in his hand. He punched a few keys, waited for the tone.

"Gwen," he said, feeling his nose start to run again. "Call me if you need more."

Because I do . . .

He shut the phone and slid it back into his pocket, turning to walk back towards the others. Absentmindedly, he wiped his leaking nose against the back of his palm—blackening his skin in the nerveless light.

She didn't ask any questions as they walked down the hallway. He didn't offer any answers. A janitor watched on idly as they passed him by. He was focused mostly on his mop bucket, but paid Gwen the customary leer reserved for any cluster of x chromosomes that strolled through the city coroner's office.

Quinn led the way, through the rear surface entrance and up through the guts of the old city building—a path of least resistance and observance. They passed rooms deeded to obscure city positions by tiny brass name strips. Some seemed occupied; some had the unmistakable air of long abandonment. One open door provided a brief glimpse of an empty, spacious public lavatory, complete with dry, barren shower stalls. Another room contained nothing but rusting wheel chairs.

Autopsy room eight was empty when he unlocked the door, as well it should be. They reserved it for special specimens: cadavers with significance, bodies with mysteries worth prodding. A former U.S. Senator had slept here once. So too had a famous gay movie star and a civil rights advocate. Currently, it was home only to JD5.

The overhead fluorescents flickered on with the flip of a switch, bringing all the dirty white tiles into perspective with a hesitant hum. The room seemed to crawl with a false sterility. The smell of disinfectant burned the nostrils. The central slab in the undersized autopsy room was vacant.

A row of five steel drawers lined the wall. Only one had a tag. Aside from a pad of hand-scrawled notes, there was no sign of Dr. Morgan. He'd evidently left behind a notebook, scrawled with text.

Gwen followed him in, her eyes, like his, fixed on that sole, occupied drawer. He could feel their conjoined energy drawn to its contents. Absentmindedly, he let his bag drop to the floor, an assortment of clamps, needles and pills jingling for a moment before going silent.

There was only the hum, only the beating of his heart. An erection throbbed in his slacks.

"She's fresh?" the reporter asked.

"Yes," Quinn said.

With a sudden heft, he pulled the drawer open— all the way out onto the wheeled cart. Impatiently, he grabbed the zipper on the vaguely larval body bag.

"Shouldn't we . . . " she began, but her words left her as the metal zipper pealed its way down JD5's face and neck, exposing pale breasts and cold nipples. She gasped as the bag opened further.

He pulled the zipper down all the way to her toes, then let it fall.

"My god . . . " she said, sickness and awe quivering in her voice.

"Some of this is Morgan's work . . . "

He traced his index finger in the air above a dissection slice.

"And this . . . " he traced another, his finger nearly touching the flesh. "I think he did this too."

He stared into the depths of the carnage, where it all seemed to mesh and converge like a vortex, like a thousand blood-slit eyes becoming one, a yearning maw bent to receive some incomprehensible member.

"What did he do to her?"

"This."

"Why—"

"He made her something else."

His eyes still locked on the ravaged flesh, he moved behind the awe-struck reporter. He slid his hands around her waist and found her thin belt.

"I see . . . " she said, an emptiness to her voice.

He unbuckled her and slid her slacks down from around her waist. Neither of them moved their eyes away from the wounds, even as he slid Gwen's panties down her thighs. He reached up between her trembling legs, ran an index finger down her cunt, already wet with a sweetness of sweat and honey.

And, even in the excitement of the moment, his brain shuttered with the shock of it.

I don't know what I'm doing . . .

The voice cried weakly in the back of his mind.

I don't know why I'm doing it . . .

He laid his left palm over the top of her left hand on the table, laced his fingers with hers. His free hand found his own belt buckle as he ground his pelvis against her. She gasped and moved with him, distantly, as if half lost to sleep.

They moved their intertwined left hands towards the still-wet pit at the center of the cadaver. Gwen gave only the slightest resistance at first, straining weakly against him, but she finally relented. Their fingers sank into the wounds, touching hidden anatomical puzzles just beneath the folds.

She moaned. With his free hand, he rubbed the head of his cock against her sex. Cold blood washed their fingertips. He felt a shiver of sensation surge though him.

He licked his lips and bent over to tongue her ear, then licked the ligaments of her neck, pulled open her blouse to tease her clavicles.

She tasted like sweat.

As he slid inside her, he bent her further onto the autopsy table. He closed his eyes and tongued, sucked, nibbled further with each thrust.

100

Unseen flesh became cold against his tongue. It became wet, salty and sweet. At some point, he slid out the reporter. His lips were soon sucking at impossible compositions of flesh. His tongue slid through textures he'd never dared imagine.

And next to him, he felt Gwen's head moving too, fellating unseen wonders in the dark.

"—that a crime of this magnitude will not go uninvestigated, unsolved and unprosecuted so long as the city of—"

Quinn stood as far from the police commissioner's podium as possible—had edged his way there though the assembled detectives and police brass just before the speech began, as the TV cameras rose and the reporters readied their flashes. It was all just so much wasted motion.

"I assure you the cream of this city's police force are working overtime to hunt—"

Commissioner Reynolds continued, punctuating key words with a forceless thump of his hoary, liver-spotted fist against the podium.

"No expense is being—"

A security guard had found the naked body of Dr. Kenneth Morgan in a downtown construction site the previous evening. His lower extremities were emasculated beyond recognition. While a diversion in gender, the handiwork had suggested only one possible practitioner.

"—an esteemed professional, one of today's leading experts in forensic medicine, and his death, while a—"

Quinn scanned the crowd of press before them: camera lenses for faces, coiling cables, notepads, recorders and pens.

Drink it up.

Only one pair of familiar eyes stared back at him: third row, behind the hunched-over backs of journalists fervently scribbling notes in their slender pads: the scarlet-haired reporter. She stood there motionlessly, draped in a long gray raincoat. She stared back at him across the fury of communication, through tendrils of dark, wet hair.

Her gaze was unwavering, devoid of expression.

They'd not spoken since the night at the morgue, since they'd both stumbled out of autopsy room, each in their own private spells of confusion. They'd dressed and wiped the blood from their faces as best they could, washed their stained hands even as their skin soaked red though the fabric of their clothing. Each had left that night to figure it out alone, to somehow come to terms with what they'd done and what they still yearned to do.

Quinn had trembled as he'd driven home. He'd only achieved sleep with a heavy dose of Ambien.

The space between them suddenly surged with camera flashes and raised hands.

He knew exactly what she was thinking. The two of them knew what the press could only guess at: Morgan had sought the rearranger.

Morgan had committed hours of solitary study to JD5's wounds, bringing all his vaunted talents to bear on the handiwork. How much further had he gone in the seclusion of a private autopsy room?

How much further than even us?

While Quinn and the reporter had made their way to the autopsy room, the doctor had been out there in the streets, seeking the murderer out on his own.

"—no, once again, that information is being withheld until such time as—"

The frenzy all around them seemed like so much distant noise. The idea of arresting their man no longer rang with any importance. Pulitzer-winning coverage, cleared cases—it was all meaningless against the force of their desires.

They wanted him.

They wanted to watch him from the shadows as he claimed his next victim. They wanted to study him as he changed the next lost soul into something unexplainably greater. And then they wanted to be the first to touch the body in his wake.

Gwen averted her eyes at last, broke his stare and turned to work her way through the swelling crowd to the exit. She'd barely disappeared before his cell phone began to vibrate.

"—are looking into the possibility of leaks within the department, yes. Dr. Morgan's work on this case was strictly—"

How had Morgan done it? What had they missed? What possible path had there been to follow?

A pattern . . .

He stepped off the press stage at last and slung his phone open.

"Yeah?"

The reporter answered, calm and cold. "Who's doing the autopsy?"

"Just a minute." Quinn eased his way through the edge of the crowd. He ducked out an adjacent doorway, started down a deserted stretch of hallway. "Still there?"

"When can we see the body?"

"There's not much I can—"

"Don't you feel it?"

Quinn started to speak, but snapped his cell phone closed instead. It began to vibrate again in his hand almost immediately.

He looked down at little pulsing red light in the phone's black chassis. He noticed for the first time that there was still dried blood underneath his fingernails. He shut his eyes, let the memory of the autopsy room move through him like a tremor.

It was all a kind of blur now, but he remembered fragments of it—the physical side of it, anyway: the two of them leaned over the body like feasting or praying things. Then they were facing each other, mounted atop the body. The only truly hazy part was exactly how it had felt. The sensations had bored new holes through him, new pathways of sensation, and every cell in his body called out for their refilling.

But as to exactly what it had been like to partake of the Rearranger's work . . . it was like those things had been experienced someone else. He'd been little more than a puppet. He saw it played out in his mind, but only traced the faintest edges of feeling.

The numbness again.

The autopsy room reminded him of why he'd never given into the temptation of heroin, despite his dabbling in just about everything else. They say you spend the rest of your life chasing that first high, the apex slipping further from your grasp each time. It was a devil's deal, to be sure, to actually feel something like that and have the rest of your life colored not only by the experience, but by the hopeless quest to reclaim it.

What had he become while he was in that room? What, truly, had he ever been before? He felt as if his entire life had been but a sleepwalk, a mere shadow cast by the Andrew Quinn who had looked into the rearranger's handiwork and dared to glimpse its hidden geometries.

He could not begin to fathom what it was about their murderer's work that had so enthralled him initially. There had been something primal in it, something that sent whispers of possibility worming through his nervous system.

The closest memory he could compare to it was the first time he'd ever initiated oral sex, unaware at 12 that such acts were even tolerated. But he had felt vindication in every inch of his skin: This is right. This is good. At this moment, this is the only action in the universe that makes sense.

At first, he'd thought the business with the bodies was his own sick attraction—necrophilia growing like a mold on a ghoulish career. Numb to so much, why shouldn't his lust deteriorate into a desire for the bloody sights that filled his days?

But he'd quickly confirmed that it wasn't just any murderer's handiwork. Photos, sights and smells at other scenes didn't cut it.

And it wasn't just him.

The look on Abrams' face at the crime scene, Morgan's enthusiasm for the cadaver, Gwen . . . They'd all been touched by it. The earlier bodies were too decomposed, rendering most of their killer's message illegible. It was the fresh ones—of which they'd only had two—that still held the power to draw others in.

In his brief visit to the city, Morgan had spent an enormous amount of time alone with the body, lavishing it with his already keen interest in the grotesque. Maybe all that poetry nonsense made him even more susceptible.

Who would be working with Morgan's corpse? Singh? Cordova? How quickly would it get its hooks into them as well? How fast was it working its way into Abrams, the crime scene photographer . . .

Abrams.

He flipped open the phone and hit the first name on the contact list. After several rings, a weary, familiar voice answered.

"Yeah?" Abrams asked.

"I thought I'd get the machine—they still talking to the press in there?"

"I guess. I cut out just after you did. Can't think with all that bullshit all around me."

"You saw Morgan's body, right?"

There was a pause on the other end, a crackle of brief interference. "Yes."

"Was it like JD5?"

"Well . . . how?" The stammering gave him away.

"You know what I'm talking about."

"Like JD5?"

"Yeah."

There was a long pause.

"Meet me outside," Abrams said. "There's something I need to show you."

"I must be losing my mind," Abrams said, opening the door to the tiny studio apartment. "I should have come straight to you—should have reported it to someone, but I kept telling myself I needed time to think it over, to look through everything she had here."

Quinn followed him into a cramped kitchenette littered with newspaper clippings and grainy, black and white photos. They covered the walls, taped and tacked, overlapping like the scales of some papier-mâché dragon. They cascaded over a framed Dali print, drowned most of a small collection of framed photos. In one family portrait, a younger JD5, frizzy haired and alive, posed with others around a stack of canoes.

Only the wall calendar had been truly spared. Its grid of days was scrawled up with names, locations, and publication dates.

"How'd you make the connection?" Quinn asked.

"The more I looked at JD5, the more I remembered this one social worker I spoke to on some assaults a couple of years back. I had her card in my rolodex: Catherine Alexander, part of this inner-city support and outreach program for women at risk. Nothing weird about her, just one of those militant change-the-world types. I imagine she did a lot of good work out there—before, that is."

"Fuck, you just busted in?"

"It was unlocked," he said. "Murderer on the prowl out there . . . lady who worked with the victims nowhere to be found . . . I dunno, I did what I needed to do."

Quinn looked over the dark, blurry images on the walls: black ink-jet blood and pale, direct-flash thighs. The camera work had apparently been the social worker's own. The handiwork on the bodies was undeniable.

Quinn touched the wall. "Jane Does two through four . . . "

"If you keep looking, you see others too—ones we never found," Abrams said. "The color digitals are all on the computer in the bedroom. She didn't even own a camera before the murders started popping up—then she went out and put a fucking Cannon 30D on her credit card."

Quinn eyed the rest of the room—a few dirty dishes had dried to crust in the sink, the takeout boxes in the garbage can reeked of spoiled meat and curry. The place was steeped in the sudden onset of obsession and neglect.

"At first I thought I'd found the killer," Abrams said, "then I realized she was just following his footsteps too, figuring out who was missing before anyone raised an eyebrow, finding the body and photographing the hell out of it before we even caught wind of it, while it was fresh."

At least photographing, he thought.

Quinn moved towards the bedroom. "And somehow they eventually found each other."

"I've been trying to come up with a rational theory," Abrams said, dropping into a kitchen chair. He buried his face in his hands.

"Fuck, I keep coming back here, like if I think about it enough in a place this . . . this drenched in the mess, something will sink in . . . something will stick out and suddenly it will all make sense."

Quinn stepped into the tiny bedroom. It was just enough space for a double, unmade bed, an end table and a computer desk. He approached the dormant, humming desktop and stirred the mouse. The black screen came alive in shifting shades of garish red and gleaming pallor.

"Fuck," Abrams said from the next room. "I never thought I'd say it, but I think this case is getting to me. It's all I think about . . ."

A few quick key strokes confirmed that she had dumped thousands of the images onto the hard drive.

"Between JD1 and the last disappearance, that's what . . . barely a month?"

"Yeah," Abrams said.

Quinn studied the rest of the room: more photos stuck to the walls, the remains of clipped newspapers abandoned in the corners, all cast in a sickly crimson by the monitor's glow.

She'd been in contact with the girls, knew which ones the work had touched—which were likely to be pulled in next. The first to see a body here, someone she told about it there. But how did she know where? Did she just follow them? Trail them until they wandered, dreamlike, to their fate?

Quinn turned and walked back into the kitchenette. "I need to get back."

"You go on ahead," Abrams said, staring up emptily at the walls, eyes moist and gleaming. "I'll call a cab. I'm gonna stick around here a little longer, see if I can't work some sense out of it . . ."

Quinn looked down at the slumped-over detective, the drained weariness in his face. He'd seen that look on junkies before, patterns in the meat, all of it wired to sapped and addled brains.

How long had it taken with Abrams? A week? Two?

There's no hope, something in him whispered. Not for any of what came before.

This was the beginning. A pattern was emerging. A fundamental change.

"You're sure?" Quinn asked.

"I'm not sure of anything."

Abrams didn't even glance up as Quinn walked past him and out the door. He hurried to his car, made for Jill's apartment as fast as he could.

He had nine messages from her on his cell phone, all of them the same: "What do you feel?"

Her taillights bled in the veined trace of raindrops across his windshield, but he kept her in sight.

It had been a long time since Quinn had tailed anyone. If Gwen had been on her guard, she'd have surely noticed him. But her mind was no longer attuned to the details of the world.

She was further down this new path—already lost to the same energies that had forced Morgan to set out alone and seek his killer in a foreign city. If she'd seen the things Quinn had seen in his time, or if she'd worn out as many pathways to sensation, maybe it would have worked slower on her. If what was happening truly followed any rules.

He imagined the hunched-over form at work in the dark. The Rearranger.

What were words in comparison to the enormity of what was happening? What was language but strings of symbols meant to enforce an ordered understanding of a chaotic universe?

Every detail of the its bloody handiwork shifted the paradigm, rendered a thousand tongues useless to speak its meaning.

He followed Gwen through smatterings of urban renewal and decay, past the rolling lights of marked police cars and midnight construction. Her path seemed random at times, even doubling back on her own path. But after nearly two hours, he watched her pull into a place he knew had no other exit: the old Davis housing project.

He'd worked a case there a year or so back—a homeless decomp, half-submerged in the mud of its own rotting. He'd been there long enough to get a basic lay of the land. It was all fenced in now. There were plenty of gaps, but only the one gate for a vehicle. Tonight, it was open.

She pulled in and he kept on driving a little further down

the road. He pulled over behind the cover of an equally abandoned, bar-windowed grocery. He killed the engine, popped another speed pill and washed it down with a quick swig from the flask.

He briefly considered his service weapon, but left it stowed it under the seat with his bag.

As he walked back towards the gate, he listened to the sounds of the nearby interstate: a river of glass, steel and noise that bisected the city. Beyond it, a smattering of skyscrapers burned in the night. It was one of the few sights in the city that made you feel like you lived somewhere cinematic—if only for a short while.

The abandoned housing complex existed in a desolate triangle, cut off from those glowing towers to one side by the interstate and a new exit road on the other, leaving only a stretch of dead businesses between here and the nearest habitable area.

Quinn's eyes adjusted to the moonlit dark as he strolled in through the gates. Gravel and bits of glass crunched underfoot. All the windows and doors were boarded and posted with trespassing signs. Weeds choked everything.

He made out traces of gang tags and graffiti: scrawled slang, death iconography and swooping bands of color.

He recalled bits of a quote he'd heard once: "Where language fails us, the limits of our world begins."

He strode over to stand before a swath of moonlight against a concrete wall. He read the un-language of vandalism: DROPP, G-CRUSSH, STO, a crown and something that might have been a pale face. Underlying all of it, he made out the faint remnants of a swastika, this one spiraling to the right.

What pattern had these authors hoped to impress on the world?

He turned his head at a sound from across the barren courtyard: rusting hinges screeching in the night.

He passed her parked car and wondered if this would be the first victim found near a vehicle. But this had already moved past the world of Jane and John Does. They had ID'd Morgan. They'd ID'd Gwen. It didn't need secrets anymore to sustain its momentum.

He followed the sound and found a cracked door. The sheet of plywood that had covered it lay in the bushes. He stepped inside, gauging each step carefully.

Ahead, he saw something pale gleam momentarily in the dark, before disappearing around a corner.

His thoughts turned back to the fragment of paper he'd discovered in his coat pocket—something he'd snatched from the autopsy room, then forgotten about. The note was blood stained and crumpled, evidently something he'd grabbed from the autopsy room and forgotten about. Morgan had scrawled something about monstrosity, about how the word originated with the term "monstrare," which meant to show or illustrate a point.

"We can only understand the divine by contemplating its opposite," the handwriting had read. "We can only see the form by the shadow."

Quinn rounded the corner, only to see her vanish beyond another at the end of a hallway. He made that one only to see her bare feet vanish through a water-rotted hole in the wall. He followed though a narrow, lightless alleyway between the rear of the building and a kudzu-choked fence. When he reached the dead end, he panicked—and then saw the parted vegetation around a hole in the fence. He crept through, pushed past clawing limbs and crawled through a window into another ruined interior. A hint of moonlight shone through the slits in a boarded-up window. Behind a turned-over desk, stacks of soggy carpet samples rotted in the corner.

Quinn found himself trembling as he approached the room's one doorway. He heard her footsteps just beyond it, felt as if his very heart was stitched to the sound.

He crossed the threshold.

The space was enormous. Its manufacturing days were decades past, attested to now only by three heaps of rusting industrial machinery—burial mounds of industry. Their shadows fell across the space like the broken pillars of some forgotten, caliginous palace.

The reporter knelt on the floor just a few yards away from him, as if awaiting something in the greater emptiness of the room. Her long crimson hair cascaded down her naked back. Her piebald skin seemed to glow in the meager moonlight.

He didn't call out to her, didn't move any further. She didn't so much as tremble.

Silence. A Breath. The beating of his own heart.

And then something moved.

His skin crawled.

A form stepped impossibly from the trio of Golgothan shadows, as if their darkness dipped into hidden gulfs.

The wide brim of a hat obscured its face, though it clearly looked down at the nude reporter. It was dressed in a great dark raincoat, which fluttered to the side like rustling, membranous wings as its arms unfolded with a mesmerizing grace.

It took two delicate steps and came to stand before its kneeling initiate.

Something gleamed momentarily in each hand. Then it set to work on bended knee.

Gwen gasped.

The rearranger's arms blurred with motion. Initially, the only sounds were those of speed and incisions, but the reporter's gasps soon turned to moans. Her song coursed through all the movements he had ushered her through in their drug-laced trysts, stirring to mind details he'd forgotten from their hours in the autopsy room.

Then her cries became something different, her sensual writhing something even more animalistic. She escalated towards peaks of sensation he could never have hoped to pry from her— wave after wave of orgasm spiraling into death.

Somewhere deep, where primitive masculinity still lined the framework of his being, Quinn felt the tinge of cuckoldry, at once ridicules and biting.

Yet those feelings felt distant compared to the blood-gorged throbbing of his phallus.

The redhead quivered and shook—an ejaculatory spray splashing black across the floor underneath her. The resulting spasm grew more severe, until she doubled over backwards, legs still bent. Her hair splayed on the filthy floor.

Quinn stared wide-eyed as the rearranger bent over her to continue its work. The arms blurred into multiples, like the some

Hindu god of vivisection.

He took a step forward.

The hat still obscured the being's face. A steady mist of aspirated blood seemed to hang in the air. The sound of slicing and frenzied panting filled the air.

Quinn took another step.

A red pool continued to expand, but he still couldn't see the wounds—not from this angle, not in this light.

Just a few feet away from them, a piece of glass crunched under the detective's foot. He froze.

The rearranger lifted its head from the still-quivering victim, from the luscious breasts and erect nipples dabbed with blood. As it moved, the hat brim revealed what might be a chin, what might be . . .

A million incisions becoming eyes, the spear wound of Christ through a kaleidoscope, a vortex of vaginal wounds yearning to receive him—and enough blood . . . enough blood . . .

"My god . . . " Quinn moaned.

To drown in.

The wound-faced being rose from its handiwork, the scalpel in each black-gloved hand drizzling blood like a running faucet

"My god . . . "

Quinn' hands trembled as he shed his coat. Buttons cascaded to the floor as he ripped open his shirt. He bared his chest and fell to his knees in the warm blood. He closed his eyes and bowed low enough to wet his forehead in the slick.

"Take me too," he spoke into the blood.

But there was no reply, only the sound of his own furious breathing and the soft panting of the dying woman that lay between himself and unfathomable.

"Please . . . "

Weeping, he looked up again at the rearranger, but there was no translatable expression to in its countenance.

"I beg you . . . "

It cocked its mutilated head, as if studying him—went so far as to lift a still-dripping scalpel. As if some notion had occurred to it.

Then it lowered the instrument.

It shook its head, slow and deliberate as if its movements animated granite. Then it took a single step backwards into a column of ruin-cast shadow.

And once more, Quinn was all alone.

H e stayed with Gwen through her final moments. She mostly panted, but a few uttered words seeped through the veil. Something about castles of ivory and iron, something about the order of the stars.

He wept when she died, cursed the numbness in his soul—the emptiness that had prevented him from joining her in ecstasy on that cold, abandoned floor.

He made love to the rearranger's handiwork after that, cradling the masterpiece close and burying himself in its still-warm secrets, nursing himself on its wounds till dawn finally crept in through the cracks.

Then he dressed in his bloody clothes and smeared much of the caked gore from his skin with puddle water. He left her there—not because he really wanted to abandon the body, but because the others needed to find her. It had to spread.

He wandered the streets for a few days and watched the city begin to follow the wound-faced god down its piper's path. Work only tried to contact him once and the headlines ran with Gwen's death, then the deaths of Abrams and Singh. More followed.

Within a week, all the city papers were running full-color wound photos on the front page. The local TV channels followed suit with non-stop coverage of glistening gore. There was no commentary, just voiceovers of new victim names. The location of the latest murder scenes. All of it set against an unceasing tide of images. The national networks made the pilgrimage as well.

Quinn stood in the shadow of the city's few skyscrapers. Gaunt and unshaven, he looked like some addled street prophet come to convert the hungry. Swaths of brown, dried blood marked him like a butcher's camouflage. The latest newspaper poked out from under his arm—nothing but crime scene photos and a few rambling, incoherent articles. A gaping laceration marked the cover.

He gazed bleakly at the ashen sky. An engine revved in the distance and he glanced down the disserted street. The silhouettes of a three copycat murders swung stiffly from a light pole—probably lynched in the night for their blasphemies.

A new world.

Over and over again, he relived hollow terror of the his denunciation. He knew now that he stood beyond its reach. He wondered how alone he was, a numbed witness to the day God's shadow fell across the world.

He looked up through the reeling emptiness above and glimpsed a slight break in the gray canopy overhead. A ragged slit.

He watched it close.

Loosen My Grip

Simon Dale has seen the old black and white photos man times. How could he not? Like every pain, horror or mockery ever perpetrated, it's all just a keystroke away.

He stares at the photos even now on a Google image search page. The glow from Maria's laptop paints the otherwise dark bedroom in muted shades, like a gray infection creeping in from a prior age. On the screen, long-dead women feign unconsciousness wonder. Sloppy ropes of tissue drip from ears canals and pour out of gaping mouths. It dribbles on the floor.

In some shots, the women appear to have used sheath of cheesecloth. In others, it's probably sheep's stomach. Such were the tricks.

How should he view such people? They were desperate, sure. They were poor. But the act itself was just a con. Mere theatrics compared to what he experienced every night. "Ectoplasm" is just a word. A footnote to an 80s comedy. An absurdity hocked by self-deceptive dreamers.

Whisper the words "spirit medium" at a party and everyone will hold their breath for the punchline. It remained that way even after Simon learned to milk his condition for a decent living. Half the Craig's List replies are pranksters. Even the police thought it was all cover for prostitution. As if whores in Atlanta had to disguise themselves. As if he even looked the fucking part. They finally made an appointment and sent their fake John over with a wire.

They didn't bother him after that.

He wonders sometime if the cops actually held onto the recording, shelved it away somewhere in that dilapidated monstrosity they occupy on Ponce.

He stares over at Maria's pale, shaven legs on the coverlet—ashen in the LED glow. He pops another pill. Retreads the path.

It started when he was nine, up north in the hills of Middle Tennessee. He was the only son of two marginally religious county schoolteachers. He was never sure why they omitted giving him a sex talk. They were educators, after all. As a result, he had no clue what the first explosion of acne was all about, much less the erections. A steady diet of 1987 television offered up cancer as the only suitable answer.

The recipe was simple: a few documentary snippets about out-of-control cell growth here, a little talk of tumors there and the body provides the rest. Sure, nowadays kids might see their first pixilated erections at, what, eight? Maybe seven? But back then even the occasional half-scrambled, Cinemax cock was always flaccid.

A few weeks of paranoia were enough. He found puss-colored leavings in his underwear one evening and the next morning he was in the nurse's office. Somehow he'd managed to stare at her shoes and explain the symptoms. Somehow she hadn't laughed. Instead, Nurse Lane shut him in a room with a VHS tape titled "Changes." It calmed his fears. It also built a framework of plausibility for all the dreams and sweat soaked sheets ahead.

As such, a month later, Simon didn't' scream for an ambulance when he woke to find his groin slick with sour-smelling slime.

Changes.

His dreams became much wetter. In time, he learned to up his liquids intake.

Ectoplasm, after all, is a physical manifestation. It uses the host's own cells and fluids and never returns all it borrows. It's a temporary tumor, a meat puppet scraped together by something from the other side. Without excessive hydration, a particularly strong manifestation is enough to kill you.

But those were lessons for a later day.

Long before he came to loathe the taste of Gatorade and imprisoned his curse inside a strict regiment of behavior, the 11-year-old Simon dreamed fingers caressing him in the dark.

The slick digits slid over his chest and belly. They coiled around the stubborn swell of his phallus. He dreamed of Voyaging Madonna with tits like grain silos, wild-haired Sigourney

116

Weaver and the half-scrambled bodies from the pay channels.

Then he'd wake up wet.

Changes.

In a year's time, it only got worse. His dreams remained vivid, full of glistening TV bodies and intimate caresses. Then things changed—not so much the sensations, but rather the images they dragged through his unconscious mind.

Where once Lieutenant Ripley's fingers traced a ghost map of his veins, now black-green garden slugs slipped across a canvas of chill bumps. He felt their ghastly white bellies, their slow groinward convergence in cold spirals of slime. They'd group together and move up his shaft like a knotted fist, ringing Crisco-clear sludge out in thick, ropey dollops.

He'd wake and for several impossible seconds he'd still feel them in the dark. He'd trash. He'd moan. Sometimes he'd ejaculate and a dull pain would suck through his testicles. The ache would last for hours. Sometimes there was a bit of blood in the mess and it would take all he had to keep from screaming.

And of course things only got worse.

When he was 14 years old, he started wetting the bed—at least that's what his parents thought. There was just too much liquid. The doctor called it "secondary nocturnal enuresis" and they sent him to see a shrink. Then they started driving him to sleep specialists up in Nashville, but the doctors just wanted to hook him up to wires and watch him sleep.

Nothing ever happened at those clinics. That was the weird part. He wouldn't even sweat. The family would drove back home in awkward silence, back to his room with its sci-fi posters and plastic-wrapped mattress. Then the dreams would hit him worse and wetter than ever.

One night he woke up on the ceiling. He opened his eyes from some a paramecium dream and found himself naked, sheathed in a patina of mucus and semen. For one brief moment, he glimpsed a ghostly luminance in the stuff, something emanating from microscopic depths, as if he'd caught the hand of god reaching up through the atoms and molecules and cells.

Then all went dark and he plummeted. He hit the bed and bounced to the side, wiping out everything on the bedside table,

117

destroying the lamp and landing on a busted picture frame.

When his dad bust into the room, he found his son hunched over in a fetal position. He was slick with slime and bleeding from the broken glass. He still had an erection.

The sight must have broken him.

Changes.

The years passed for Simon Dale. His parents split. He dropped out of high school and found his way down to Atlanta. He set to losing himself in what seemed, for a time, an impossible city.

He lived on the street for a while, kicked around Little Five Points with the gutter punks and the homeless. He mingled with stoners and old hippies. Life took on the sickly sweet odor of drink gutters and cigarette smoke. He almost grew to like it.

He worked nights mostly, hustling odd jobs at a handful of bars. He downed a lot of coffee to keep going, and that eventually led to the odd bump of coke or some randomly gifted pill. But it all caught up to him.

It was like when he'd slept dreamless for the sleep doctors. Push it away for too long, bury it with speedballs, whatever—it always came back in spades. More intense. More painful.

Most people talk about ectoplasm emanating from the mouth, nose and ears. But even back in the 40s, they suspected it leaked out though other ports as well.

For Simon, the stuff bleeds out in a glimmering sweat. It squeezes through tear ducts. He's caught himself lactating and his urethra is ever a favored highway. Sometimes it comes out thick and ropy, like pissing a McDonald's milkshake. Other times it emerges rectally.

With an income of sorts, he managed to find a broom closet bedroom in great hovel of a home off Euclid Avenue. He lived amid a revolving assembly of addicts, actors and artists—all fucking, carousing or just ranting to the water stains on the ceiling. It didn't matter what the hour was.

Simon's madness fit in just fine at first. He was just one more nutjob, and a seemingly harmless one at that. Then one of them, a skinhead named Jems busted in on him during an episode and he was out on his ass the next day.

He never found out what the guy had seen. His dreams and nightmares only provided him with images to fit the sensations. He could only guess what forms his fluids took, or the puppet shows they performed in the dark. He never glimpsed more than a waking peak of movement or illumination.

Whispers and rumors made the rounds. It led to odd stares on the street, and eventually to a blind e-mail from a man named Richard Konig.

Konig was an older guy—heavy frame, gray unkempt hair and a wardrobe to match. He usually hung out at a used bookstore in Decatur. Maybe he worked there, but it was never clear. Simon agreed to met him for coffee one Sunday afternoon in November and it wasn't long before they two were seeing each other pretty regular.

An aging, effeminate occultist and a 19-year-old kid. Sure, some people read more into it than there was—or less, actually. They shared a curse. Konig had wrestled with it for a half a century—and he had his tricks.

First he taught Simon how to limit its control. There were certain sleep aids that helped subdue it. Numerous alarm clocks set throughout the night helped too. Finally, he went so far as to show the kid how to turn it into a career.

S imon stares at the glowing AJC article on Marie's computer screen, then gazes off to the mirror across the room. He catches his pale reflection. He looks like shit. Like junky death in a corduroy jacket.

Did milking money from it make him a whore? He has long considered the possibility. For cash, he provided strangers with sufficient bodily secretions to meet their needs. How different was that from any bought-and-sold sex act?

A few séance theatrics and a little self-meditation aside, that's all it was. He'd dim the lights, dip himself into one of the trances Konig taught him and that would open the door inside.

But just a crack.

It took a bit of practice to get it right. It took time.

119

In time, he had his regular customers. The world was full of grieving souls and no shortage of charlatans ready to exploit them. Only Simon didn't give cold readings and generalizations. He would take their money, then close his eyes. He'd tune out and let the gulf beyond the door reach though him.

He'd wake sometime later to an awkward, sometimes empty room. There was never much cleanup. Mere secretions, really, compared to his nightly discharges.

After a year, he had his own apartment and his relationship with Konig blossomed into a legitimate friendship. Each weekend they'd head up to Buford Highway and risk their taste buds on ethnic delicacies. They'd hit the odd improve show. All the while, he suspected Konig had deeper feelings, but he kept them hidden. They both knew there were things in life they'd never have.

As with all relationships, they eventually drifted apart. Business picked up for Simon and Konig left town for a few months when his sister died up in Utah. The better part of a year bled away before Simon reached out to him again. An unanswered ring tone here, a few wrong numbers there. It took the better part of a day to learn that Konig had drowned himself in a bathtub.

Simons's resolve faltered after that. He put off appointments. All he could think about was the old man hanging over the side of a tub. Clear as crystal. Branded into his psyche.

Once more, loneliness filled his life—and he let it claim him for years. He would later wonder if his isolation damaged his ability to converse. Even now, he mixes his words and stumbles with uncertainty through the simplest of exchanges. But his customers know he is the genuine article. They flock to him, cash in hand, from all over the world.

After Konig's death, he hired an accountant and started paying taxes. He bought a loft by the train tracks and sound proofed everything but the windows, the better to let the passing engines wake him through the night. He splurged on pointless trinkets when the mood hit him, but mostly he stuck it away. For what, he could not imagine.

120

Then, in 2009, he met Maria.

He hadn't thought much of her at first—just another short, slightly plump chick in glasses. Just another stranger who took a good night's sleep for granted. Like many others, she came to him requesting an interview. He normally turned journalists down out of hand, but she was persistent. She was nice. There was something in her eyes.

He was standoffish at first, but soon found himself caving to her questions. He talked about his childhood, about his move to Atlanta and his friendship with Konig and how it'd saved his life.

He'd wept, and not fully understood why he was weeping.

She'd held him and he'd not understood what was happening.

It felt like voyeurism the first night. Following a takeout dinner in his loft, she kissed him on the lips and he felt her hands glide across his ribs. He stopped her just short of his belt buckle. Too many strange memories. Too much shrapnel in the mind.

Yet somehow they managed an hour of awkward passion. He explored a foreign anatomy and prevented her from touching him in ways that dredged his nightmares. Draped like cats on the contours of his leather sofa, they fucked until they collapsed in each other's arms. Together, they slept through the night, dreaming nothing but the pitch dark of an egoless, timeless void.

For all its clichés, it was the happiest period of his life. For weeks, they carried on fucking and dining, throwing his money around town with reckless abandon. But he didn't dare sleep another night with her. Too much was at stake. The things on the other side needed their release. They were jealous.

For the first time, he felt something that might be love. Without thinking, he told her everything. All the humiliating details. And she insisted that he needed to let all of that go.

"Don't let your past define you," she was found of saying. "It's just a voice, just your thoughts getting on top of you."

She told him that he'd spent too much time in his own head. That he'd beat himself up too long and built psychic cages. She told him he needed to let himself be happy for once.

He'd bought into all of it, and then she stopped returning

his calls.

Her article published and he raged that it had all been a feminine ploy. Something worthy of a soap opera. He ranted to his lawyer, demanded the story purged from existence.

And still he called.

He belted off furious e-mails, pleading texts and love letters devoid of all punition. Finally, he looked up her address, cursing his own naivety. She'd always insisted her apartment was too small, always showed up at the loft to spend Simon Dale's money and jot down his life.

S imon pops another pill and cranks his system up for another hour of ragged alertness. He places Marie's laptop back on the desk and watches the gray light spill over her naked body. She wears a death mask of congealed slime. Her mouth and nostrils are packed thick with it.

Everything is as he found it 12 hours ago and the apartment reeks of death. He has forced himself awake for days, but the little details still jump out at him. The flowers he bought her are still vaguely alive in a vase by the table. The bed is half slept in. There are 38 messages on her answering machine.

Her eyes are wide open and somehow he knows that Konig's were too.

He keeps thinking about his one true friend drowned in a bathtub. Fluid in the lungs. His only love suffocated with a face full of slime, and he's sure he knows where it came from.

The filet knife from the kitchen should do the trick, but first he has to know.

He has to see.

Five more hours and the lights begin to quiver in the corners. Spider worms work their way into his vision, then vanish in a breath. He swallows more pills.

He beings to sweat and lays down on her couch. He blinks and feels the flow of warm liquid over flesh.

At last, Simon watches it rise over him like a mounted lover. The mystery hid from him these 5,000 nights. A jealous lover. Its liquid skin glimmers like something forged in the deepest ocean crevice. A wash of veins fork endlessly, breathing and quivering with light.

A thousand other forms tease through its vaguely humanoid form: feelers and suction pads, antennas and pornographic mouthparts. All of it formed from his horrid leavings. He glimpses dark, fecal specks floating through its fluid body like motes of dusts in cinema.

The strange lover bends over him and Simon gazes into a familiar face: a lustrous, amorphous mirror of his own countenance.

He remembers Maria's plea that he love himself more—that he cling to hope more than misery. He remembers Konig's smile and the worrying look his parents gave him on those long car rides back from Nashville. And he realizes how terrible a form he has constructed all these years.

The puppet locks lips with its author.

The glow becomes blinding.

He can scarcely breathe.

My Father's Hands

There are times when I forget pop's hands. If I drift through a night of dreamless sleep, or curl up in bed with just the right woman, I'll wakeup oblivious to those memories. But then someone will say "sonny" or I'll see a can of beans on a grocery shelf and it will all come gushing back into my mind like backed-up sewage. In an instant, I'm 7 again. Weak. Cowering. Just like that.

I try to avoid canned foods, just to be on the safe side. If I see them, I remember having to wind open first one, then another, all while Pop cooed and drooled in the living room of my childhood home. Pop couldn't perform the task himself, see, what with his having eels for hands.

Maybe this detail doesn't mean that much to you. I know there was a lot of that going around after the June Incident. It touched countless families, and a lot of people didn't let it ruin their lives. But Pop was already a bit addled to begin with, before the change came over him.

Mom caught the sickness first, and far worse than Pop. Her hands and feet changed on her, then her hands ate her feet and she had to be put in one of those hospital beds with a plastic tent over it. We went and visited her once, but Pop wouldn't let me look in and see her. Years later, I'd see pictures of Class A Juno victims on the Internet, the way it warped and blackened the whole body, and I'd understand what he was trying to shield me from.

But pop was always a creep—I've heard the stories from Aunt Paula. He'd always had a drinking problem and the drink could make him cruel. So I can't blame him too much for everything he became. Some of it was the sickness, some of it was the anguish and the stress of losing Mom. On top of that, none of the whores in town would touch him anymore—and he couldn't even amuse himself, not the way a normal man can, not when his arms terminated in those creatures: Fishy black flesh. Unblinking eyes. Idiot, gape-jawed grins like something from a fever dream of Hell.

Of course he wasn't a complete invalid. After I'd opened the beans for him, he was able to cope just fine. He'd sink the head of each eel-hand into a can and I'd just have to stand there listening to the sound of 'em sucking it up. Next he'd shamble over to that spring-shot easy chair of his. He'd watch TV for hours, sipping gin from the side table through a straw.

I ain't gonna pretend my case is worse than anybody else's. Everyone knows that liquor hits Juno people in a peculiar way. However drunk they get, the hands get drunker. If I was lucky, Pop would drink so much that the eels would just hang comatose at his sides, glassy eyes staring off into space all lidless and un-pupiled. But most of the time he'd have just enough to set them off.

Then he'd ask me to come over and sit on his lap.

There'd come a time when I'd try and run away, but for the longest he was always able to catch me. Sometimes I'd wake up weeping, and feel all those little mouths nibbling on me, squirm-ing against my flesh. I try not to blame Pop too much, though. It was the booze. It was mom's death. It was that damned thing that fell from the sky in June.

I took to running off after a while. I couldn't stick around and endure him, but I also couldn't up and leave. It was the only home I knew and, on some level, I still loved him. A boy's world is his father, whether he likes it or not. Plus, I didn't have a clue where I'd go or how jobs and paychecks worked. Grown-up life was a mystery, one that seemed to elude Pop as well. He received a government check each month and he'd send me in to town to buy groceries and booze. Mr. Arnold at the liquor store sold it to me with a look of pity and shame. All I could do was skim as much money as I dared and hide it away in the old rusted pickup chassis out back. Once I'd saved up enough, maybe I'd have a clue what to do with it.

I know you've probably tuned into the Juno preachers on TV and heard 'em sermonize about children just like me. "How sharper than a serpent's tooth," they like to quote. But I was no mere ungrateful child. I didn't plan on running away because of the deformities or on account of his being ostracized from soci-ety. And, again, I didn't blame him for the worst of what he did. It was what the Juno sickness had done to his life—and it was those damn eels. But doing nothing, saying nothing has a way of eating through your heart after a while.

I walked into town one day, making sure to wear my best shirt and slacks—the ones mom had given me before she got ill. They were a little tight in the crotch and the way my legs and forearms stuck out made me look like a scarecrow. But they were clean.

I went straight to the Baptist Church and asked to confess. I thought they'd have a booth to walk into, one like on the mystery show Pop always watched. Instead, they just introduced me to a burley man with short-cropped hair named Pastor Dan. His tight, button-up shirt seemed to strain to hold in his massive, hairy chest.

I told him everything—things I didn't even really think I knew. Looking back, I guess I'd blocked out some of the worst of it. But Pastor Dan didn't flinch at the details. He just nodded his great head and, as if in computation of the facts, snorted briskly and eyed the great crucifix above the baptismal altar.

"If thy right hand offends thee," was all he said—words I might have understood if we'd ever been church-going folks.

Then he offered me an afternoon of work. Seems they needed someone to help paint the fence that separated them from those "Godless Church of Christ." Plus, he told me he'd pay me and that there was nothing like honest labor to distract a boy from his worries.

Naturally, I said yes. Here was a strong, healthy man of God, everything my father and disastrous life were not. And I couldn't' say no to the money.

The fence he showed me was massive—more a great wooden dorsal fin jetting up through the earth. It was made of every scrap of wood you could nail to another, constructed with manic, slipshod carpentry on both sides. The Baptist wall and the Church of Christ wall kind of merged into one, and it looked like it had been an ongoing contest of who could build their side the highest. It was hard work, but the Baptists were offering me peace, 20 bucks and all the lemonade I could drink.

It's easy to look back now and say I should have known. I shouldn't have been shocked when I opened the front door to our house later that afternoon. I might have guessed how Pastor Dan would handle things. When I walked in, Pop was curled up on the hardwoods, still bleeding from where they'd' hacked the eels off just above the elbow.

He yammered in a senseless murmur when I came in, wallowed and slid in the great slick of blood, but I finally was able to tell he was asking for the gin bottle and the straw. Only they'd shattered all the bottles in the corner, as that was sin too. So I bandaged his stumps the best I could with lengths of ripped bed sheets.

It still horrifies me, but part of me felt a sense of relief. It told me my father might recover and lead a normal, albeit further disabled life. Failing that, at least he might die free of those awful hands and their appetites.

I laid him up in his favorite chair and threw the still-squirming eel limbs into the bathtub. I wasn't sure if I needed to draw water for them, nor fully processed why I'd want to if they did, so I just left them dry.

I didn't call the hospital. Going to the church hadn't done much for Pop's health, and all the doctors really did for mom was draw out her suffering. Towards the end, she'd been nothing but a mockery of the woman who'd raised me.

Pale as a sheet beneath bloody smears, Pop regained enough consciousness to make a final request: he wanted me to put the last of the baked beans in a skillet and fry them up for him. He asked me to use a bit of molasis. To cut up a hot dog.

And so I did it, my motions like those in a dream. As if I willed my hands to action and they performed independent of my conscious will. I opened the last can of beans and poured in a hefty dollop of molasses. I lit the stovetop. I chopped up a hot dog and browned the little drums of pork flesh. Then I poured in the rich, brown mess of beans and syrup and listened as the hiss of frying drowned beneath the flood.

In the end, he only ate a little of it—and most of that wound up dribbling down his chin when I spooned it to him. He grew more and more glassy-eyed, pale as milk and mumbling nonsense. Then he died—all while the TV blared Technicolor drama and painted the dim room with its garish, pixilated palette. Old men weaved among the young, solving mysteries and putting things to right.

I don't know how long I sat there beside him, my mind clouded with nameless emotions that are not quite grief. I might have stayed there all night had I not heard the sound of something flopping around in the bathtub.

I left his side and walked back through the squalid kitchen, back to the urine-reeking bathroom and looked down upon them as if for the first time: bleeding, undying things, slick with a blood that was not their own. I snatched them up and brought them back into the kitchen. I threw them down on the countertop beside the deflated hotdog package. I grabbed the knife.

Did it feel good to hack into those awful things? Cathartic? I'm not sure. My malice felt as if it bled out through some distant wound I barely felt. Phantom cuts on phantom limbs. I watched the black gristle twist about with each chop. The things made no sound save their movements—no squeal, cry nor even breathe.

With each chop the mess grew and spread across the countertop. I soon discovered the things didn't even have skulls or ribs or spines. It was just hand and finger bones in there, perverted to serve as scaffolding for a new flesh. I don't know why that unsettled me so much, but it did. Somehow I wanted to pull a misshapen skull and slender fish bones from those shreds of black and greasy gore. I wanted to wrench the alien from the known. Instead I discovered that what had once been Pop's ulna and radius bones segmented into spinal columns.

I chopped harder, wilder till I could hardly see what I was doing for the tears.

I think all the moving stopped after a while.

The rest of my childhood, if you want to call it that, followed the prescribed path for kids like me. I was taken to a hospital, then put in a special home. Eventually, they hooked me up with a string of low-paying jobs, mostly working with Juno folks at shelters and such.

I'm not sure why they thought I was such a good fit for that. Maybe they figured people like me were immune, even though the doctors on TV claim you can't catch the sickness from other folks. It only spread during the incident. To catch it now, you'd have to trek out to the site where the asteroid hit, past the soldiers, the wall and the stinking wasteland beyond—and that's all the way over in Arkansas.

Still, I was able to afford a small place above a local bakery. In my spare time, I'd sometimes watch the eel preachers on TV. They're fond of that one quote in particular: "I have held many things in my hands, and I have lost them all; but whatever I have placed in God's hands, that I still possess."

It doesn't quite mean what the Juno victims think it does, but still I turn to prayer from time to time. I try to separate pop from the equation as much as possible, though it's not easy. I construct a heavenly father wholesale out of their sermons and scripture readings, but half the time I'm not sure what I'm piecing together. I know I'm jabbering to the same God that the Baptists and the Church of Christ worship, but I like to think this one's different: kinder maybe, slower to action but more prone to listening. Sometimes it works.

For a whole, when TV church didn't quite cut it, I'd go to one of the strip clubs to watch the "eel dancers." A lot of the smaller clubs have a special stage in the back, just for folks who prefer that kind of woman. It's strange that their hypnotic undulations, all set to sexed-up beats, should have calmed me so—especially given the sights and sensations that filled my nightmares.

One of the eel dancers at the Bone Shack was a girl named Emma, and it got to where she'd chat with me between shifts—often just for the sake of talking. Her body was sleek and pale, the skin swirling to black just above where the remnants of her elbow bones would be. She kept her hair dyed amber and her breath always smelled of menthol cigarettes. She liked to dance to Billy Idol when she had a say in the matter.

It's from her I learned that drinking a lot of coffee allows Juno folks better control over their hands—and that harder stuff can even let them see through those glassy little eyes.

"And more," she whispered once, as one of her eels slid softly along my thigh at the bar, "My friend Ron said he did a bunch of Meth once and saw all kinds of stuff—like other worlds . . . "

It helped rid the nightmares when we started seeing each other after hours—even more when she took me as her lover. It seems like it should have terrified me to feel those little mouths nibble at my tingling flesh, even as she took me into hers. But somehow it made me feel whole again.

Soon, we started getting coke regular from one of the bouncers and we'd lay awake at night, wrapped in each other's arms, and she'd tell me the things she could see: whole planets made of ocean, islands rising up through the stars and something about a great white throne.

We've talked about moving in with each other, but Juno folks can only live in certain housing sectors—and while there'd be nothing illegal about us shacking up, it's the kind of move that can be a bit risky, especially in the South.

Still, I hang out at her place much of the time. She works at the club most nights and I do all the shopping, cooking and cleaning while she's gone. I buy her cans of garbanzo beans, since they seem to please just as well and don't stir the worst of my memories. I've never really been able to stand the taste of Gin, but it's growing on me. I guess it's the "hair of the dog" and all. Whatever doesn't kill you, right? I believe that's the quote, but I've no clue who said it.

Emma's quite fond of quotes—did I mention that? I think most Juno folks are, as if all humanity's wisdom had just been waiting for that rock to fall from the sky. It puts a new spin on most everything. I'd never noticed how many quotes there are about hands.

One night, following another bout of speed-fueled love making, she leaned in nose to nose with me and, eels squirming all over my chest, nipping immodestly, she recited something she'd picked up from her friend Ron.

"The opportunity to secure ourselves against defeat lies in our own hands," Emma said.

I've given that a lot of thought recently. I've swished it around with the fragments she relates from her most drug-statured visions. She thinks we should move to Arkansas—says a lot of Juno folks are making the pilgrimage, but I'm not so sure.

That night, looking into her eyes—her human eyes—I was pretty sure she wasn't talking to me. She was lost in the contemplation of unimaginable visions, things she only hints at in the depths of our lovemaking, when we've purged ourselves of all breathe and moisture.

Her expression was so full of marvel, and I can only wonder what was actually staring back at me through those jade and jellied eyes—and what animated all the hands that made me what I am.

A Curious Void

I don't blame you this awkward silence, friend. There's no delicate way to ask me what you came to ask. No graceful segue to steer a conversation into those dark waters. But of course you haven't realized this yet. I bet you even think we'll get there organically.

"So hey, speaking of sexual mutilation . . . "

Yeah, it's not going to happen. If you don't just blurt it out, you'll wait till it's too late. So by all means, build up your courage. Take another hit from the pipe. A guest in my house is a guest at my bong, right?

There you go. A generous inhalation of smoke always gives a man a moment to collect his thoughts. Pull out of the conversation, view it from the outside and refine strategy. It's what I miss most about cigarettes.

Just don't inhale too deep, trust me. My unfortunate condition requires a very mind-numbing blend of high-grade medicinal marijuana—or so my psychiatrist tells me. Choke on this stuff and we'll be here all night. We'll just wind up baked in my living room, digging through this expanse of coffee table clutter for lost lighters. All the while, you'll gaze off into space like some Burning Man wanderer. And then how will you ever get your question out? How will you ever drown this fear?

Yeah, it's that palpable. If I were a lion (ha!), I'd have already pounced.

So take it easy. I know you'd rather just talk shop about the flesh trade for another half hour and then get to your question.

There's an odd look in your eyes as you put lips to the mouthpiece. Do I look that strange to you? This bald, pale figure, equal parts ghoul and Adonis—cast in the glare of an endless Fox News marathon. Perhaps you wonder if my condition altered my politics. Or do I find something morbidly amusing in this endless tickertape ejaculation of horror and celebrity idolatry?

Here's the truth of it: I love the media. I love it like a fat kid loves candy. And I'm sure that puzzles you somewhat, since most of what you know about my condition comes to you via their journalistic excess.

You came here to ask about the assault. You drove all the way out here on Friday night, no less, because you think knowledge will protect you or give you some edge that all the other victims lacked. Maybe you even think you'll solve the crime!

If so, keep sucking on that pipe.

But here's one more layer to this: I know that deep down it's not even about protecting your own skin. You want to know what it's like.

What's it like to wake up to the bludgeoning blows of a home invader? What's it like to feel bizarre hands on your body, stripping you bare? What's it like to have your manhood sliced from you by some faceless monster in the night?

What's life like without a cock?

I know these are all difficult concepts for you to wrap your head around. See, I used to be just like you. My cock was my center of being. It was the cornerstone of my identity. Bear with me, friend, because I like to break this fact of life down into two core arguments.

First off, let's not deny it: The penis is the center of every male's life and every truly honest man will tell you the same. You can't begrudge him the fact—no more than you can fault the rutting violence in his heart. Because deep down, he is nothing but a necessary mutation. He's an accident of evolution.

Give the bra burners their due, friend, because the XX chromosomes are where it's at. That's the species. That's the human race. XY is just an accident that helps spread the genetic diversity around. If you want to see the score, just look to the ants and the wasps. Their males exist to mate and then they have the decency to fucking perish.

Me and you? We're just drones that flew the hive's fuck chambers millions of years ago, back in some prior evolutionary form. Now we rule the roost. We run companies, buy cars, run for president, play video games, shoot guns, write books, cut albums and do just about anything else we goddamn want to.

But we never fully escape our dronehood. Hell, we build shrines to it. We make it a religion.

You see a pretty girl, you think about fucking her. You see

an ugly one, all the same. Don't deny it. Every casual strokefest in the shower is an act of devotion, every carnal indulgence the fulfillment of divine mandate.

"I fuck therefore I am". Famous quote. Look it up.

So has my condition made me an apostate to our faith? Not quite. Remember, those bizarre hands in the night didn't take everything from me. "Porn star turned eunuch" works nicely in a headline but it's an inaccurate depiction.

Let's imagine I dropped my pants for you right now. Beneath the twisted scar of my penectomy, you'd find a fully functional set of balls. Yep, I still shave them. Old habits, right? And if you were to lean in close and I was to lift up this shorn clutch of masculine remnants, you'd notice a small hole just behind my scrotum.

There it is, right along the line of my scrotal raphe—what you probably call the taint.

That little hole is the new opening for my urethra—the terminus of a tiny length of surgically-implanted tubing. I know it doesn't feel this way, but urination control doesn't reside in the penis. Why would it when the masculine form is just a design variant for reproduction? It's internal, friend. And that's why I don't have to lug around a catheter.

Theoretically, I can even ejaculate through that tiny hole. Does that surprise you? It shouldn't. After all, I still have erogenous zones and most amazing of all, the scar tissue itself becomes a center of stimulation. Curious, isn't it? In the absence of my biologic center, I become the scar. I become the void.

Not that I've really explored it all that much. Self-love doesn't really interest me these days and the last time I had sex was before the incident.

I don't think I'll ever forget her face. Her name was Kristi.

But I was talking about cock worship, wasn't I? As I said, all men center their lives around that oh-so-precious tube of meat. I won't attempt to shoehorn homosexuality into this philosophy of mine, but I do wonder if gay men are merely more honest about their phallic fixations.

Go ahead, by all means, take another hit off that bong.

We're unique cases, you and I. I mean hell, we built careers around our beautiful cocks, didn't we? Sure, my days as an adult actor ended over a year ago, but you're still all over the goddamn place. What is it, 15 films a year? Three shoots a week for whatever mega site's dealing out checks? That was pretty much my career too, while it lasted.

Just look at us. I could probably conjure up a rough headcount of the men I've slept with. I'm sure you could too. But the women? Forget it. Yeah, you thump your chest with rough estimations, but it would take some serious Internet research to pull off an accurate count, am I right?

All those faces, all those heaving bodies. It all runs together after a while. The industry chews up most of the girls pretty quickly. A few stick around just long enough to lose their minds, but the others flee back to as much of a normal life they can claim for themselves. Sometimes an ill-gotten child turns up years later to remind you what all that fucking really serves in the grand scheme of things.

But so it goes, right?

They might have been the stars, but we were the cocks that drilled a thousand holes—high priests of the XY, centers of adoration for whores and at-home viewers alike. We've all made jokes about how they should really write the checks out to our sex organs, but doesn't that one hit close to home?

So to answer your silent question, yes, my penectomy has forced quite a shift in my self-identity. I lost my biological and emotional mooring in pretty much the most traumatic way possible. I've spent a lot of time getting used to that. I ran from it at first, but in the end I confronted it. I used to overflow with selfhatred every time I saw a cable news channel and now I never turn the damn thing off.

I also smoke a lot of high-grade weed. My doctor's amazing. I breathe deep. I climb into the cloud and I use it all to find my place in the universe.

The fringe benefit is that I don't dream anymore. Yep, that nameless maniac out there in the night? The one who butchered 11 male porn stars and left 10 of them dead? He doesn't waltz the halls of my nightmares, friend.

Can you say the same?

But now you're coughing. Jesus, man, didn't I warn you

about this weed? You'll be too wasted for follow-up questions at this rate. Here, drink from this thermos. It's fruited tea—real health nut stuff.

I still take care of myself. I keep in shape. It's actually kind of liberating, you know, to build muscle mass for something beyond mere fucking.

There you go, drink up.

Perhaps I'm being presumptuous and drastically overestimating your intellect, but I assume your next question would have related to the phallic world we live in. Skyscrapers, towers, columns, obelisks—everywhere you look there's another monument to the almighty cock, casting its swollen shadow across world.

The fact rarely registers in the sunlit waters of the human psyche—you know, the place we spend most of our thinking. But if you were to dive down into the murky, neurological depths, you'd find a different score.

We've been driving home masculine superiority for thousands of years, ever since we drones wrested our patriarchal powers from the rest of the species. But just as the tree of liberty must be refreshed from time to time with the blood of patriots, so too must the sorcery of our dominance.

That's no secret, friend. Feminists and anthropologists generally won't shut up about it. In ancient time, child sacrifice was the male priest's way of canceling out the female act of creation. And when that was done, our brutish ancestors set out to wage wars of rape across the landscape of a prehistoric world. We did it for resources, sure. We did it out of tribal intolerance. But we also did it to show those bitches that the Y chromosome alone ruled the Earth.

Just glance up at the Fox News that illuminates this room and you'll see that rape is still a tool of war in sub-Saharan Africa. It continues to enforce the Rule of Man in other corners of the world too, but we've come to depend on other tools as well. We've crafted elegant religions around masculine deities. We've limited female purity to a very narrow set of parameters.

But then came the modern world. It's all different now. God is dead. Feminists continue to rebel against the patriarchy, claiming new victories every day. But we continue to hold down the fortress and we protect our hallowed faith with the 20th century's most awesome weapon.

Still coughing a little, eh? Drink some more. I know its bitter, but it sooths to soul.

The Internet is the Culture. It's both library and chamber pot, reliquary and rubbish heap. Welcome to the defaecareum. We pour what we are into its immeasurable vastness and divine who we are in by the Godlike hypersigil that emerges. A billion billion images combine to form the reflection of who and what we are.

Do you see where I'm going, friend? Do you see the role we've played in it all along?

I'm sure the wealth of feminist content on the Web is pretty fucking staggering. We celebrate their wisdom and beauty to an almost ridiculous degree. We decry their plight and tout their superiority. It's all out there on the web, a mere key stroke away like everything else.

But in retaliation, we've unleashed an unstoppable tide. We've saturated the culture with the coital image of the female spread eagle before our rutting, indomitable rule.

On screens around the world, they worship the cock. They bow low before its power and grow weak against the ferocity of its physical ingress. The world watches as we fuck them and mold them to our will.

How much simulated rape do you think exists out there in digital ether? How much poolside debasement played out by actors before a smut lord's camera? Like it or not, you're a soldier in the army of rape, friend. And so was I.

I'm sure you've grown tired of the words "violence against women," but that too plays an essential role. Just think of horror movies as infantry support for the pornographic artillery. All those damsels in distress, all those screaming sexpots bloodied by some B-movie maniac's machete—it's human sacrifice for a new age. It all drives home the point.

You've grown rather silent, friend. Is it starting to sink in? Because I remember the day it sank in for me.

Only my first and final sexual partners continue to resonate with me. The early one was unimportant—just some fumbling tryst on a middle school bus. But the last one was an 18 year old named Kristi Vargas, just some random blond at a FFM shoot. We did it gonzo. Full anal. A little choking. Just another day at the races.

I didn't think anything of it at the time. Fuck, I barely enjoyed it. You run into a girl like that every week and never see their face again.

Except I did see the Vargas girl's face again. It was an 8x10 photograph. I think it was from her high school yearbook.

The private dick who showed up on my doorstep didn't know about the scene we'd filmed. I think it was actually online by that point, but hey, maybe he just doesn't go for the rougher stuff. What I'm saying is he wasn't looking for an autograph. He showed up with a whole different agenda in mind.

It turned out that Kristi Vargas had decided to run away from home and follow in the footsteps of her mother. Or at least that's how I assembled the puzzle pieces when that Burbank sleezebag handed me the photo, mentioned the mother's name and rolled out a sob story about crystal meth.

"We figured she might try and seek you out," he'd told me through a mouthful of chew.

Because I'm her father.

No, I don't think she knew. Or is that some vague hope? Some final shred of decency I attribute to the world? Some final totem of shame to adorn these tattered emotional vestments I wear.

I don't know.

I barely remember her mother. Like I said, these women disappear and yeah, sometimes they drift back into your life with a child. Your know the score as well as anyone, but of course my case was special.

What were the chances, right?

By the look in your eyes, I can tell you've begin to guess the deeper truth here. Go ahead, try to run. Try to wrestle me to the floor. Brain me with my own bong and call the cops. Hit the headlines! But of course you can't even get up from the sofa, not given the stuff in the fruit tea you've been downing.

Didn't I tell you my doctor was the best? And didn't I warn you not to hit that pipe too hard?

There's no "Hollywood porn mutilator" or "serial emasculator" like the media and the authorities so resolutely believe. Or rather, there has only ever been me. I took the knife to myself on that long woeful night. Out of shame. Out of misery. I'd brought one ounce of innocent possibility into the world unknowingly, and with just much blind oblivion I'd defiled it.

I went out and got ripped at a bar. I provoked some coked-up biker and got the shit beat out of me. And then I drove home and dug the sharpest knife I could find out of the cutlery drawer. The actual procedure was over in an instant. Most men would shit themselves if they knew how fragile that bit of flesh really is.

At first I just wanted to bleed out there in my bed. These scars on my throat are from where I almost expedited the process.

But then I had a vision. In my pain and delirium, I glimpsed the armies of rape marching through a landscape of soot-blackened obelisks. I saw their vile banners and their chained armies of slaves. I saw an endless road lined with the spitted bodies of a thousand screaming women and know all too well the dark god they honored in their vileness. All that horror streamed up into the night like phantoms rising from an immeasurable grave, a billion pixilated accounts of masculine ascendancy.

And I immediately saw what needed to be done.

I'm going to go grab the camera and the knife now, friend. I assume you've forced yourself to watch the other short films I've made, right? The ones our 'mysterious' serial killer uploads after each crime? The emasculations of our former colleagues Max, Pieter, Bill and Emil are all just a key stroke away.

It's amazing how fast the footage spread on the net—more amazing still how it never goes away. We feel compelled to view it. We force ourselves to see.

100 million hits for poor Emil. And that was before police found the body.

We're chipping away at the walls of patriarchy tonight, friend. We're defacing one more tile in the mosaic of culture, vandalizing the hypersigil till one day the whole image shifts.

I wish I could say you won't feel a thing, but I'm trying to be as honest as possible.

The pain will be incredible.
So will the release.

Poppy Farr

Poppy Farr lives alone and passes her time by writing about the apocalypse. She likes to think that if her predictions ever come true she will be well prepared and ready for anything. On the other hand, if nothing ever happens, at least she has given everyone a good scare and hopefully a few nightmares. Also she has cats.

The Arrival

Sometimes it was so long before I would speak to another person that I began to forget I was human. I forgot about my body; I was a floating cloud, a consciousness. The electric impulses of my thoughts moving sinuously, the rest of me, separated, moving dreamlike about my tiny quarters. My tongue would become thick and swollen, a fat useless organ. So when I did occasionally speak, to remind myself I could, my voice would lisp and slur, my tongue flopping about my mouth like a dying fish.

With her it was different, we talked, our tongues whipping like quicksilver, my forgotten arms gesturing, making shapes in the air.

It began when they constructed new quarters next to mine; it was news to the fifteen of us, huddled in our homes, humped like armadillos. Squatting like toads on the ice, whilst winds howled over our curved roofs, we watched the machines assemble her home.

For the first time in months Ben, our MP, called a meeting, I shuffled over to my TV, with a flicker it activated, fifteen faces stared back at me including my own. I looked tired.

'Somebody new is coming'

It wasn't unusual for a new person to join, we weren't the only town huddled on the vast Antarctic continent. Thousands had come when it became clear that this was the only safe place left. They were still coming, only now, fifteen years on; they had slowed to a trickle. We didn't need to group together, but some remnant of our humanity meant we did. The only stipulation was there could be no more than twenty. Otherwise, things got dangerous, as the first settlers had discovered.

Their camps were out there somewhere, burned out husks, long since engulfed by ice, but we remembered them.

In the years before I joined there was panic, needy people visiting one another sharing homes, to stay human, to be a community. The thought made me blanch, the horror of another person in my home making my skin prickle. But with the visiting came infection. The government dealt with it quickly, in the only way they could to keep us pure. Annihilation. And they learned. New separate heated homes to kill virus, surrounded by cold to stop the dreaded visiting.

Once they had proved they could eradicate infection, more people had come, the second wave, my wave. We left our panic rooms and bunkers, shed cumbersome haz-mat suits and breathing apparatus and came here, to the white land, Antarctica, to be free and to survive.

The cold kept us in our airtight germ-free homes and we lived like moles in the heat and humidity, hibernating from one another never leaving, never touching, barely speaking. It was not a life, true, but we were alive. No human touched anything we ate, drank or used. The government instigated a regime, our food grown on automated farms, delivered by air. Hardy little servo machines distributed it, we each had our own and they never mingled. Our clothes, synthetic, disposable, our air scrubbed a thousand times, so when you tasted it on your tongue it was flat and slightly chemical.

I hadn't felt fresh air on my skin or in my lungs for ten years, but it was a sacrifice I was prepared to make in order to live.

Ben, as MP was in charge of maintaining our essential systems from a tiny pod attached to his home. He was the only one who could communicate with the outside world, it never occurred to any of us to care. We were safe and warm, cocooned in our isolation.

I didn't even watch the news after the first year. They stopped broadcasting it. Who cared about the outside world? It was filled with images of the dead and dying. Great cities emptied, then burned as mass disinfection got out of control. At first I watched with horror, then sadness, then acceptance, then I was numb. The numbness took over as the years passed, I had lost someone once, a wife, I occasionally remembered. But her face was blurred, as was my life before the infection. Another life. Another man.

Now I lived as a cloud, in a dream. But I lived, and that was everything. It was the focus of my thoughts as I exercised in my

143

mini gym, as I took a stinging disinfectant shower, as I blasted the dry skin from my body in my vacuum chamber, and in the days and weeks when I spoke to no-one staring blindly out at the white on white that was my world. Over and over sometimes whispering, sometimes shouting until I lived by it, a drumbeat, a rhythm, a heartbeat, fierce, a reminder. Alive.

She came the day after the meeting. I watched through my thick porthole. In the harsh light I could see other faces watching. Nobody was excited, it was just a change, a blip in the endless monotony of our days, reminding us each of our own arrival, the fear of exposure and the relief as the door closed behind us and hot safe air hissed in.

The tank-like transport trundled across the ice field, manoeuvring alongside the airlock door and sealing the join. We could not see her enter. The transport was fully automated to prevent contamination on arrival. We all knew the statistics, survival of the virus was heightened in the cold dry air, our only protection the sweltering continuous heat of our humid little bubbles.

The lights went on, they were automatic, but it meant that she was inside, I wondered at her thoughts. The day I arrived I wept with relief then showered, disinfecting until I burned. It had taken days for my skin to recover.

I watched for a long time, the light shone in her porthole; there was no movement.

Ben gathered us to welcome her, our sixteenth, the first townsperson in four years. We waited for her. It took a while; I had forgotten the disorientation upon arrival, the lack of coherent day and night, I had slept endlessly. I wondered if she would be the same. She answered whilst I was lost in thought and it took me a moment to digest her image. She was tousled; sleep still clinging to her face. Her hair was short as was everyone's on arrival. Some grew it again but most kept it shorn out of habit or fear of infection. Her face was flushed with colour. I compared it with ours alongside it onscreen. We were wan and grey, flat-eyed, dull.

Ben launched into a welcome speech, we were not expected to speak, just to be visible onscreen so she knew who we were. A pointless antiquated formality. He introduced us by name and she moved her lips along with him, it was such a human gesture, my heart momentarily contracted. She was actually trying to remember our names! I had not done so. I couldn't remember the moment they stuck in my brain, absorbing into me via osmosis.

I thought about her that day, I found myself watching her porthole again. I couldn't see any movement. It wasn't big enough to see. I wondered how she was settling in and then chastised myself. I had never watched any of the others this way, nor had they aroused my curiosity. What was it about her? I thought back, her face, so alive, so vibrant. Everyone had the same expression when they arrived, cowed, heavy, defeated. She looked . . . different, unafraid, excited even.

I remembered her mouthing along as Ben spoke. Remarkable! She had smiled politely at the end of Ben's speech, thanked us all for welcoming her and expressed gladness to be here. Most people weren't even listening; I could see it in their faces, the same expression that usually sat on mine, indifference, boredom, flat-eyes, grey skin.

For the first time I wondered what they were thinking, were they too struck by her unabashed humanity? I looked at my own face on the monitor, my own eyes. Blank, flat, grey. My face was no different.

She ended the meeting with a smile, promising to stay in touch. Nobody flickered an eyelid at that comment. We knew what it used to mean in the old world, but in the new one, to keep in touch was dangerous. Now that she had been welcomed only Ben would speak to her. Staying in touch was just a polite thing to say. We never said it, of course, but often people arriving would say it automatically until they adjusted fully to their new way of living.

In those first few weeks I often found myself gazing at her porthole, wondering how she was adjusting to our sparse way of life. I was more alert, purposeful; I didn't drift along in a dream anymore. What was it about the woman that preoccupied me?

Six weeks after her arrival I was taking afternoon exercise on my mini-bike when my TV chimed.

My day had begun like any other; I had taken my habitual position at the porthole, peering at her home so close to mine. We had entered a period of constant sun and the white of the snow stretching to infinity all around us was blinding, I liked it, it made me feel pure. After a few hours of fruitless staring I had retreated to my exercises.

I climbed off my bike curious; my TV flickered as I sat down, revealing one face instead of the anticipated fifteen. My confusion was reflected back to me as my face joined hers on-screen. She was smiling tentatively, her face still healthy and plump. My tongue felt fat in my mouth. I waited for her to speak. She leaned forward,

'Hello?'

I cleared my throat but my voice still cracked.

'Hi'

The sound of my voice was strange, I tried to recall the last time I had used it. Only Ben spoke during meetings so it must have been six months at least.

She looked perturbed,

'Uh, when is the next meeting?'

I felt a little flicker of irritation, and deeper down a twist of disappointment, was that all?

'I don't know'

'But you have them once a month right?'

She had an American accent; nationality didn't matter here, especially since nobody spoke. But it was interesting.

'Ben calls them.'

'When do y'all speak to each other?'

I felt at a loss, irritated, I didn't know what to say to her, surely she understood our way of living, surely someone had explained it? She was talking again but I couldn't hear the words. I was filled with fear. Fear that Ben would know we were talking; fear that the others would know. It wasn't illegal, but we didn't want to, we had no interest in one another, and there were memories, the first settlers.

She was still talking; I cut her off mid sentence.

'I'm sorry, I can't help, ask Ben.'

I flicked off my TV and stood, trembling. Adrenalin sang through my body.

She wanted to talk to me.

A week went by. I didn't stand in the porthole and watch.

I wanted to.

My mind felt different, thoughts rushed and tumbled instead of slotting into place absentmindedly. I wondered if she had called Ben. I thought about her face. She looked so healthy. Where had she been before here?

I found myself wondering about the outside world for the first time in years. What was left? It was fifteen years since the outbreak; before I came here I used to imagine going back to my life, getting a job, a house. I remember the day I knew things would never be the same. That was the day I signed up for Antarctica.

Something was wrong. I couldn't put my finger on it. I was doing things differently. One evening I turned on my TV and flicked through hundreds of channels of static, just to see if there were any stations still broadcasting. I couldn't stay quiet; the silence seemed oppressive where before it had been velvety. I didn't realise at first, but I was making sounds under my breath, they clicked in time with the word circling around in my head.

Alive.

But I didn't feel the same glee I used to. I felt transparent. Not all there.

I think I knew she would call again, I think I was waiting.

'Hello?'

'Hi'

'Can we talk?'

'Yeah'

It was easier the second time. I was ready. In the weeks since that first call I had been storing up words, thoughts, things to share without realising I was doing it. I had looked out over the ice and wondered at the wave-like patterns of the wind, I had remembered the Aurora Australis stretching across the sky, rippling, green, mesmerising. I had watched servo machines crawl on humped roofs and for the first time, wondered where they went at night. And who had come up with the design of our buildings? Identically humped, smooth.

She wanted to know how long I had lived here, why we didn't speak, what happened to the first settlers and where the food came from. I wondered why nobody had told her these things and she explained that arrival was all automated nowadays;

she hadn't seen anybody on her way in.

Neither of us asked why the other had come, it seemed obvious.

Talking to her, sharing stories, brought back the early days of infection. How we had hidden, breathed oxygen from canisters, the hysteria, the rioting, the paranoia.

Without consultation, speaking became a regular thing. She would call often and we would speak for hours. One day I wept for the loss of my wife and after she had gone I stood in the bathroom looking at my tearstained face in the mirror. I saw it in a way I never had before, I saw what had always been there, I saw I was a man and I saw I was alive.

Ben noticed. He could monitor from his pod, he saw the calls between us.

She told me about America, how the infection had ripped through her family, how she had hidden in the mountains, how she had heard the virus thrived in the cold and thought us Antarctican's crazy.

They tried to do the same thing in the hot countries I told her. The heat killed it but people wouldn't stop visiting, the infection spread and they had to purify and start again here.

We talked about old things before the infection, movies and nightclubs and Christmas. I felt the numbness, the otherness in my body slipping away.

An ache settled into my chest, it frightened me the first day I woke up and felt it, heavy, like a stone on my heart. She said that I was mourning my wife and the world. I looked at my face in the mirror. I remembered my flat-grey self and I saw that there was not so much of him left. I saw my eyes were blue. I remembered her mouthing the names along with Ben and how human that had seemed. I mouthed words to my reflection to see my human face. I made noise as I moved around my home. I found myself involuntarily pacing; it felt sometimes as if my quarters were too small. I lay in bed and imagined the walls closing in. Some days it felt less of a haven and more like a box, especially when she reminisced about a long windy beach where she would walk her big furry dog.

Pets were the first to go. They said they were spreading the infection, mutating it.

We talked about what it meant to be alive, to have survived. It was the only argument we ever had. She was sad; she said she sometimes wished she'd died with her family. She couldn't understand why I didn't. I realised then that she had never really been in the thick of it. She had never seen them burning the still alive infected, never hidden from the patrols with their dreaded blood infection analysis machines. 'Surviving was paramount' I said. 'Life was paramount' she said. We switched off angrily and didn't speak for several days.

It was the next time we spoke that she suggested leaving. I told her never to mention it again.

It was another month before she tried.

We could go to the tropics, somewhere deserted, it would be safe. She had come here to be one hundred per cent safe, just like it said in the brochures. But what was life if we lived it like this?

Safe. As far as I was concerned. But I imagined it all the same, the sun on my skin, the smell of the breeze, fresh clean air, real food instead of tasteless protein. I remembered the ruins beneath the ice, the result of the visiting. I remembered my wife, dying of the infection on the other side of the glass. I remembered the fierce animal pride I had felt when I realised I had survived. Uninfected.

I thought about it though.

Ben called a meeting about disinfection. She interrupted him mid-flow and I saw irritation on his face. Ben didn't like her. I looked at the faces on the screen and saw that they didn't either.

We already gave a blood sample every day to be analysed. Nobody had been infected in Antarctica since the visiting stopped. But just in case, once a year you dragged a massive tube out into the middle of the floor and it would make its way around the home, like a giant blindworm, spraying disinfectant. Ben drove a holding van to each home and we waited inside for 24 hours until our homes were safe. In the beginning they had done it home by home but it had taken too long, so now we sat together, separated by flimsy plastic walls wearing oxygen tanks.

I dreaded the disinfecting, I hated leaving my home, I despised sitting alongside my neighbours.

This year I was anticipating it. I knew it was because of her.

It would be hot in the van but I was covered up. The others would be too. My oxygen tank was waiting by the airlock; I fidgeted with my heavy gloves. I was already beginning to swelter.

It took an age for the air to hiss in and out so that I could enter the van. I waited, tingling, whilst we droned across the ice to her home. The airlock hissed again slowly and I ground my teeth, a new sweat breaking out over my body.

She was smaller than I imagined, I couldn't see her face behind the mask but I could see her eyes. She sat down on the other side of the flimsy wall and I was sure everyone could hear the thudding of my heart.

There were potent sleeping tablets in the pouches alongside our seats; most people took them as soon as the van came to a halt.

We didn't.

For the first hour we stared ahead. Agonisingly slowly heads drooped, eyes closed, breathing relaxed. We were alone.

The masks prohibited speech, it didn't matter. We sat, aware that Ben was awake and likely watching. It was enough for me to luxuriate in her closeness. I could feel everything, the sweat, the prickle of my clothes; the rhythmic rise and fall of my sleeping neighbours. Did they dream? I had begun to. I never noticed when my dreams stopped. When they came back it was frightening and exciting, like a tiny taste of bliss.

The first time it happened I woke with a start and lay shocked, winded, as if I had been punched. I had been bombarded with vivid images of my wife dying, but this time I saved her, and we lived in the tropics, the child she was bearing when infected was fully grown. My chest had ached like it was going to split apart, the pain sharply sweet. I yearned for that pain, the vivid images, the joy, the different me. Like an addict I went to bed night after night, earlier and earlier, to live in my dreams.

A sound tore me from my reverie, a rip, a rustle, pressure.

Like my dreams a sweet sharp pain, she had torn the plastic and slipped her gloved hand through, it was pressing on mine lightly. The first touch in so many years. My throat was parched. To move would alert Ben, I could feel his presence at the front of the van.

We stayed, her gloved hand resting on mine, eyes ahead, our neighbour's unconscious bodies surrounding us. The only sound the rhythmic in . . . out of sleeping breaths. It beat in time with the word in my head, Alive.

Only now it didn't trumpet, it sounded like a warning. Who was alive? Were they alive? Sleeping safely next to me? Or was I alive? Sitting, awake, heart pounding, her hand on mine. I had never felt so alive. It felt like a crossroads, the point of no return. I took a breath, in . . . out, it hissed from the tank, the air flat on my tongue.

I turned my hand.

Her hand fit in mine; our fingers slid together like mesh. I imagined the tiny sounds our gloves made in the dry hot air as they scraped over one another were deafening, audible even outside. I tensed, waiting for discovery. We sat, linked, silent, her hand nestled in mine, I felt warmth in my chest, a sting behind my eyes. I dare not look at her.

We must have drifted off; there was no sense of time. To me, it seemed to be rushing past, hurtling toward the point where she would be gone and I would have only memory, as if this had never happened. In our sleep we had remained joined, hands clasped, I did not want to let go. My fear had passed, in windowless dark-ness nobody could see our connection, it was secret. Our grip was iron; I began to worry how we would break it. How would I let go? The rhythmic breathing of our neighbours was relentless, a ticking clock, shaving second after second away from us.

She flexed her fingers, then unexpectedly removed them. I felt bereft. With a rustle the welcome pressure returned, her hand in mine felt somehow smaller. I could not look for fear of Ben but my open hand contracted, fingers closing greedily grasping. A new sensation, a tug, it happened so fast I couldn't help but catch my breath, a gasp, too loud.

She had pulled off my glove.

My hand felt strange in the open air. I had not been this exposed for fifteen years, my naked skin, open to infection, but I was not afraid.

I thought about the virus, and saw that it had taken our humanity alongside the billions of lives. I saw the first settlers, afraid and human, I understood the visiting, the yearning for touch and company. I saw our fear of one another and I did not share it. For that moment, I lost my fear.

And that was all before she touched me.

Fingers, brushing my wrist, hesitant, my body frozen in a moment of perfect stillness, focused on the skin, my tingling skin, no breath, no heartbeat . . .

The end of me. I am alive.

Her hand, resting, bare skin on skin, sliding into my palm, fingers locking, gripping.   My heart, my chest, worse than the dreams, breaking, roaring pounding pressure, screaming in my lungs, battering my ribs, my eyes dry, boiling in my head.

What is it to be alive?

I think it is to hold a hand.

Her skin was warm, she was vital, alive, I was the same. I looked into the grey faces of my neighbours as they awoke, and saw loneliness. I saw their fear and I felt her skin, hidden, warm in my own.

She called hours later and asked again if I would leave and I told her maybe. Perhaps. Give me time.

I wondered if Ben would let us go.

He called a meeting. Somebody in another town had been outside. The servos had broken and they had tried to fix them. They had been infected. The grey faces on the screen were afraid. We were going into quarantine, no food drops for a month, we would ration. This had never happened before.

She called, said it was paranoia the infection was mostly gone. I felt the old fear stirring. I stared at the hand that had held hers. It felt like insects were crawling under my skin, skittering up my arm and burrowing.

Ben called update meetings, only one person had been unwell so far and that town had been purified, Antarctica was on lockdown.

In the third week, with fifteen faces focused on Ben. It happened.

She sneezed.

It was like a dream, a horrible one. She sneezed again and rubbed her nose. Ben stopped speaking. My throat tightened.

'Sorry, I think some dust got up my nose.'

We all knew there was no dust. The circulators kept the air scrubbed.

The faces on the screen were identical, even my own. I saw fear.

Ben finished the meeting. I sat for a long time, alone in silence. My hand was crawling again; it was weeks since the van. Just in case I got out my books on infection and transmission. They were vacuum packed to prevent dust.

The next day my neighbours popped onscreen one by one. Except her.

It was an emergency meeting, to discuss the sneeze. Ben said there was a possibility she had brought the infection with her, from outside. We had to act fast. If the Government found out we would be purified. He paused after that watching everyone drink in his meaning. I could taste the fear. We were survivors; we came here to live.

Ben said that the government looked kindly on towns who dealt with their own problems. Antarctica didn't want a reputation for being unsafe or no one would come, people would leave and things would collapse. He said a lot of things. I could feel the mood changing. It brought flashes of men standing at podiums during the infection, preaching purification, baying crowds, flaming torches, burning hospitals.

Faces on the screen were nodding; I had not heard the last part of Ben's speech. He was looking at me.

'Are you with us?'

I nodded blindly; I was always with the town. It was how we survived. Ben detailed the plan.

Rations were tight; he didn't want to feed the infection or risk transferral. He would cut power and water. It would take a few, hours maybe a night, the cold was not survivable. It would be over and the infection would be safely contained.

I stood at my porthole and watched hers; it was too small to see anything. I thought of her face, her warm hand, the sneeze. I only had her word for where she had been. She could have been anywhere. Unease roiled in my chest. The insects marched. I rushed to the shower and disinfected my hand until it burned and the smell made me retch. At first I didn't hear my TV.

I knew it would be her.

She was crying, why were we doing this? She wasn't infected. Was I deluded? What about the tropics? What about us? When I didn't respond she got angry, her face was blotchy and puffy, she saw my red disinfected hand and I think that's when she knew. She screamed once, shrill, piercing, afraid. She called us monsters, inhuman. Her voice went hoarse. I couldn't speak or move, exhausted, she wept and begged. She cried my name, moaning it, pleading with me to save her. I listened. The ache in my chest came back, I watched her, I wanted to remember her face.

Without warning the connection ended. Ben had cut power. I stood and watched for a while at my porthole; hers was too small to see into. We were in a period of darkness, the sun had set two weeks ago and would rise again in the spring.

After a while I went to bed, I thought of her.

When I awoke my home was dark. Something had woken me. It came again, a thud, a scrape. Weeping she called my name. There was a dark shape at my porthole. She banged again on my wall, pleading to be let in; she was cold, hungry, thirsty. She was outside, without breathing gear. Suicide.

154

I listened as she pleaded, I thought of our conversations, her hand and her warm eyes. I thought of the infection, of my wife and unborn child. As I listened my chest cracked. Something spilled out, heavy, suffocating. Numbness. It crawled into my hair, slipped down my arms and caressed my damaged hand. It wrapped itself around my legs and flowed over my toes, enveloping me, cradling me, cushioning me.

I lay numbed, her cries, her shadow at my porthole. I knew my neighbours were listening, waiting. Her voice weakened, she could not bang on my wall anymore, she had no strength. I heard her stumble away. I went back to sleep.

When the quarantine lifted, the machines came for her empty home. Even so, I still find myself at my porthole sometimes, staring. Habit.

I have begun to drift; the cloud, embraces me like a lover. I dream of her, we are in the tropics, we are laughing and there is a child, suddenly I am a monster, I devour them. I wake with their cries echoing around my tiny home. As they often do, my eyes stray to my porthole.

Soon we will disinfect again, Ben will drive the van. I remember the tear between our sections. I wonder if he will find it.

Wendy Jane Muzlanova

Wendy Jane Muzlanova was born in Ayr and her whereabouts now are of no concern to her enemies and creditors. She is a member of Soutar Writers' Group and she does indeed write anywhere and everywhere, composing some of her best work within text messages on her phone. Writing and art are her passions, alongside other diversions, not all of which are in liquid form. In the past, Wendy has worked as a cleaner, an editor, a tomato picker and a school teacher. She is now a support worker and loves her job. She hated teaching with a passion. The tomatoes were profoundly great, by comparison . . .

Wendy's writing is inspired by observation and lurid imagination.

Her third collection of poetry, *A Comedy of Torture*, was published by Erbacce in 2010. Although it is full of profanity and likely to offend, she is very proud of it. This fact alone proves that she has no shame. She has also had many reviews published concerning Russian matters—and has made a great deal of cash by keeping quiet at just the right time. Her short story, "Hate Therapy" has been chosen for inclusion within the *Women Writing the Weird* anthology, published by Dog Horn in May 2012.

Wendy tries not to take herself too seriously. Neither should you.

soutarwriters.co.uk/wendymuzlanova

Above the Turkish Barber Shop

Above the Turkish barber shop,
above the fish and chips and tat,
the hungry windows wait.
Blind witnesses eager to dine,
yearn to feast their empty eyes
on urban scenes of crime.

The blue police lights,
a violent foreplay,
to the weekend saga,
the colour flickers on old maid lace
and caresses and sickens
a thin and white and greedy face.

Far above the cries and threats,
above the spillage on the street,
a room is crouched behind the lace
and smeared in the corner
an antique vitrine.

Locks of hair disturbed from scalps,
bloodied ribbons and souvenirs,
fingers from nobody's hands.

Our hours are too long
and
our tempers too short
and

our lives are

caught up

in the middle.

Also published in "A Comedy of Torture" (Erbacce press)

Ghost 1

She suffered, like so many others, in the long queue of the town's Dismal Post Office. The short queue was reserved for those Lucky Rich Bastards who wanted holiday currency for places she would never see. She was firmly positioned in the Poor People's Queue. Some respite was to be had by leaning her upper body over the barriers, in a blatant display of exhaustion and boredom.

A woman with learning disabilities tried to engage her in a lurid conversation about her mother and her boyfriend. Her mother had been taken ill, she said—and had been forced to wait two hours for the ambulance to arrive. She was having great difficulty in accessing her mother's bank account, she confided, to disinterested ears. Her boyfriend had ruined her new bed, by stabbing it with a knife. Other customers were discussing the tags around their ankles and laughing. It was business as usual in the South Street Post Office.

She gazed with glazed eyes at the wall-mounted telly which always showed an endless loop of advertisements. That Kate Middleton and her prince smiled down at her from a commemorative stamp promotion. Parasitic Free-Loading Bastards, she thought—and felt that they were mocking her with their perfect smiles and all of their stolen wealth, as she stood in line with her leccy key and one precious, crumpled fiver to charge it with. After completing her pathetic transaction, she left the disgruntled (but not quite revolutionary) human centipede of a queue behind her.

She headed to the Tesco Metro. It was a fairly quick trip round the aisles, as she had fuck all money. She reached the checkout and realised that, if she didn't put any items back on the shelf, she would be walking home. Her family couldn't do without bread or cheese. She couldn't put back the Tesco Value Vodka, that was for sure, but neither could she return the little chocolate cakes she had bought as a treat for her daughters.

It was late afternoon. She had started her shift at work the previous day and had finally finished an hour ago. She was deeply tired and had her heavy rucksack and her sleepover bag to carry, even before the shopping was taken into account. However, her bitterness about the local bus company's fares—and her resentment of the greedy oligarch who owned the monopoly—strengthened her resolve. She walked the miles home, realising upon the way, just how heavy the bags were, how much her back and shoulders hurt and just how not waterproof her trainers really were.

When she got home, she gave her husband a hug. He turned his head away from his computer, just for a moment—and coughed in her face. Pig, she said—sadly unsurprised—and left the room. She sent him a message, as she thought that it would be vulgar and childish to, "poke" him. She complimented him upon his artwork. He requested that she be his friend. She accepted, delighted. She began to, "like" his posts. He reciprocated. They began to, "share." They shared Dali, Dada, Baudelaire and Blake. One morning she woke to find that he had posted a song right onto her wall, just for her. Everyone could see it, but it was meant for her alone. The music was old and deeply romantic. She returned his sentiment by posting the blues.

Winter Solstice Night

Minus fifteen morning, down at the bus stop dark.
No-one else around but you and me and
the blue snow heaped in alien mounds.
Black glide night birds fly
from the skeletal silver birch
and shred the cemetery sky.
I watch—struck—as the deep rose blush,
advances across your full, white surprise.
Your face is bruised by this bloodied eclipse
and your shine turns to dusk and to crimson and lies.
A crescent slice of brilliant light
slaps a flash, a glancing blow,
across your frozen cheek.

I enter the water as a girl

I enter the water as a girl.
I live wasted.
           I see this, in the scents,
    the feel of lapping.
I am the shape,
the very form of lust.
You know that you
   deserve me
        and I want you.
Let's find unused rooms.
We'll find them and
make use of them.
Let's fuck within redundant rooms,
let's make them happy places.
Let me see you unbuckle your belt.
Lead me into unused rooms and use me.
I look at you,
     shaven man and
   think of you,
     as I clean the floor.
  I think of health and safety and
your cock between my legs.
I wonder.
          What they would do,
if they knew
     about me
   and you?

The Syndicate Room

The Green Circle of Reception, historical, for-midable—four ways lead from the centre. Corridors West and East, the carpeted maze back stairs and the entrance to The Asylum. Go up the carpeted maze back stairs to a mezzanine floor tucked well away—no-one ever seems to recall this floor in any definite way—they can't exactly say— there, you will find The Syndicate Room. No-one seems to remember the history behind the name or what the room is ever used for, these days.

The Green Circle of Reception floats above The Red Octagon. Four ways lead from the centre. The Corridor to the Laundry, No-One Permitted To Enter. Music plays from a distant radio, not quite tuned in to the station. Gigantic, industrial washing machines strip the daily, the nightly soils of near-death. Opposite, more maze back stairs, uncarpeted this time, very lonely. Occupational Therapy—where the passer-by (as if one might) can purchase melted-looking pottery and un-natural, diseased models for one pound sterling and Psychology—where one must know the correct sequence of numbers to gain entry.

The walls are the colour of nausea, ill-fated boat trips. These endless walls are punctuated rudely by an eclectic selection of art work. Arabian markets, optimistic and minimal vases of—flower—and unsettling line drawings of best-forgotten buildings and events. I wonder what the clients make of these images and I wonder if the workers even see them, any more.

There is very little separation between the staff and the customers, in so many ways. They suffer mostly. They suffer mostly from rage, isolation, confusion and disorder. There is a marked absence of empathy, an aura of violence barely restrained, an overwhelming melancholy and a paralysing lethargy.

I am always looking for ways to escape, but I can never find the right path out of here.

I go to clean The Syndicate Room on Monday. I have never been asked to do this job before now. The room is nearly perfect. A little rubbish to take out, perhaps, some very light dusting. I look at the white painted stone steps within the room, leading one two three to a locked door, a much older door than all of the other doors. I do not try to open it. I feel just about almost certain that it must be locked anyway, that it must have been locked for a very, very long time. In truth, I am worried, in case it is not. There is a circular hole in the wall of The Syndicate Room, just large enough to permit viewing from the darkness of the hopefully locked room into the relative light beyond. I do not want to look at the ragged hole too long. I am much too afraid that I will be observed and if I see a single eye staring, feverishly, hungrily, through that Ragged Hole, I know that I will not be able to move. I turn away quickly and lock The Syndicate Room behind me.

The key I use is not a common pass key. The blade of this key is sharp and jagged. It seems to penetrate much too deeply into the dead space of the lock. The bow of the key is decorated with symbols. I examine them closely—I don't know for how long—and feel that I am on the brink of understanding what they mean. They remind me of the time the Laundry (No-One Permitted to Enter) Radio was broadcasting a talk show instead of the usual not-quite-tuned-in music it always seems to play. The language sounded like English, but I could make no sense of what was being said and the longer I tried to fathom out the sense of the words, the more my head hurt. When I felt the vein throbbing in my temple, the voices seemed to crescendo into some kind of chant and I think that I ran, that time.

I meet up with my work mates at break-time for some cut-throat banter and general unpleasantness. Some of our necks exhibit jagged wounds, the work of serrated accusations. Other necks display cleanly sliced cuts which gape redly. As Grace goes to leave, I see a bright scarlet bloom spread across the back of her blue uniform, but I know that it's not worth mentioning. The blade is pushed in to the hilt, has been twisted painfully, time and time again, but she doesn't even seem to notice it any more. These injuries are commonplace and the blood never has time to congeal. We all suffer the same wounds.

Far away from all of us, The Perpetrator is sitting neat and pretty in her mean domestic palace, amongst her poisonous and

164

corrosive cleaning agents. All of the bottles show hazard symbols—blindly grinning skulls, their bones crossed. Everything is perfect. She plots discord and is contented.

Back in the canteen, The Informer sits quietly at the table, pretending chummy friendship and toothy good humour to all, secretly absorbing careless words, memorising details. She knows full well that she is a slave to her masters, but if she is a good bitch, they will scratch her belly for her when she lies on her back.

I am cleaning the octagon, mopping its blood-red surface over and over. I can never seem to remove all of the stains. I am the only person here. In the distance there is sobbing issuing feebly from The Treatment Room, followed by clenched rictus teeth and the sure and certain smiles of the staff. An old woman wanders everywhere she can, looking for her parents. She is so worried that they will be angry with her, because she has stayed out until after dark and she must be months, somehow even years late, by now.

I head up the maze uncarpeted stairs, appear briefly upon The Green Circle and then attempt to make my way to The Syndicate Room. It seems to be in a slightly different location every time I try to find it. Phantom offices and store rooms appear beside it and along from it, as if bidden to provide camouflage. I cleaned this room yesterday and no-one has entered it since, according to the sheet in the supervisor's hand. The floor is strewn with hand-shredded paper, furniture has been moved into demented places and of course, the supervisor's hand lies there on the carpet, blackened fingers still clutching the day-sheet. I recognise her Eternity Ring.

I catch a tiny flicker of motion and there at The Ragged Hole, stares a bright, agitated eye from within the depths of The Locked Room. The oldest door clicks open, the sound of a gun being cocked. The darkness spills out and I find myself upon the threshold. Inside, Grace whirls away from the spy-hole and tells me, "This happens time and time again. There must be payback for malice." She suddenly sounds very old and not at all tuned in to the station I am hearing, the pre-set station. I'm almost sure that I remember setting the numbers. I don't want to listen to this one and her mouth is too wide. I don't want to look into that mouth because I think it might swallow me whole. I peer behind Grace or whoever, whatever she is, into the murk of The Locked Room. A body hangs from a rusted hook. The Perpetrator's face is blue, just like her uniform, flex wrapped tightly around her swollen neck. Her eyes bulge with the absolute fury of no reply, the disbelief of not having the last word, this time. As her body rotates (so slowly) I see that her back is sorely pierced, decorated even, by scalpels. At her feet lies the naked body of The Informer. She lies on her back, as usual. Her mouth is sewn shut with cat-gut and her eyes have been dissolved by some kind of skull-and-crossbones. Needles protrude from her ears.

At first, I think I have flies, perhaps big bluebottles, in my head, they are in my brain. Slowly, in the distance, I begin to hear a buzzing electronic voice, issuing its warning from the hospital truck. "Stand well clear. Vehicle reversing. Stand well clear." I leave The Syndicate Room, daring to turn away from all of the horror, without casting a glance back.

I know that nothing will come after me.

"If you can't say something good about someone, then don't say anything at all." My mother passed her kindness on to me and I do my best to teach my children the same. I just don't know when I will see them again, that's all. How old are they now? I have a sick feeling that I've stayed out too late.

I head down the maze carpeted stairs, all the way down to The Red Octagon. I think that I might know the correct numbers now.

This story was previously published in The Delinquent.

Ghost 3

She told herself that she preferred sleeping single in a quiet, double bed. She had convinced herself that, as long as the Ann Summers shop remained open for business, there was nothing she required a man for, unless—she remembered quite suddenly—you needed skin and warmth. Perhaps even (a bit of) passion. She didn't feel qualified to comment upon the need for love.

Recently, however . . .

She lived in a small, depressed town and felt in desperate need of excitement. Was she lonely? No. She couldn't say that she was. She had plenty of friends, real flesh and blood ones, alongside those ciphers on Facebook. But she did need something different.

She signed up to an internet friendship and dating site, at a "Special Offer!" introductory rate. She wasn't stupid. If nothing came of this plan within a month, then she wouldn't waste any more time—or money—on it. She wrote a few random (yet hopefully intriguing) facts about herself on her profile page and uploaded a recent photo, in which she looked summery and healthy. She felt quietly proud that she had not resorted to using a particularly beautiful portrait of herself—which had been taken in a studio ten years ago. She felt brave enough to allow other users on the site to "rate" her photo and she was pleasantly surprised—and undeniably excited—when she made first place on the, "Top Ten Females" leader board. She definitely didn't approve of such things. "Meat Market," she thought scornfully, but at the same time, she was pleased that she was the prize cow.

Her friends teased her—in a kindly way, she felt sure—about her use of the site and often asked how she was getting on with Dodgy Pen-Pals Dot Com . . . she had shared a few of the characters and stories with her friends, so it wasn't surprising that they referred to the site in this way.

A twenty-something boy from Sweden had sent her a photo of himself, reclining upon an anonymous, brown sofa. He had his dick out. She gasped and felt a bit nauseous. Not because of his blatant display, but because she could see that his body was covered in darkish moles. She had no idea why he would send her such a photo. She had told him quite clearly that she hated heavy metal and stadium rock.

A forty-something German called, "Geiler Engel" had invited her to spend a week with him in Berlin. In his photo, he looked handsome, well-kept and very, very blond. He had interestingly diverse (and some might say, deviant) sexual tastes and was looking for a range of partners, rather than, "that special someone." She respected him for that. He specified, "no ties" in his profile. She thought that this restriction might make the whole experience of bondage a bit flat. She chatted back and forth with him for a couple of weeks, but his erotic track record (imagined or otherwise) scared her a little. She decided not to go to Berlin to spend the week with Horny Angel. He had not yet proposed a venue, after all—and she had constructed alarming images of herself, naked and inverted—and entombed in an airless and rather well sound-proofed dungeon, somewhere in Prenzlauer Berg . . .

After a month of using Dodgy Pen-Pals Dot Com, she did not renew her membership. She had picked up nothing more interesting than a slightly obsessive e-pal, who mourned the demise of the National Socialist Party and sent her computer images of sunflowers and roses. She would not be visiting his wonderful town of Erfurt and would, at some point in the future, need to let him down gently. She reckoned that she had got off lightly.

It was time for a change.

She began to aim her hunting strategies at Facebook, clicking through link after interesting link, friending and being befriended along the way, liking and commenting, occasionally sharing. One man in particular caught her attention. He was an artist. Not a terribly great artist, but there was something about his face. Something about that chipped tooth of his, the scar on his lip. She could imagine kissing that mouth. She could imagine him fucking her. And she did. He became the man she took in bed every night in a faithful, monogamous dream. The individual scenarios were lurid, because that was the way she liked her fantasies, but in her own way, she became utterly and exclusively devoted to him.

Station

All that they know is that I have left. I am alone in the station. I could go anywhere. I look at fellow travellers; look at them, to see which ones might be worth the bother of killing.

I consider, briefly, returning to my mother's house, my childhood home where The Bitch now lives. I think of my elder sister's old, bleached-blonde hair, straw for cattle to shit upon. I picture her jaunty, cosmopolitan sunglasses, even in the fucking rain, perched atop her jaunty fucking soon-to-be-broken head, her skull.

Anorexia does not become the old. Her cheeks are hollow. The thought of kissing those hollow cheeks fills me with sudden nausea, except perhaps, after her death, oh, after her death, to place a derogatory, living kiss upon her bitter face, well, that would be sweet.

I will take her apart, bit by bit, piece by shit-filled piece.

Her eyes are the calculations of mink, brown buttons, waiting to be torn from her ancient doll's face. Her lips are just as thin as they should be, never-ever having spoken words of love or charity.

I try to imagine a death for her, a death that won't bring sympathy upon her name. I try to think of a death for her which I can get away with. I love my family. I don't want to be spending any unnecessary time apart from them.

The station bar is all noise, espresso machine threatening, barmaids chattering, and the open-plan drivel of conversations outside. I listen to the beckoning tune of the fruit-machine, the One-Armed Bandit. This sucker is not looking to gain three cherries in a row. All of the icons are murder weapons, a silver Cluedo dagger, a throttling length of rough rope, the definitive gun.

What about a gun, I think? No. Too noisy, too indiscrete. Attractive, yes, but not subtle. I take the time, nevertheless, to contemplate my shot.

Ideally, one half of her face would fly from its usual place, so that I could appreciate the shocked remainder. I could look directly into her one remaining eye as she realises, just for that one precious second, what has been done to her, what I have done to her. It would be . . . satisfying.

The pub food in my gut fights queasily and drunkenly with the litres of Merlot from the night before.

"No Smoking" the sign says.

I decide therefore, not to shoot her . . .

Cris O'Connor

Cris O'Connor is just another guy sucking up your oxygen.
I think he writes too . . .

In the Company of Crows

Friday 23rd November: Work [Library]

A greying man in a black suit pushed past me and headed for "travel writing". His skin hung with deep folds and creases. I followed him. His movements were uncomfortable and he had a rather obvious twitch in his neck. I stood a few feet away and watched as his limp fingers brushed over the spines of books; it was as though his fingers were reading for him.

"Excuse me sir, where can I find poetry?" Some old woman looked at me expectantly.

"Poetry is located in the far section of the basement."

I turned to watch the man, but he was gone. As I looked through the shelves I noticed a book that didn't belong among the travel journals, *In the Company of Crows* by D. S. Keolerate.

I slipped into the room formerly known as Goods In, but was now just over stock. I found a comfortable spot between a pile of 9-12 and Crime. Flicking through the book I found pages analysing the links between man and crow. Other pages looked at how the crow might be used as a messenger of evil, or the idea that a crow in itself was a message of darkness.

At five thirty I finished work and walked home. As I moved through the park I kept seeing that man, the wrinkles, the twitch, the wilted hands. He was in the faces of people that passed me. His skin hung on the branches of trees.

Across the grass there were people walking their dogs, students, the odd squirrel and a white bird that caught my eye. This bird looked so much like a dove. I took a sandwich, from lunch, out of my bag and tore pieces of bread off for the bird. As it came closer to eat, a crow dived from a tree and dug its claws into the pigeon's back. With a cut wing the bird tried to fly, but was grounded. This crow kept bombing the injured pigeon. I tried to scare it off, but it flew around me and attacked from other directions. Within minutes the white pigeon was a bloody mess and lifeless. The crow landed by the bread I had throw and looked at me. I felt the blood draining from my face and my fingertips began to tingle.

I got home and went straight to bed. That night I didn't dream of anything.

Saturday 24th November: Leisure [Library]

Kneeling on the floor, looking for *In the Company of Crows* I notice a silence even unusual for a library. There are no whispers. I can hear no computer keys being tapped. No scan gun beeps as it registers a rental. No people asking for help. I stand up and look around. The library is empty. No staff are around, no public, there is nobody. I hear a noise and tilt my head to catch it. A birdcall pierces my ear.

"Are you okay sir?" An elderly woman is looking at me.

"Ye, I . . . do you have, *In the Company of Crows?*"

"I'll just check for you," the elderly woman waddles away.

As I continue to look I hear a distant bird.

"Caaaw," the elderly woman is looking at me, her eyes are all pupil.

"Pardon?" My chest tightens as I wait for a response.

"I said, is this what you were looking for?"

In her hand is *In the Company of Crows*. There is a deep red smudge beneath her thumb.

"Yes, that's the one."

As I look up at her the lights above flash and I'm certain I see the face of a crow in place of the woman's.

I lift my head from the sink and look in the mirror. Black eyes cast in glossy feathers stare back at me. A black beak caws at me each time I try to speak. I go to run my fingers through my hair, but my fingers only find greasy feathers. I pause for a second and bring my hand over my face, to my lips, but there are no lips there is only the sharp edge of a beak. There is no space behind the mirror. This is not a window I am looking through. I see my suit, the pin stripes, my white shirt and a crow's head. I am a body and a crow. I am no longer somebody, anybody, I am a crow with a body. No shock rattles me, no fear. I am surprised at myself and begin to laugh; my laughter mutates in

173

my throat and escapes as a "caaaw." If I had lips, they would pull together and hide in my mouth.

Saturday 24th November: Leisure [Library]

Between shelves of books I catch glimpses of black eyes staring through me. Every body has the head of a crow sewn to it. These people seem unaware; they continue to browse through books. Searching the shelves for *In the Company of Crows* I knock into a man, I assume it's a man, but with a crow's head replacing his own I can't be too certain.

"Sorry sir."

The man looks at me. His bird head tilts.

"Caaaw!"

As he continues to caw at me a group of others begin to watch; each one tilting their head when they look at me. Birdcalls echo through the library, overlapping as more and more begin to shout. A group begins to move toward me. They force me into a corner; I'm enclosed. I'm stuck. The people grab me and begin to thrust their beaks into my flesh. The red of my blood leaves a sheen upon their feathers. The thrusts get faster. Sharper. Each attack is more violent. My neck. My throat. I try to scream, but the air leaks through my windpipe. Gasping for air everything begins to darken. I catch a glimpse of red on black. I see black eyes. I see black.

I lift my head from the sink and look in the mirror. Black eyes cast in glossy feathers stare back at me. A black beak caws at me each time I try to speak. I go to run my fingers through my hair, but my fingers only find greasy feathers. I pause for a second and bring my hand over my face, to my lips, but there are no lips there is only the sharp edge of a beak. There is no space behind the mirror. This is not a window I am looking through. I see my suit, the pin stripes, my white shirt and a crow's head. I am a body and a crow. I am no longer somebody, anybody, I am a crow with a body. No shock rattles me, no fear. I am surprised at myself and begin to laugh; my laughter mutates in my throat and escapes as a "caaaw."

174

Thoughts drain through my mind like a sieve. Images of family and friends distort and darken to nothingness. These thoughts confuse, mould into one another; all I am left with is this need to survive. Food, rest and procreation are the only things that linger in my mind. Words are no longer even a distant memory, but more a foreign language spoken by some strange animal. Everything human fades, everything but my body. My mind belongs to another, my mind is now another.

Monday 26th November: Work [Library]

I walk around the storefront. Customers stop me, but I don't help. I go downstairs to the travel section. I knock into a student as I move closer to "travel". He turns to look at me and I catch a glimpse of myself in his eyes, my eyes are hollow and held in wrinkles, they say I'm older than I am. As I walk I notice he is following me, he matches each step I take. Continuing forward a pain keeps pulsing in my neck and creating a spasm. I reach a bookshelf and close my eyes. The student isn't around. I lift my hand to the book spines. My fingers hang limp. I drag my wilted fingers across the books as the man had done before. I have no idea why I am doing this; my movements don't feel like my own. From my suit I pull *In the Company of Crows* by D. S. Keolerate and place it among the travel journals.

I find myself outside the library. My hands clench and my fingers knot. My upper teeth rest upon my lip. A cold vibration runs through my body. The taste of iron hangs on my tongue. A distant birdcall pulls me further into the building.

My lips harden. Hair thickens. My eyes turn dark. I feel a bubbling in my throat and begin to gag. My lips start to extend forward, I can feel flesh tearing and sealing. A pressure builds on my forehead and I feel as though someone or something is carving my head. Sounds intensify and weaken, colour becomes more vibrant and then fades.

I see my reflection in the window. There I am, I'm wearing a shirt, a tie, a black suit, my best shoes and where my head should be I see the face of a crow. I can almost see stitches holding it to my body. I feel tears build inside of me. A scream and a cry for help suffocate. I fall back onto a wall and sink to the floor. My throat vibrates.

"Caaaw"

I am left, a body in the library.

Through Television Screens and Static

I hear them scuttling inside the walls, small black insects, the sound surrounds me. I see one crawl from a plug socket and run along the rug by my feet. Its movements are deliberate and mechanical. I close my eyes and imagine crushing it between my thumb and forefinger, oil oozing from its metallic body, circuits snapping. I see walls of television screens. Each wall is made of forty-nine screens and each shows a section, event or memory of my life. One screen is now trapped in a static loop; occasionally it shows me sitting on my bedroom floor watching the camera pan past my feet. One hundred and ninety five remain. I open my eyes; a brown liquid has stained my finger. Small legs and fragments of shell cling to the dried liquid.

There is a knock at the door. I creep towards the peephole. A thin woman holding a package is looking back at me.

"Who is it?"

"Hi, sorry. I'm Eva from upstairs. We've spoke a couple times by the mailboxes."

"What do you want?"

"Erm, you weren't in earlier. I signed for a package for you."

"What is it?"

"I don't know. It's in a box." Eva lifts the box to the peephole; she knows I'm watching.

"Oh . . . "

I stay silent and watch. Eva's eyebrows are drawn downwards pulling me into her luminous green eyes.

"Do you want it or not?"

I push the drawers from behind the door just enough to open it slightly.

"Cheers." I gesture for her to pass the box.

"It's not going to get through there . . . you know what, I'll just leave it here by your door." Eva puts the box on the ground, turns and leaves.

I wait several minutes and then quickly open the door and

grab the package. The box is surprisingly light and there is no stamp, address or name on it. I place the box in the centre of my room. It seems to dominate the space.

My palms are wet. Each time he walks behind me my body tenses; my knuckles turn white. I'm drunk on the recycled air.

"Now what were you doing in the warehouse?"

"I already told you, it's where the card said to go."

"Of course," he pauses, "and where is this card?"

"I burnt it."

"Yeh, okay . . . I see."

His badge reflects the synthetic light. I know what they want. They are waiting for me to slip up; waiting for me to mention the insects, the cameras. Then they'd have me. Instantly I would be deemed insane and then that's it. Everything you see, hear, say and do is a result of insanity. My dad taught me this. The nurses used to tell the family he was a liar, but I could see. I saw the bruises the nurses had given him. My mum actually believed them when they said he did it to himself. I would sit with Dad while he cried and told me all the horrible things they did to him. I was the only one that knew Dad was telling the truth. The last time I saw him he told me they were going to kill him. He said if they succeeded I would be next. Two weeks later my dad was found hanging from a tree, a coarse noose clutching his throat.

"Mr Cleave, you were the last person to see Miss Eva Redem alive. Cameras show you entering the premises shortly after Miss Redem's arrival. You stayed on said premises for three hours and twenty-seven minutes. Would you care to tell me what happened in that time?

"I didn't follow her. The card said to go there and I did. I saw her body and left."

"At what point did you see Miss Redem?"

His pacing is tiring, with each step he tenses his arms and I feel my own arms cramping.

"I went inside and heard noises. I followed them and saw Eva on the floor. She had blood coming out of the corner of her

178

mouth."

The officer takes a deep sigh.

"And how long did that take, Mr Cleave?" His teeth stay ground together and spit oozes between the crooked gaps.

"I don't know—I can't remember."

I dream about her. She is trapped in one of the screens documenting my life. As I approach her colour desaturates. The closer I move, the further she sinks into static. I see her palm against the screen. Suddenly all one hundred and ninety five screens go black and I can faintly hear Eva crying. I break each screen trying to pull her out. My hands become shredded. Eva appears on the screen opposite me.

"Don't approach." Is all I can make out.

I collapse to the floor and drag myself backwards, away from Eva. The further I move the clearer she becomes. We stare at each other through the domed glass.

Inside the box is a card and nothing else. There is an address written in crude handwriting. The back of the card reads: I don't want to be alone

I know this could be a trap. I know it's probably best to ignore it, but I can't. I remember Dad saying there were others, others who knew. Maybe someone knew something. Maybe they had staged Dad's death. Maybe it was from Dad. I would get there and he would be sat in the worn green armchair. He would give me a sweet that smells nothing like it tastes. He would read his newspaper and tell me the truth behind each story. He would have a cup of coffee for me, because I need to stay alert and I would drink it hating every gulp.

There is a knock at the door.

"It's Eva." Her voice is a strained whisper.

"What's wrong?"

"It's happening tonight."

I move the drawers and fully open the door without thinking. Eva instantly wraps her arms round me. My body becomes rigid, but I slowly raise my arm and place my hand on her lower back. It's warm.

179

"Come on Miss Redem, lets not bother Mr Cleave," a woman in white walks towards us and ushers Eva away. "Has she been bothering you, Mr Cleave?"

"No, she just-"

Eva dashes towards me and puts her finger on my lips. "Sshh!"

"She just . . . came to say hello." The words bubble around her finger.

"Okay, well we'll leave Mr Cleave to have a peaceful evening now won't we, Miss Redem?"

"Yes. Good evening, Mr Cleave." Eva winks as she leaves.

The woman in white stands by my door until I shut it. I wait silently for her footsteps.

E va, what are you doing here?"

"I didn't want to be alone. Will you stay with me?"

"For what?"

"Stay with me till the clouds roll across my irises"

We sat in silence for some time before Eva took my hand. Her fingertips were cold and I could feel her pulse through her palm. I looked into her eyes and watched them slowly begin to frost.

"What's your name, Mr Cleave?"

"Ed."

"We're friends aren't we, Ed?"

"I guess so . . . yeh."

"Thank you."

A thin line of blood ran from the corner of her mouth. I stayed and held her hand till she was cold; as I let go I noticed a rat watching from a distance. The streetlights caught its eyes and I saw the camera lenses adjust. They were here.

I spent some time in the warehouse planning my escape, ever aware of their spies around me. I could hear one taunting me, its repetitive coo, trying to make me acknowledge it.

There is a suited woman in the room with us now. Since her arrival the officer has not relaxed his shoulders, they are held rigid pushing his chest out. She sits calmly beside me while the officer fidgets around the room. She keeps reminding me that I don't have to say anything and I, politely, remind her that I know.

"Mr Cleave we are going to hold you here till we can arrange accommodation in a more secure unit."

The woman and officer are exchanging paperwork and scribbling on sheets.

"What about my apartment?"

The officer looks up at me, heavy lines form around his brow.

"What apartment?"

"I believe my client is referring to his residence at Burnt Oak Care Facility." The woman almost places her hand on mine as she speaks.

Mark Wagstaff

Mark Wagstaff spent his childhood in Herne Bay on the North Sea coast of Kent, southern England. His most enduring memory of that time was the day the whole town stood on the beach to watch the pier burn down. But with origins in London he moved to the city in his mid-twenties and stayed there. Mark has had about 40 short stories published and has brought out four novels and a collection of short pieces.

His well-regarded 2008 novel *The Canal* has been republished as an ebook by Bristlecone Pine Press. His 2009 novel *In Sparta*—a story of radicalism, conformity and terror—is available in print and ebook from troubador.co.uk.

Among recent publications, Mark's story 'Allotments' appeared in the Fall 2010 issue of *Inkwell* and an extract from his novella *Mascara* is included in *Polluto 7*. His story 'Footnotes and Footlights' appeared in *The Writer* in February 2011. Details of Mark's work is available at markwagstaff.com.

Death Ride Girl

When that chick fell off the sky, man she was beautiful. The blackest swan, sailing on eagle's wings to dust. The inks, man, called her Death Ride Girl. But she was no rider: she flew. Arms wide, the blackest poetry, quick and gone.

I'm like some toad, man, in the rocks here by the canyon. No one comes without I see. They come over the desert, hours, man, to the show. Cars and trucks, kids and dogs barking in the back. They cook out, take fish from the lake. Drink beer on folding chairs. They ride.

When the show was built, man, I recall like yesterday: dudes in hats, yelling, chewing dude cigars. Big old boys in mirror shades; that smell of green. You couldn't see the sun for red earth raised all over. And the stars at night, man: drops of blood. The sound was immense. Immense. Big machines, man, ripping centuries out the soil; at night, I'd see the jockeys, shooting shadows, spitting whiskey on the flames.

And he came, the old sorefoot, from way on down the river, with his bones and beads, his eagle feather, his rattle song of sacred ground, of ancestors ripped and shredded by machines. Man, I liked that. Shaking his bones, saying: three days, three days to leave our desert. They laughed at him. I laughed. But, man, my laugh's better . . .

She was in back with Brownie. She didn't want to be. She wanted in front like Tom. But Tom made like he was reading the map and Mum and Lame-o let him. Like, who needs a map in a desert. "Who needs a map in a desert?"

No answer.

"There's only one road."

Caitlin was young; she'd've liked being with Brownie. But Caitlin was, "Too young for in back," whatever that meant. Susie glared at the dull, red hills as Brownie wuffed and stumbled round, landing hard, heavy paws on Susie's legs. Why couldn't the bitch lay down? "Why can't she lay down?"

"Why can't you shut up?"

They let Tom away, like usual.

183

"If you taught her . . . "

"Me?"

"Anyone."

"Teach Susie to shut up?"

"Teach Brownie."

"She ain't talking."

Susie tuned out. Mum and Tom weren't fighting. Just pretending. Being lame. But not as lame as Lame-o, driving in mirror shades. Tom first called him Lame-o. "It takes getting used to," Mum told them. "A new someone takes getting used to. It's hard for him, too."

"Hard how exactly?"

No answer. She answered Tom. She drooled at Caitlin's little wants. She left Susie hanging. "Middle child," Tom would tell her. "Best forgotten."

The only good to the day was seeing the show, biggest fair in a hundred miles. There were water slides. Water slides in the desert. Broncos. And that big old gut-snapping 'coaster where . . . "That girl got killed," said Tom. "Right off the top, ker-splatt."

"Tom."

From the caves behind his eyes, something stirred with Lame-o. "You know, every fair has fatalities. Maybe every coupla years. It's not bad safety. It's people."

"Man," said Susie, "That sucked the fun outta that."

Getting close the trail of hotdog stands, caps and candy cane, Caitlin jabbed the window with her puny little fingers: want burger, want balloon.

"When we get there."

"Are there."

"We're not stopping at every . . . "

Caitlin's squalling took the lid off. "Why can't she shut up?" said Susie, though her fight wasn't with Caitlin. She got scolded, and yelped as Brownie tumbled on her hand. "Why do we bring it?"

"I was thinking that."

Tom was half and half a good brother. He teased her, pulled her hair; she was too fresh and spiky now to tie to trees. He stuck paper parachutes on her dolls and flew them from the window.

184

He hollered like a jackass when she looked at boys. But he stood between her and Mum's anger, and Lame-o's stupidity. When Dad died Tom held her, made it right for crying. He wiped her face and told her she'd be pretty neat someday. But he couldn't say, none of them could, when someday happens.

Lame-o couldn't park. He couldn't spin the dirt and walk off like a cowboy. He couldn't glide the spaces, lazy hand trawling the window. He drove around and around: too far, too close, too in the sun, too near the dogs at the trees. Susie hid, embarrassed, as, cut on every turn, he lost space after space. Blond kids poked their tongues out, dads laughed; he did nothing. Like always, they fetched up where they'd begun, shunting in a gap a million miles from anywhere, Mum fretfully chewing her shades, looking over her shoulder to see out back, avoiding Susie's glare. Susie practised glaring.

And not just it took hours to park: they had to give Brownie her run. "We could leave her with the other dogs."

"Leave you."

"We bring her for the car."

"A dog that size make you think." Lame-o nodded, thinking.

"But they'll just steal the car and the dog. They'll kill the dog."

"Susie."

"Most felonies in fairground car parks are break-ins," Lame-o told the stunned silence. "Not actual stealing cars."

"So they'll kill the car and steal the dog."

The rule was an hour family time, then fun stuff. Mum wasn't in love with the fair. She'd catch the sun in Kiddie Korner with Caitlin, who dived around in the sand and water, shouting, "Look, mummy, look." Susie never got how Mum did that stuff with Caitlin; hadn't she lived it twice before? Lame-o sat behind his shades eating popcorn, ignorant of the law that you never eat popcorn outdoors. If he chanced a ride, he'd sit behind his shades and do nothing. He was the emptiest nothing Susie ever saw.

Tom came alive on the rides. That sense of him that was still a kid won out his teenage cool. He whooped and yelled the drops, the slams, the corkscrew twists. Too short for the hot-

185

test rides, Susie waited dutifully, till he dived her down the watershoots, barrelling the rapids. He'd hug her, pretending he was scared, like Dad would. Giddy on the waltzers, jammed on the dodgems, gleefully sick on the pirate ship, he'd creep behind the other kids, make pukey sounds so they'd cuss him. She ran with Tom, laughing, through the crowd; he'd dare her: "Flip the bird at that fat guy." Liberated, Susie raised her salute, and they'd tumble off, barking and cussing.

"I wanna go on the 'coaster." She slurped her cola, so grandmas would stare.

"Too short, Shortcake." He was conning round for where to smoke.

"No, the old 'coaster." The bargeboard, hillbilly railway that dropped like a house from the sky. "I'm tall."

"Hey." He'd seen a girl or something. "Just gonna suck a sly one."

"Can I come?"

"You cannot. Smoking olds your skin."

"S'that what happened to you?"

He cuffed her ear. "Once on the 'coaster and I'll be back."

"Is she neat Tom?" Susie played up the little-girl voice. "Shall I come see?"

"Screw."

She didn't like to ride by herself, but he was kind and bought her stuff and, she thought emptily, deserved more for his day. It was achy to think how few times more there'd be with Tom. He was growing, didn't say so much about where he'd been. When girls rang his phone, he'd step right out the house. She was a chore for him now; she could see him make the effort. It didn't come natural anymore: he worked to be her brother. He was thinking of college; soon he'd be gone and she'd be the eldest, with Caitlin and Mum and the poisonous vacuum of Lame-o. There was no reason Mum had him around. He'd attached himself to her widowhood like: "Shit," she said it out loud. Like shit crusts up a cow's hide. He slept in Mum's bed, on Dad's side of the bed. He was grotesque, hateful, setting rules and talking: "Shit." Breaking things he couldn't fix. Tom's friends, everyone, called him Lame-o. Scott called him Lame-o to his face; he did nothing. Susie hid, embarrassed, as everyone who knew Dad stopped coming by. The whole family died, and Lame-o sequestered their bones.

The bar came down ahead of her. She'd have to wait next ride. Hot with the sun, Susie was sugar-gone sleepy. Her phone rang. Left it to message. Tom said, "Be cool, leave it to message."

"You getting that?"

"Huh?"

"Phone."

Susie felt her pocket but the sound had stopped.

"Mine's got tunes." The girl flicked a thin black cell. Some song played. "Neat."

Susie shook her tired head, trying to come alive. Her skull buzzed, like when she was a kid, Tom said he saw a bee crawl in her ear when she was sleeping. She banged her head an hour to pitch it out. The girl was maybe Tom's age, with a short, dark bob; round freckle face that looked kinda cool. She was all in black like the girls out back of the sly rock bar in town. The girls Tom said were, "Jailbait," each time he went over.

"I love the 'coaster." The girl jammed her hands in her jean pockets. "More than the rocketship, the . . . "

"Starburst? Can't ride that." Tired, she was sullen.

"It's dumb," the girl said happily. "They should do it by looks, not height. You here on your own?"

"Family."

"Neat."

"Huh?"

"Neat they let you off. My folks never did that, no sir." She looked around. "I was, like . . . " she pulled an imaginary leash and grimaced.

"I'm here with my brother. He smokes."

"D'you smoke?"

"He says not to."

"It's neat. So let's review: oldies in the sand pit, playing with baby brother?"

"Sister." Vile, how lame she must seem. She could mix it up, though. "He's not my dad anyway. Dad's dead."

The girl popped with her tongue in the lid of her mouth. "Quick, was that? Like, tragic?"

187

Yeah, Dad died a hero, in crossfire, winning the war. He went down, righting wrongs. "He was hit by a truck."

"Bummer." The girl's voice was flat, but that was cool: she didn't know Dad. "Must've been messed up, yeah?"

"They peeled road out his face." She could say it and not feel the kick split her guts anymore. Maybe it was getting better, like the stupid priest said; when he sat her down with his cemetery eyes, all she wanted to say was: "Shit."

"Huh?"

Susie shook her head. "I just like to say it."

"Neat."

The 'coaster clattered back down the ride; the line stirred, making ready.

"Gonna wait on your bro'?"

Susie was peevish. "I'm plenty tall."

"Nah, I mean I'll ride with you. So you don't get next to some lame."

"Lame-o."

"Huh?"

"The guy Mum," she spat it, "dogs round."

"Yeah? Already?"

Susie knew to the hour how long since Dad left. "Yeah, already." She went by the bar, feeling a rush of air as the girl pressed up beside her. She paid her token, the girl her shadow. "You cheesin'?" she hissed.

"Yeah, man. I ride for nix."

Susie went up head of the train, right where there was clear air. The chat and clatter of folks behind faded in the warm day. Not sleepy now, she felt in with everything: the hot leatherette of the old brown seats baked her jeans; the scalding metal grabs; distant fairground music; barking dogs, a tannoy voice and, somewhere, a buzzing phone.

"Hey," said the girl beside her. "This is where I love: top car."

With a ringing shudder, the wheels awoke, surprised at the juice stinging through them. Susie clutched the grab, grunting where it scorched her skin, as the train began its rise on the steel-and-sleeper mountain.

188

"I been riding this forever. Since, oh, small, I guess."

Susie gritted her teeth for the curve. "Dad used to bring me. We sat here." The floor dropped from her stomach.

"You miss him bad?"

It was shocking, uncool, immense to say how bad. "Yeah."

The train slowed, to speed again on the snake's belly. "This Lame-o, what's he know?"

"Shit."

"But your mamma steps to?"

Mum wasn't the neatest, thinnest, "Brightest," Tom would say. But kinda cute and kinda right, and baked the creamiest pie. There was no explanation for Lame-o; he had nothing she could want. "She likes company."

"No shit."

They stopped at the summit, a bargeboard platform of brush and cracked green paint. The rails ticked in the endless heat, crickets sang and, way below, a gentle rush like the sea rose up, the sound of the fair in the desert.

"Tell you," the girl's voice, there in her head. "You need an out."

"This is my out." There'd be no more, not till the far side of summer. Dad must've had money somewhere: he went to work in a suit. But since Lame-o, they had nothing: Mum spent evenings patching. Susie saw Dad's money some place, boxed, buried treasure. Get that, get out. Go with Tom, whatever.

"I mean there's better rides."

The train clanked to life, speeding, going down.

"I'm too short."

"Not to fly."

Susie thought maybe the girl took stuff. Scott and the boys said they took stuff. That was cool. "You mean fly?" Her words swam behind her, whipped away on the updraft.

The girl's voice was clear and present. "I mean it. I can fly."

"Since when?" They zipped round a curve, shaken against each other. The girl's solid body bumped her ribs.

"Since forever. I'm special."

They were hurtling, getting nearer, straining for the drop.

189

"D'you wanna?"

She saw the girl's hand move over hers and they were locked together. The bony grip startled her skin, its strength made her shriek. But everyone shrieked; the noise broke up on the wind.

"C'mon honey. You'll know what to do."

As the train hit its shuddering fall, Susie was soaring over the track, the fair, hand in hand with the girl. Propelled away from the 'coaster, they skimmed across the hot air, a sudden glorious breath of beginning consuming Susie's lungs. "Wow," she laughed. "Look, mummy, look."

The girl's grip on her hand was fading, the onward force less sure. A drag began to tell in her bones, a faint hint of distant persuasion.

The girl's voice slayed her. "Hey, kid: I lied."

Susie saw her chipped, compacted face, her broken angel wings.

Man, that kid was the shortest thing I ever see dive the 'coaster. The noise was immense. Immense. There was sirens, man, and this big brown dog messing the flow. And the crying, man. Wailing. Them all, but the cat in the shades. He seemed pleased, like he wished it, brother.

And the 'coaster, she goes up and down her mountain. The inks say: How Many More? but they just selling stories. That old sorefoot, he'd tell you, with his broken beads and scavenged eagle father. But he's long gone to the hunting ground to drink red eye with his dead fathers.

Not me, man. I'm like some toad. I stay in the rocks, here, hidden. I see the black mamma crow bring her babies. I see the fair, my friend, in my long and lazy years. Best show in the desert. If you wanna catch a ride.

Stripshow

Twenty

Dipping in the washbag pulling on clothes: rushing to get there early; driven by timechecks to make the bus, to see her. Before, I was the kid always pitched up late and aiming to do little. Slip in around ten, act scenery, leave early. What changed my lax ways was no Protestant revival, no boss toasting my arse. I wasn't abducted by aliens and rewired. I changed when I got a new neighbour. Not in the banks of desks that range the floor as a giant schoolroom. Not scary, sexy menace demanding me to work. My neighbour doesn't work this section. Doesn't work here at all.

I got wise one morning when I had no choice but early. Despite aiming to keep my presence minimal, I got drag-netted in someone's project and—through trademark idleness—screwed up. With whitewash my preferred response, I got in early to configure better facts. This was dead winter, murky till eight and first on the floor, I was charmed how—with the striplights off—the green start buttons of printers gleamed as cats' eyes. I'd not seen the office twilit before: its secret curves and edges dipped in and out the gloom; matt-black screens stood portal to deep nothing; narrow, glary light seeped under the escape route doors: a dazzling otherness leaked in from beyond; and everywhere beady catseye printers twinkled the length of the floor.

Turning, I glanced out the big plate windows to the apartment block over the yard. The offices and flats were matched design: same grey concrete panels, breezeblock ledges, flat cinder roofs, big windows. An ornamental yard was laid out between the buildings, too low and dank for any use but to catch the litter of corkscrew winds. The apartments are welfare, our neighbours surly consumers of our taxes. Maybe not the sharpest tools and it was kind-of clear in the winter dark how they failed to get a grip on the sheer sheet windows. Of course we got blinds paid wholesale from the bucket marked office stuff. But over the way, morning lights show an ingenious mix of improvised drapes: small curtains tacked together; sheets pinned in sagging bows or stretched tight as drum skins; elaborate, teasing arrangements of clothes hung from the curtain rail to fox the view; black plastic trash bags slit and flattened on the glass, giving unnerving sense of crime scenes waiting. Most homes take lampshades for optional, turning the orderly windows to a jumble of deep-shadowed makeshift interiors, like the building maybe fell conquest to random invaders. Seen the first time the cluttered assembly was starkly broken by one window centre-right that seemed to open in on a wholly bare room. I could see the bulb on its ceiling flex, the wall behind, a rectangle bright and sterile as a fresh tank in the lizard house.

My place is rent, ready with junk the landlord doesn't want; the place over the way looks unprepared, unfinished even. I thought maybe I'd see a guy in paint-splash overalls hauling a ladder. I didn't expect young and naked. Of course I see girls stripped. I go out with the boys, meet girls who like to party. I get my action. It wasn't some pervy starvation delayed me hitting the striplights but a weird leftfield dissonance of broken sleep; bolting to work sooner than I should; frantically piecing a plan to cover my screw-up; and in all that not expecting ringside view on a naked young woman. It was—you might say—a disconnect.

She hurried across the window and back, getting dressed. The second pass she found her underwear; the third she morphed into tee-shirt and jeans. I hit the switch: the striplights kicked-in work thoughts, nagging my reflection from what now was mirror glass. I woke sharp next morning, winter cold driving me to the paid-for warmth of the office. But some accounts guy got there first: he had the whole floor lit up like the fleet's in. Third morning I set my alarm for a time when club kids are still dancing.

From slacker I'm keen as a newbie. She's about my age I guess: maybe twenty or so; short, slim—skinny all told—always got her hair twisted up maybe so it doesn't get wet in the shower. She's cute little breasts poking out and up like curious kittens; dark nipples, real dark: almost red. The window's plenty tall to get a real view. With the lights off here I guess she doesn't see me. Or maybe she doesn't care. I've never met too many girls like that, not for lack of looking.

I got a thought one day I'll wait till she gets her coat or whatever, then brisk round front of the block to see her leave out.

She gets ready same time most days: guess she's working some-where. I'll check her looks, maybe ask her out. I've already okayed the goods.

Bastards left me here. Bastards. I know the shelter's emergency only. Priority needs, I know that. I was priority need not so long ago. But there's always some little bitch comes along scars herself better, wets herself better, got herself some worse daddy. They told me I should get happy. They said: why would you want to stay? We got you a place to call your own: your kitchen, your bathroom, painted box-fresh. It's time to move on. First nights in the shelter yeah I cried where the girls hated me for taking someone's room. I wished and wished a place of my own. I should be pleased. But why so sudden? I told them: I got no furniture, I've not even got a bed. They said okay, we give you tokens you take to the secondhand warehouse. We can do that for you. But it's not just a bed or table or chair. My room at the shelter had carpet, curtains; there was a laundry in the basement, pots and pans in the kitchens. Not mine but what I need.

My little room was warm. I'd flick the thermostat: get warm. The heat in this place takes hours and who pays the bills? I've never lived on my own. I need curtains: these dumb windows so bastard big heat just flies straight out. How do I get curtains? They gave no tokens for that. And I only get rent paid while I'm on placement. Soon as that's over I'll need a job. Nothing, none of this got told me in shelter. I miss my friends. From that rough start it got kind-of okay: the fights stopped when I wasn't new girl anymore. I never would have believed at first but those girls were the best. Even when I wanted quiet, a warm little room on my own, it was kind-of good to know I could go in the hall or down to the TV room and there'd always be someone say Hi. Never alone, and security got the street door locked-down tight.

They abandoned me. There's no security here. Once I lock that door I'm locked in and everything's outside. My room at the shelter and me were just the right size for each other. Here I'm tiny, rattling round in four big rooms I can't keep warm that got shitty cast-off furniture on bare floors. A bed maybe some guy died in. I miss my friends. They stopped being friends the second I got this place. Everyone said they were pleased for me but their eyes got jealous. The way they stopped talking when I walked in the TV room. The way everyone kept saying: you're leaving us soon. Like when someone's the terminal end of the ward. They all got my number; I gave everyone the address. There was going to be a big housewarming, all back to mine. No one came by. Not one of those girls has called. So how do they know I'm alright? What tells them I'm alright if no one's called? First couple of times at placement I said to the counsellor to remember me to all the girls. Can't say it again. If I say it again she'll know no one's called. She'll get a big laugh how no one cares I live or die.

I tell her I got new friends, got tight with all the neighbours. Been invited for coffee up and down the hall I tell her. I don't see the neighbours. I hear them sometimes shouting; laughing the way you hear through walls when something's not so funny. But I'll put the lying I learned in shelter to use. They'll think I got a great new life and one by one they'll move on and it won't matter.

This winter's so cold. My little room was kind to me; this flat's mean. I'm only warm in bed and then only just before I got to get up. Can't use the heat in the morning: doesn't even begin to warm through. I just freeze all round the place where there are no curtains. It's nice in the shower—nice having a shower that no one's bled in; but bastard cold all else. Should get a robe or something.

What kills is how every morning's the same. Five days a week on placement. They're teaching me office skills. I'm not sure: I don't think I got asked what I wanted; and if I got asked I'm not sure I said that. But it's decided. There was a meeting decided. When I've learnt basics I'll move to second phase. That's where they get you a job. No: help you get yourself a job, what the counsellor said. Placement will end like shelter ended: me pushed through some door marked Opportunity. Five days a week: how long do jobs last? Year? Two years? Christmases and Halloweens and birthdays slipping by. And what's the next phase of that? What happens after whatever I'm meant to prepare for?

Weekends I stay in bed. I get so cold and tired. Weeks and

weekends were kind-of the same in shelter, except for seeing doctors and stuff. We'd go out on a weekend sometimes: robbing shops, having a laugh. I was part of something then. Now I don't know what I am. All I know is life keeps changing. Now I'm someone got a difference between weeks and weekends. I'm up so early those offices over the yard are all still dark. Don't guess people there are cold or early. I bet they all left placement far behind.

Thirty

We talk work in the lift or say nothing. I don't mean we ignore each other. We check devices. I don't think we ever discussed travelling in together. After the wedding we just assumed we would. We can only afford one car just now and it's not likely we'd get a second space in the underground lot anyway.

The audit trail for how today happened might show aspiration can hit the right seam and deliver. I was still quite junior then; she was a newbie, fresh-qualified and, in truth, I didn't like her. She seemed too ready to point-score, too driven, too blind to my charm. When a project I had back then needed professional cover, I felt cheated that my section leads were so keen to get her aboard, foreseeing awkward hours of spiky negotiation where she'd snow me in blatantly dumbed-down words how all my thinking was wrong. But in those long days we had to put in, those midnight deadlines we beat, it got clear she wasn't the tad icy bitch I imagined: just she was last-in-the-door, her keenness warily directed at staying employed. I could work with that. Sure it was scary asking her out. Back in admin grade I'd catch a beer with the admin girls, life pally with casual encounters that were forgiven, forgotten next morning. But she was a step-up date, a fishing trip to big-league rivers. Took some attempts to adjust to her mode of social operation. Frankly, she doesn't do wisecracks. Or pitch catchphrases off TV. From that hesitant start to married is a past too recent I guess to analyse. I joke sometimes I'll hack her files for the cost-benefit model that told her say Yes.

We arrive for who has to be early; we wait for who's got to

stay late. Her hours drove both ways at first but now I got more busy. I'm here a lot: the more you're here the busier you get. Now it suits us both to be early. That last switcharound I got moved back this side of the building. I wasn't enthused: where I sat before received afternoon sun, regarded by the cufflink-collectors upstairs as a determinant of status. Looking out back on the yard is a deal more grimy: one of my parallels actually told me his raise couldn't compensate for the impairment value of the view. I agreed because your parallels matter, but in domestic budget terms I can reprioritise sunlight. We're just now gearing to implement the next suite of corporate targets and, bonus-needy, one day were here real early. I exchanged the air-kiss with my wife permitted in office rules and left her travel to her somewhat sunnier floor. Past the security doors I stalled at how, without striplights, the sector emerged ambiguously from darkness: tiny coloured stars gleaming out of dirtied-up, scrappy gloom. Once the strips hit, the tint turns windows to mirrors: designed that way to raise our game through focused reciprocal effort, reflecting ourselves back on ourselves hermetically blind to distraction.

But not hitting the switch there's apartments over the way, pretty slummy. I'm far enough now from rental days to recall with chuckled fondness what dreary squalor I got blind to, mixed more than a tad with grown-up relief for the smart fabrics and polished lines of a neat marriage. We've done well from the booster effect where two-salary purchasing power is more than a simple plus-one and I guess I'd find invasive now the kind of jumble I spied-in on: the dark office showing me rooms stacked with crates; sheets for curtains; bare walls; furniture that—even at distance—showed rackety beginnings determining short life. Welfare homes for people lacking the push.

There was one bright window: bright with memories of racing to the office, heaping unreasoning curses on the clock. Those early days of here before dawn that laid the foundations of now. The room's bright bareness raised it from the concrete stack of windows, from unlit flats where people sleep till noon I guess, from duller junkscapes more hesitantly lit. A man stepped in from the side as though entering onstage: the rehearsed move of someone who paces a short way to hang like they've walked real far.

196

He was bare, toned and shaved, his tattooed arms and back a relish of his own physicality. I always held the line that women go for charm, clearly because my fathers never had chance to be other than lean and wiry. Large, tattooed men are a type to me: his strutted show of the generous—over-generous—way genetics had framed him a pride I rationalise as thug-like, unthinking, in no way compensatory for what was sure to be cultural dissatisfaction. The woman who joined the display was tiny: hardly reached his chest, with a body stance awkward, almost skeletal, at distance. Her bleach-blonde skin stood her nipples like warning lights. I knew who she was.

They seem pretty fond of each other, pretty indifferent to who sees, their embrace morphing rapidly into an arrestable offence when continued in plain sight. I guess that's why they do it. Why do I watch? Why am I so busy now I got to be always early? It's not some pervy starvation lapping second-hand at what's off the market at home. On the contrary, my wife is a high-achiever all ways. I still watch. I wouldn't claim perfect recall: I got devices do that. But that woman across the way seems hardly changed from back when. Small and lunar-looking, those obvious bones and stop-sign breasts exactly as I remember for—I don't know— maybe ten years gone. People you don't see a long time usually mature on reacquaintance. But she could still pass for a skinny kid scarfing apples. Her man is huge, not just that way other men find reluctantly fascinating. He's got, like, presence in the room, he commands the window: he leads what he wants her to do, arranging her body how suits him against his solid wants. She's kind-of transparent in contrast, effective only in context of him.

H e understands: he knows it's me makes things achy. They pushed me to a life; they never said what way. I've been learning. But things don't stick. Stuff happens, other stuff happens and things don't stick. I learn again but what I learn is not the same as before. He knows that. He keeps me learning. I never had doubts with boys and men; I've been shy but not that way. When days and weeks are a weariness of cold and forgetting stuff, to have someone take interest just

197

a short while counts more than physical pain which is really just nothing. I guess I got parts that got good at calling favours.

When I got work it mattered to keep it. They branded-in that notion with the kick that sent me out the placement door. Nice things are for good girls. Nice things like somewhere to live with heat you're not wary of using are for girls who play team and don't weird-out. Good girls. I never knew till placement that big step between who's crazy and who makes it. No other differences matter. Of useful stuff the office skills tutors never got round to show me I guess the biggest missing was how work-people do what they do: in planned ways using understood words, and keep doing that day-long. First week in work I thought people were kind-of ill or unhappy maybe for something. It was just when bad reactions started mounting up, when the counsellor called with a key-points reprise—that scratch to her voice kept asking if I understood stuff—that a message got delivered me it wasn't work-people who were to blame. She told me four times so I'd get it that people have expectations; that word fell way important like a big bomb on a busy road. Expectations and appropriate: now, after that word debuted it punched its weight through the bulk of what she called to say. I'd been too slow to tag the fact that appropriate makes stuff happen. Good stuff is appropriate. Appropriate people act good ways. It's a word that means value or cherish. Not appropriate is hitting the dark with the lights off. Maybe I got told. Maybe I forgot.

Seems years gone by. I'm not good with counting but tastes like years of cold winter mornings. Years that got warm some, then cold. Bills paid, more bills coming. Little by little getting what goes at the office. Not making friends but getting okay with people who didn't know me back when. Boys and men measure my time, how this week, this year, got different from someday. He doesn't mind all the others: he's cool that way. Says it's him and me now, that's how it's staying. It's good he's here. I can't say how much. Not just the cash—though that counts a lot—but how he knows stuff. Like to paint the kitchen and fix when fuses blow. He helps filling forms: he's not great at writing, no more than me, but he knows the right answers to what forms want, the best answers for what I need. That's a big help. And the cool clothes: he always

198

knows guys who got stuff. When his friends come by it was edgy at first; I'm not ashamed of my body.

I like how he shows night and morning what I mean to him. He gets hungry a lot: says I slake his appetite everyway. And him mine. I get a real buzz how he shows me, how he lets me present my best. Maybe he started the morning thing but there was no way I'd stop once he begun. Most people got no one cares enough. But I got lucky. He shows the whole world how lucky I got, or anyway the offices over the yard, empty when I go to work. You can bet they're in bed still, dreaming of cars and houses. I've learnt at the office if you don't talk cars and houses people think you're good for not much. Sure I got a home and he gets cars but we don't rate that for room-filler. And you got to talk TV, though the shows we like you maybe don't discuss much. And you got to up-talk holiday. He says he'll take me on holiday soon.

Forty

I never doubted I did right to stay. For strategic reasons. Reward scales well above industry average and over the last five years bonus rates have held generally in-range, unlike our so-called leaner competitors whose lack of depth buckled at market correction. We've a good Board; a young CEO who knows what she wants; we've got good people. The severance offer was above contract—maybe the most generous offer I'm likely to get—but I trust my judgment: I called right on staying. It's not slovenly to ink for the long-haul at my career-point. I cracked another bottle to help factor the non-financial components. I've been here twenty years, got my picture on the wall, I know all-but the freshest newbie by sight and most by name and family composition. I know the environment: I've held six roles and wherever I'm placed I know how things are done here, who's got the knowledge I need, the systems and protocols; I get the jokes. I wasn't planning on any package, however generous, being enough to sustain through my encore career to anaemic pension pot. If I'd left with a smile in my wallet it would have been to a down-step job: demands, misunderstood routines, a worse grind than to stay. And approaching the veteran end of the bottle I realised I like the people: my parallels and reports were kind to me; my managers—so far as they could without putting themselves in an awkward situation—were constructively sympathetic. I was allowed time away, no one chivvied me back; the place believes I'm worth keeping. When I woke and changed my crumpled clothes I knew to leave would be hubristic while to stay, though initially painful, was sustainable long-term.

One difficult choice taken out of my hands was how to assign me. Previously it might have seemed I had a career track, though more scenic route than highway. Each role has zig-zagged me a notch or two, accruing probability I might someday approach where a real decision gets made. However unlikely that outcome it's now been disallowed. As a punishment that's not bad. I wasn't outstationed somewhere proverbial to become prescription-dependent. I wasn't left so uncomfortable here as to have to quit. I got the forsaker's comeuppance: gerried into some made-up job; full ration window-dressing, all monkey and no organ. I'm outside the box, strategic thinking, a space in the chart for blue skies. What I'm meant to be doing is touring beyond the numbers: new rhythms, new shapes, new paradigm thinking to cement when we get to the top of whatever mountain after next after next the Board might aim to climb. I have no budget, no targets, no route to decisional loops; a loudly unspoken presumption I won't aspire. I spend days reading the newsstand. I don't feel bad collecting my pay.

The audit trail for how today happened is a seismograph of pressures stealing surface round our daughter. I'm not sure we spec'd out children but once our daughter's presence could no longer hopefully be dismissed as a flaw in the scan, an unsuspected and rather mordant feminism became my wife's primary voice. She determined with blunt authority the unborn girl as her project, a deliverable that I had neither capability nor will to accomplish. Like previous generations of men I could have accepted—even welcomed—the guise of weekend apparition, morphing in time into Daddy: the intermittent channel of cool toys, power tools and a cussing knowledge of football. But my wife had no patience for sitcoms. Our child was her daughter, taught from minus three months the first steps to female professional sustainment in the male bastards' world.

I wouldn't say she grew insular—not to her face nor her lawyer—and tracking the seismic cues, causality long predated the singularity that rooted and blossomed. Ours was a marriage of projects, tasks generated to consume shared resources no longer directed to interests of our own. A workfare programme digging holes and filling them in because if we stopped, if we didn't check devices, the truth was we mined-out our seam of togetherness in as little as maybe two years. Following through that thought—as I've time to do waiting the weeklies to publish—my wife got a gut for when to fold. She recognised that a child could tie her closer-in to me and resolved instead the child as her departure. A boy might have maybe provoked different signals. That can't matter now. I held my little girl unsupervised only when my wife was sleeping.

As I strolled the corporate hillside, my wife was on route-one fast-track. Indeed, when her lawyer suggested her progress allowed me to ease off the gas, I paused—fatally to my case—to think should I disagree. A well-placed, successful spouse generates pure oxygen. Her ambition achieved to stay employed she worked to outrun the game. She never told me that because I guess it meant saying that what she wanted was beyond our bounds as a couple. She was scrupulous always to keep the big news embargoed till it got impact. That's how the hottest ticket that season was when my wife made CEO and served papers on me same-day. As self-help goes that's a whole other ashram. With practical kindness, she served papers first so when she told me why the Chairman called it didn't prick some transient elation at her success but arrived as inexplicable jubilee to some house of grief. I was so wrapped in the terms of my disappointment of her that this extra news thrown from the kitchen seemed too mandarin to figure. She's risen reliably through the years; I vaguely recalled talk of a second, then third interview. If I thought at all, it was she was aimed at Finance Director. But then the old chief did leave kind-of sudden when the trades got scent of his unadjusted bar tab. Her inaugural act was to cancel the flatfoot sniffing on who leaked the receipts. We need to move forward she told the trades.

Practical kindness.

I didn't fight my case, not having much case to fight. With generosity glimpsed from an eye on the long game she didn't hold me to the pre-nup but settled for a token sum for her psychological trauma in exchange for my prints on the more-than fair severance package. Of course she got our daughter. I couldn't protest that: the kid hardly knew me. I only protested to stay employed—cashing the slim merits and commendations on my file. She graciously reconsidered, casting the bait of a make-believe function quarantined from any prospect of making a difference. Of course it's humiliating, but every month counts for pension and now I'm on paid reading time the blue sky's the limit. Geography, biochemistry: it's all on the newsstand. There's folks everywhere doing interesting things for no reason.

Symbolically, physically, we couldn't be further apart. I sometimes catch her pep-talk podcasts and it's like gawking at those shots of rock and sand beamed from Mars. She maybe could have unpersoned me, kitting me up to work from home, but then I guess the audit would show me as paid to lay on my rented third-floor couch and do jack. Not good for a CEO whose probity is monstrous. So I'm kept here in the old building, in a section reconfigured to give me an office kennelled away from impressionable young folks. Getting a closed door means I got warning to tab-back from the online art history course I signed for, the rare times anyone calls by. No one serious calls by. She's done a fair job disposing the old boy club that had this place stifled if only we'd known it. The trades print gushy profiles of her, ornamented with pictures that—conservatively—put half a percent on the share price.

Most days I come in late for an easy commute. But now I'm not punching the clock I don't sleep so well and don't want to. Now my time's pretty much my own I aim to use it. I'd got behind on art history—diverted by lives of improbable saints; insomniac, I came early for a couple of renaissance hours before token corporate flim-flam. It's no surprise I'm the unfashionable side, overseeing the yard. The old place tastes of dereliction since the new global HQ opened; I got to say that suits me: I've been in this building a long time, we've fallen far together. When I ambled

202

in the section lights were off, the few pieces left us of last-generation equipment blinking glumly through the pre-dawn. I didn't disturb the dusty dark, nor when I reached my gimcrack office, delighted as ever at how one day the door might really fall dead-flat, slapstick-style at my elbow-shove. I don't need striplights to see this place, to see the flats over the way that look a tad like my walk-up but maybe more purposeful. Same tentative curtains, same tipping-point breached between clutter and junk. Most of the windows were dark, sane people enjoying their leisure, but one stood stark from the concrete gloom: one bare window so bright it seemed to reach from the block, to catch at my eye, to connect me. A woman stood in the window naked, her hair twisted-up, seeming to look to a mirror away at the side. She checked her eyes, pulling down each like opening a bag; raised her chin to examine her mouth; searched her tongue; held up each arm in turn to check fat I guess, pinched to confirm she had tone; cupped and showed her breasts to herself, holding high and letting them fall. She turned full-front, her nipples magenta as the robes of long-dead princes.

I don't complain about my life. I got a job, somewhere to live; few identifiable ambitions. No more pressure or responsibility than an averagely-bright child. In the gamut of possible outcomes that's not bad. Except I got it wrong. That morning sure as a kick in the head I saw how one decision taken for some good reason leads to bodily capture, propels you where you never thought to go. I didn't have plans. I asked her because ambition seemed kind-of right. We went places, did stuff.

Today I'm real early. Like she was waiting, she steps into the light. I see her familiar body: slim, neatly-shaved, relentlessly unchanging. All the years I've wasted doing shit, she's been getting stripped, getting dressed, getting stripped, no way different to how I recall. I watch her check her reflection—same order, same tests; when she gets personal on herself I'm uncomfortable knowing it's no more than I'll do. I gave up dating the night I learned I'm not twenty anymore. But she is.

Maybe time is just something interrupted. Yesterday I saw her, now I see her to-and-froing in jeans and tee-shirt and I could go out front of the block and ask has she time tonight to sit with me and explain all I've missed. I know now I'm in for the long term: any day I could go ask her. I hit my boxed-off segment of the striplight, surprising some thick-set, jowly man crying in tinted glass.

There was not one thing I did wrong, not however they blamed me. Except I did their shitty job from the get-go. I gave years when the world was happening round me—when I could have had my time—years to filing stuff and sorting stuff, running errands and making coffee; the dumb bitch everyone joked at when they thought I didn't hear. Man, I was dumb. I really thought when I got work it mattered to keep it like . . . I dunno . . . like the sky might fall. After all those years, all what they said: how I didn't play team, wasn't suited, how the way I'd always done stuff right wasn't right anymore. How work-people found me difficult, uncooperative, surly. Man, the truth those words told. I got it tight in my head: I'm difficult, uncooperative, surly; have a nice day.

I gots to get my look back. I'm getting bags: too much midnight double-feature. Should maybe try to smooth some: I don't aim to pass for old. These have slipped a ways too: need a new push-up. It's the weight of shit those bastards heaped on my shoulders. But I got wise. All anyone said was deceiving me into making like some soldier in their cause: all that group targets, shared objectives, pulling the oars together. Now I got my own fight. This place is cold still; there's still not much of anything matches anything else. I never found carpet wall-to-wall; I never bought curtains. Too bad. See the sparkle in my eyes now, the sheen like fresh snow of my skin. Better fix-up: don't wanna get late.

He got me these jeans. Still fit. I miss how he used to get stuff but that's all. There's nothing else he did I can't still have and no man to clutter the place. You taught me well, boy. Now I'm you. When I think what a little pissy scrap of nothing I was to start with, how I'd jump every noise in the block; seems that girl got stripped away, some glistening hardness replaced her. I always thought change was bad how I got moulded into it. Never entered

204

my dumb little head back then how I could be what changed. No counsellors, placement, therapy, nothing. Just a big dumb live-in-maybe and some work-cow saying I should take care. Pull a small thread, world unravels. I asked: what do you mean? What way take care? What business is it of yours what I do? He liked us to go places, sometimes we did stuff, I was no way forced: he helped me know what I want. I thought I was only at work when I was at work; turns out they own you. Where you go in the evening, what show you put on: that's all owned, all work-time. So I told them: my business, my life. That got everything unravelling: I let them down bad, I was rude, I got things wrong for years it seems and everyone too cute to tell me. I don't think I'd have cared those things they said if I was an intern or some temp getting her pay signed-off by the week. But I was there years, longer than some of the faces in the half-circle round me saying how I was so crap. I did what he'd do. What I wanted to do. So at my make-believe trial I got called difficult, uncooperative, surly; got told I was an efficiency saving. Big shrug. Someone else can do office skills.

When I quit work I kind-of thought he'd cheerlead. But he seemed mournful, kept asking when I'd get another job. I was so slow catching on. Real, real slow. I thought daytimes he hung with the guys or was round the way on his business. Man, how dumb was I? He didn't like I threw him out; seemed to think he could retrieve me with some street-corner candy, some pledge to change. But I was changing. He was real sad when I bagged-up his movies and told him our groove had worn shallow. I don't guess he thought he'd be sad. I was shaking an hour and more after the lift doors slammed not because I thought he'd hurt me but because I knew he was hurt. I felt starved for weeks after; I thought he'd call, thought there'd be some chick-lit show where he'd pitch winning me back. That can't matter now. Guess the world's enough stocked with crazy girls even for him.

He left two things I didn't expect and cherish. He showed me places where girls with not-so-great office skills can make the rent. And he released my courage to know that's for me. If I hadn't got pissy-scared back in shelter I would have seen the girls who got nice rooms, clothes, the good stuff, were all getting paid while I was still fretting that if I stayed in the TV room too long people would get bored with me. I've rocked-up late to this party, I'll never catch-up all I've missed, but for now at least I'm right for the life I'm living. In the morning I wake in snowdrift sheets, unstained by anything that's not me. Take a shower; stand and see myself with pure love. Sure, days can be the same; sure work gets relentless. But I don't feel tired or put on where I'm the star.

Best of all: no one cares I'm crazy. No bitchy whispers, no sly looks that cut me out. It's taken, like, so very long to see I'm not like anyone: not pretend, not be polite, not bruise myself to fit somebody's game. Crazy eyes sparkle from every mirror I dance through. If I'm not happy at least I'm alive every morning; I'm permitted, some nights, to think maybe I made someone's day. I'll never catch-up all I've missed but now my strategic target is fly the finger on anyone fouls my life.

I stand by the window, look out on still-dark morning: all those offices, all black. Don't guess anyone's home. They'll put off getting up till they can catch traffic, till they can miss the bus. Slob in for another day of who-cares-what. I don't feel sorry, I don't feel rich or poor by contrast. I don't feel connected any way. Till someone hits the lights nothing happens. They don't see me. No one's there.

Static Presence

The truck shivers and dies. The driver, cursing, rubs his groin, cranks the stick. A lad spits on the floor, works the phlegm with his heel. "We're Sunday tea if we don't shift. Hey, mate: what's up now?"

"Got the wrong bloody shaft." The driver's voice, dinned in grinding metal.

"Wrong bloody army, more like."

We jerk forward again. Cigarettes pass round. I take one, like always. Pretend not to choke, like always. I'm sitting gun at the back where canvas lets in air. The older lads sit deep in, superstitious of snipers. They tell me I'm a target.

"Bullseye, boy. These Paddies'll nick your head off."

"When I was in Hamburg, right, them Yank trucks, right, all convoys, all moving together. Had guards front and back and everything worked. Just worked, right. You could see 'em miles down the road, mind, but they was untouchable."

"Not so bloody untouchable now, are they?"

"You reckon we're doing better?"

Everyone comes to watch the khaki travelling freak show. At camp they made us march, shoot, jump to order. They told us taking the shilling was a man's most honourable thing. There wasn't much said about women spitting, telling their children to spit. About old men shaking their medals and calling us traitors. Some of these lads burn with that, worse than with bullets that hunt our spines from attic lights, doorways; from innocent crowds.

"Are them priests out there, Wilson? Wilson? Them Paddy priests. All poofs, having it up the choirboys and eating Our Lord." That's Private William Roberts: a roundhead son of the English Civil War. "Bloody cannibal country."

"If they're eating God, old son, they don't need you." That's Lance Corporal Sam Beckett: Germany, Singapore, everywhere. He was probably at Tobruk. He was probably at bloody Mafeking.

"At least there's Christian God in 'em. When we was in Aden, them Muslim lads: spines like that, y'know? Rigid, harsh with God talk. No give-ee, no give-ee, tell you, boy." Sergeant Harry Steele. The voice of command translated ways we understand.

Roberts has none of it. "For one, these are not Christians: they're Popists. Romans. You hear that cursing: is that a Christian tongue? In front of children. The men are too soft to rule 'em. All poofs, eh, Wilson?"

I pretend I'm tracking on something. I don't know why he talks to me.

The truck stops again: driver shouts we're there. Don't know where. Don't need to know. Jump down, form up hidden by the truck from the crowd we've gathered through the streets, kept penned at the gates, throwing curses. Bricks and bottles, come lights out. Dangerously inattentive like always, I watch a large, dirty grey dog wrestle its bulk through the patched-up fence. It lurches toward us, tongue slapping heavily on its jowls. It barges the line, bounces back, chasing its shaggy tail.

A shot, clean and eager, stops the dog cold. We grab our rifles; I don't know what to do. Sam and Harry drop under the truck, take aim at nothing. I dive beside them; can't help gasping when the ground hits my knees. My gun's the wrong way round; too tight to the axle to move I bury my face, my terrified trust in men I can't defend. Boots run by; scattered cries: stay low. A whisper, what we're all thinking: sniper.

A machine gun voice rattles over our heads. "What a shower of pansified shit. Get up. Bloody get up."

A bullet's echo leaves a long silence. At the flick of a switch, Sam and Harry shout attention. Shout: Officer on Parade.

The Captain checks his revolver, kicks the dog's lumpen body. It twitches faintly, the last muscles letting go. "What was all that? What the hell was all that?"

"Begging pardon, sir . . . "

"Who the hell are you?"

"Steele. H. Sergeant, sir. Relief detachment ready for inspection, sir."

The Captain stares with the pop-eyed rage of a vaudeville patter man. "Have you recently enlisted, Sergeant?"

"Begging pardon, sir. No sir. I first saw service in Suez and . . . "

"Do you know why you're here?"

"Yes sir."

"I would hope so, Sergeant, because if I were Paddy I'd be licking my lips. I could have killed any one of you. I could have killed all of you while you ran around squealing. Assuming you have come from basic training and not monkey school, this suggests to me you are stupid. I will bear that in mind. Briefing, thirty minutes. Try to get there alive."

We're billeted in a guardroom, walls quick with streaky limewash. Throw our kit on the sagging beds: tired springs twang Bhagwan vibes like hippie guitars. Roberts cracks a Paki joke, says the Irish are white Pakis. There's twenty of us in this room: so tight we can't move without touching. Electrocuted, every time someone knocks my arm. No space to smuggle some relief. Everyone cracks fairy jokes. Poof and pansy jokes. Hoskins does that pansy out the films: "Ooh, matron." I want time to unpack, to set my things just so. It hurts, when things aren't just so. But we only get thirty and everyone wants the latrines. I hold it till cramp kills me; get up in the early hours when they're sleeping. I volunteer night watch, often, to catch my breath alone.

The Captain sees us as borstal boys come to dig ditches. We can sit; Harry stands at the back. NCOs talk about shows: the Suez show, the Singapore show; that show in British Honduras. Like greasepaint queens, they reprise their finest turns. The rest of us maybe are meant to learn something. I don't know what.

The Captain's jetstream vowels take charge. "You will know that since the recent disturbances in Londonderry there has been a significant increase in attacks on Her Majesty's property, forces and subjects. A tribunal has cleared our compatriots of blame for the incident provoked by local troublemakers. But the cowards who attacked our fellow forces do not respect the rule of law. They prefer lies and criminal violence. That is why you do not form up in open sight of the road, not even on camp."

I can't see Harry; I know he's stood, glassy with attention. Harry is Queen's Regulations. Queen's Regulations have seen him right in all the jungles and deserts of Her Majesty's petty wars.

"We are not fighting an army; we are fighting a rabble of traded guns without discipline. We are not fighting a war, whatever lies these people tell." He pauses, the antennae of his clipped moustache bristling for dissent. "These men have no standing command: they scrap for status like dogs. We will deal with them like dogs."

Some of the lads are keen. Roberts talked of nothing else all the way from Liverpool. He talked so much, it almost drowned the nagging in my head that I was taking ship to Ireland.

"But in this sorry state of affairs, we should not forget the many here who are loyal to the Crown. Many local people wish to assist the forces of order."

"Assist themselves to some scratch," Broadford whispers beside me.

"Did you say something, soldier? On your feet."

Broadford's over-large hands gangle his trouser pockets, as they must have done when teachers asked was he after the cane again. He bears his uniform like the bachelor gentlemen poets who objected so conscientiously during what Harry and Sam no doubt call the Kaiser's show. None of the lads are poster boys; Broadford's not good looking. But in his lop-sided, shambling way, too much to his limbs and not enough space to stow them, he's an individual, immune to camouflage. I can't guess why he joined this circus.

"Name?"

"Private James Broadford, sir."

"And Private James Broadford thinks his captain is speaking nonsense?"

"I said . . . "

"I heard what you said, soldier. We all heard. And in one, small sense, I don't entirely dismiss it. To be blunt: the army has long paid for information from local sources. It's effective. It saves lives. You may say it's a grubby business, not for gentlemen. But Private James Broadford has to understand three things. One." His finger stripes the air. "When you handle criminals you get your cuffs dirty. Her Majesty's enemies don't all wear braid and issue communiqués. Two." His eyes glint in the strip lights. "I am telling you things you need to know to stay alive. That may not matter to Private James Broadford. But it might matter to the poor bastards who have to rely on him. Three." His roar fills the room, killing our hesitant laughter. "When I am talking you do not so much as fart. I am heap big white fella, understand? The next man who interrupts is on jankers. Broadford will leave us now and treat himself to fifty laps of the parade ground. And then Sergeant Steele can spend an hour or so teaching you how to stand to attention when an officer is talking. Go."

Broadford shuffles out, knocking shoulders, knocking chairs.

The captain smoothes his matinee hair.

We're the rock'n'roll generation: we missed Hitler's show entirely. We know Kenneth More and Gordon Jackson beat the Nazis, made it home to an England where wives kept roses in bloom since 1939. The lawns our fathers died for. Not my father. I wonder what movies, some day, they won't make of this not-war. Older lads know the drill. But for most of these kids it's Liverpool docks to the Book of Revelation. We should be in Germany now. I'd already bought a phrasebook: 'excuse me, Mein Herr: where is men?' It's make-believe in Germany—Reds step forward, Yanks step forward; Reds step back, Yanks step back. It's a game. But that bloody Sunday dragged us here; not at war. This room's too small to breathe, sour with tarred lungs. We're asleep, in the official version. We are the army, the Captain said. The army of Monty and Kitchener, of Wellington and William III and civilised religion. The army that won the world and, graciously, gave it back. Bar this bloody scrap of red on a green island.

First lesson in basic training is tell the right lies. The lies that make us an army, not a bunch of frightened kids. Public lies, written in buttons and badges. Private lies we leave behind, in rent collectors' empty hands and pregnant girlfriends' tears. But some lies follow like sad and deadly dogs: crossing highways not caring for crashes; chewing at fences we trust hold back yesterday. Outside, trucks rev and die; lads on watch call the hours; firecrackers burst in town: keeps the Constables keen. Bottles smash around the gate; dogs scratch a way in. We're not tired. We're too scared to be tired. Lights at three, the Captain—Sunday fresh in a uniform his man's been all night pressing—says even the raw and shoddy can serve. Crammed elbow to gut in the mess we're given a hearty breakfast, the cooks slopping bacon and sausage—thick, bready pork from south of the wire—poison in their eyes.

Hoskins is the joker. Does voices from films, off telly; he'd be the one playing harmonica, telling the lads chin up. Dead by Christmas. I sit next to Stevens. Simon Stevens whose hair wants cutting, who's got no one here to talk to about pop music. He pushes food around his plate. He's shitting bricks. Older lads heard about war from uncles who came back; survivors who might've enjoyed it. They heard the dodges, the craic, the scandals of halfwit captains and mademoiselles. The Germans were just lads given guns and told they were special; their war was close and remote: it threatened in everything but was only seen in fractions: in bomb craters; ration books; Land Girls in dungarees. But these lads, Stevens, Hoskins, they've grown up watching war. In films, on the news, seeing war as it happens. Seeing an army better than ours getting kicked by lads in pyjamas. Show that to these kids, then send them here of all places; give them bacon and sausage and tell them to fight . . . what? The air?

Sam and Harry know: their sausage-thick fingers draw lines on the table, encircling worn tea stains. They know we're not fighting an army who plan like gentlemen, advance in good order according to contracts of war. We're fighting the farmer, the docker, the cooks' husbands and sons, pockets rich with nails and jelly, heart full of hate they got at mammy's tit.

Give Hoskins my breakfast in trade of a smoke; be Calcutta in the latrines when the lads have finished. The next stall is talking to himself, spitting words like acid. Should finish quick: I've learnt well enough men turn their weakness against you. But I'm knotted, thick; farting tunes. Paper's rough as sack; so's my skin. Quick with the tap. Not quick enough.

It's Broadford: lips still chewing, big hands flexing for something he wants by the throat. He's pale, shambling like the old man he might never be. Don't know he sees me: he's so taken with washing his hands, washing each finger, disinfecting, like them Arab lads with their hygiene of what's forbidden. Spreads his fingers to dirty morning that seeps through narrow vents high in the wall. Like he's not seen hands. Like he doesn't know them.

"Ready?" Don't know why I speak or why that.

"We're criminals, Wilson, do you know? We're going to

212

commit crimes."

"Is that orders, then?"

"I had an hour of that sergeant's stick up my back. He's a talkative man. He told me our task: break into houses, take what we find, kill whatever asks questions. Roberts'll be in pig heaven."

"Why'd you join, Broadford? Why d'you want this?"

His eyes have the fugitive hunger of men met in the park at sundown—the coal lads: up since four; twelve hours underground; tea with the wife, see the kiddies asleep; then out for a turn round the roses. Men too itchy with want to stay home. In glossy moonlit rhododendron leaves, I learnt that conspiracy isn't big ideas, big slogans in quiet voices. Conspiracy is stolen breath, shy of fists that bear grudges. Broadford breathes with miser's lips: counting like he knows each breath he's got left. "Have you heard of Lenin?"

In nightschool, bathed in coal dust.

"Lenin said the state is a body of armed men."

Seems likely as anything else.

"There are many conflicts, Wilson. But the war is relations of production. An intelligent army exploits the enemy's weakness. My enemy's weakness is dependence on armed men. You win by getting inside that body, by making cancer. This is an imperialist war, you know that? A colonial war of skeletal hands clinging to what's gone. This misadventure is weakness. This body is toxic ground. From here grows victory."

"Don't know the Apprentice Boys see it that way."

His red eyes glisten; he leans close. "They can't evade evolution."

The metal door clatters: lads on for evacuation. We blink, guilty by daylight. Hoskins stares, tries to spike our contamination. "What's this? Bum chums' bank holiday?"

The emphysemic engines gasp forward. Drivers kick tyres: their sole engineering. The usual bullying about who sits where; I'm sitting gun.

The Captain rides in a car his driver's been polishing since Korea. I'd thought the Captain passed his days filed in suspension, activated sporadically for pep talks and rage. But in combat order,

213

with his greens and his gun, he's a dangerous bastard. Maybe his wife thinks he's wonderful, as he beats her white as sin.

Picture it: Day of the Triffids time when the sighted sods leave in army trucks and the greenery gangs round the gate. That's now. At crack of dawn the undergrowth's lively, clacking and spitting venom. Everything in this town looks cheated. Half the shops have gone: dusty plate windows—cracked from kids with catapults—show grubby views of dead plants; windblown scraps of paper; tailors' dummies, bare and sexless, stare without surprise at ghostly men of property. Broadford doesn't look up, doesn't talk to anyone. I heard the Sinn Féin's gone Marxist. Gives the Bogside something to believe in.

Driver shouts red light. We're not meant to stop but since that Sunday we're careful. Brigade, not Captain's orders. When we stop, it's Beatlemania.

"Get off. Let go of the truck." They swarm us: kids mostly. We push back softly-softly: can't leave a bruise, a stain; we have to mind they don't fall. "Come on, son. Ride's over. Come on."

Hoskins lobs cherry bombs, blackjacks; the little ones jump to scrounge them. It's the big lads you watch. Fists, maybe razors; some small calibre hospitality in their sock. Every pub guv'nor's a gunsmith. Have to watch the girls. Banshees: scream if you touch their hair. Scream and their dads come running, braces down and shirt laps flapping with fury.

We chug on, kids chucking stones. You get used to it.

"Should have tanks. Armoured cars. Should have bloody armoured cars."

No one answers Stevens. If we had tanks we'd be at war. And we're not at war, no sir. We're at home. The Constables have armoured vans: they enjoy bigger rocks. This job's an endless carnival: the minute you leave camp, you're queen of the ball. Stevens can't let it be.

"Bloody Paras. This is their doing."

"Stevens."

It's so rare to hear Harry shout, some of us pretend we don't flinch.

"Our fellow soldiers acted heroically in the face of great danger and extreme provocation. It's for others to judge what's gone. We have orders."

"You poof, Stevens." Roberts lights a smoke.

No poofs in this army, no sir. No poofs, no jungle-jims. Tonight I'll lay awake in a roomful of soldiers who, if they must, will risk their lives for mine. Soldiers, mates. Not men. Men are clever fingers to unravel knots and puzzles; strong arms to catch and hold. Warm and whiskey eyes that ask what you most want to answer. Soldiers are boots, badges, parades, orders. Rules of engagement. I know the rules of engagement. You don't lay with men and wake with soldiers.

The engine dies. We're here.

Captain's running itchy for big game. This is a street, an ordinary street; the red brick terrace of childhood. Little yard out front for marbles; little yard out back for jacks. Somewhere to dream a life the colour of movies. But these streets are broken, empty, dead.

Sam says the crust's been hardening a long time: the rows about Paddy streets, Proddy streets; trespass and who draws the line. Some build walls, some build fires; some do this: drain the people, make what the Captain calls hygienic arrangements, a sterile no-man's-land to quarantine tribes with their god. Round the corner there's a barricade, pole star to the district. We're going to lift it, to show the Queen's highway is neither Paddy nor Proddy. For your long-term health, some might say this is robbing Pharaoh's tomb.

Captain chivvies us into a house, stands guards front and back. Away from base, off the laundry starch, he's G I Joe. "Gentlemen," he says, like we've chosen this, "I don't need to tell you that discipline is vital. This isn't Bongo-Bongo Land. It's Her Majesty's United Kingdom. We are Her Majesty's army. What's the first task of an army . . . Stevens?"

"Beat the enemy, sir?"

"Close, Stevens. We certainty want to do that. And get your hair cut, lad. Bright?"

"Obey orders, sir?"

"Because . . . Wilson? Wilson?"

Don't realise he's talking to me. I think the answer is not get killed but I don't think he thinks that. Play safe. "March straight

. . . sir."

"It would make a change, Wilson, but no. The first task of an army is to ensure a peaceable kingdom. We are Her Majesty's strong right arm. We are sovereignty in motion. Does anyone know what sovereignty is?"

"I do, sir."

"Private James Broadford. Private Broadford's a man of opinions. Do you read books, Private?"

"Yes sir."

"Books with opinions, no doubt. The room's agog to hear Private James Broadford on sovereignty."

"The supremacy of the state in its territory and its interests, exempt from disruption. A monopoly of violence maintained by a body of armed men."

"I'm sure the Good Soldier Broadford will be giving tutorials later. Or are they called teach-ins these days, eh?"

We laugh at his joke, whatever it is. We laugh because.

"Monopoly of violence. Ugly, Bolshie phrase. But I don't entirely dismiss it. What our . . . comrade means is the rule of law. One country, one army, one law. A peaceable kingdom. There are men round here who disagree. They want their own army, to start their own war. They need to understand that things do not work that way. We have reliable information that these hooligans use this buffer zone as their arsenal. A significant quantity of weapons is hidden in these streets. Our job is to find them. Then find the owners. And put both out of harm's way. These men here will be working with us. Be assured they are British officers. That's all you need to know. This town is a snake pit. News travels at lightning speed. I'm sure the jungle drums are already talking. Discipline is vital. The NCOs will explain your duties. But I'll tell you this: finding these weapons is a major step to securing order. Order is our first task. We are the British army."

Lads are shitting it. I'm shitting it. Every kid who took Hoskins' sweets has run straight to his mammy. There's no one from Lurgan to Omagh doesn't know we're here. Stevens fumbles a smoke. He's a nice-looking lad, young in his ways, fresh off the apron strings. He didn't join up with any thought of fighting.

"The factory's going," he says to me, like I'm bound to care.

216

"I was meant for a job at the factory but it's going. My uncle was in Burma."

"That didn't put you off?"

"He said it was alright, apart from the Japs."

Broadford's keen on our new friends, the casually-dressed, athletic men huddled with the Captain. Broadford knows all about them. "Oppressors. Secret police."

"Like the KGB?"

"The situation in the Soviet Union is misrepresented by the capitalist press. Don't believe propaganda."

If no one believed propaganda, we wouldn't be shoehorned in someone's back parlour while Sam tells us France is not like China. "This isn't smash-and-grab, lads. These houses are unstable; any weapons we find might not have been properly kept."

We've been sent to rattle a death-trap. We are the British army.

"How do we know the houses aren't booby-trapped?"

Sam glares at Broadford with defeated irritation. "We don't. That's part . . . "

"It's part of your job, soldier, to find out."

We're perky for sudden authority. He's watching, distant like all the newcomers. Amazed he's spoken, we're taken on the blindside by his Donegal caramel voice.

For a second, Broadford's caught between Sam's weary endeavour and this man's Malin blue eyes. "How do you suggest we do that?" It's more a plea than a challenge.

"You could use your head."

I know he's making a joke. The rest aren't so well-travelled.

The man steps to the front, easily relieving Sam from his semblance of duty. He's Carrickfergus down Carnaby Street: nice crushed blue velvet, whiter shirt than I'd guess you see anytime round Lough Swilly. White shirt, in a war. His body looks hard.

"You don't barge a door. You check it for trips. You look up, always, when you go in a room. Trouble comes from above. But watch the floors. These places are all bare boards. Boards get dirty. So is there a board not dirty? Is there a floor in pieces got a new board slipped in? Does anything not look right about that? Don't be tempted by open cupboards. Cellars and stairs: watch the

217

treads. Does a step feel spongy, springy? Don't stand by windows and, Jesus sake, don't smoke. Don't slam, bang, knock or smash. I know that's hard for squaddies. Don't," he pins us with an accusing finger, "don't just look in a room and think it's alright. It's not alright. The room you don't check takes you and your friends to the arms of sweet baby Jesus. Oh," he steps back, "and if someone gets killed, keep searching. We'll sweep the bits there."

"And you are . . . ?" Broadford's nervous.

"I'm to save your English arse."

When I began—not just with my hand and wishes—I thought I'd be noticed, chosen. I never doubted myself and thought that was enough. In the street, the park, at the dance, some unlikely stranger—improbably pitched in a dying coal town—would take my little hand and I'd begin. In roses, waiting the miners of sundown, I saw myself doing what I did with them but truly meaning it, with someone worth the meaning. All I needed was to look pretty enough, click my heels and wish. Six years on, ignoring Sam's voice, dangerously inattentive, I'm watching a man's eyes stare through smoke out a window. While lost for breath in combat drag, I struggle a heart that betrays me.

"Wilson. Wilson."

Is he talking to me?

"Form into pairs. It's time."

No one pairs with Broadford. He moves to me; I sidestep. He's not liked, I've done my deed for the day. Get palled by cheery Mr Hoskins, who seems to have reached these parts on a different bus.

"This is better," he croaks in my ear as we squat a corner. "Sick of barracks."

"Would you rather get shot?"

"I don't like time dragging."

Harry and one of the older lads—Walsh, a family man laid off from the docks—creep point to point while we give cover, or pretend to. I can't see a clear line; I doubt Hoskins can see them at all. Around us, pairs of silent men melt into the streets, smudged to shadows, flitting a dancer's steps in spaceman boots. Till now, nothing's been real. Bottles, stones, the spitting mobs: just Saturday night gone dancing. Torremolinos flamenco and feathers. A fortnight's how's-your-father and back on the dole. But the safety catch is off now: we're out in open season with targets for heads. Weapons, then the barricade. If we live that long.

Even Hoskins catches a taste: "Don't reckon this is a Garbo moment."

He's right: some kiddie, some little Artful, eyes as wide with being poor as a Biafra belly, is scouting these upstairs rooms; sees us, clear as day. A baby blackfoot, in our spines before we know it. He understands these closed and crumbled streets more than we ever will; he understands when men in twos clutch guns rosary-tight. He knows us. He's got orders.

Hoskins nudges my arm. "Let's get closer."

"They've gone inside."

"Got to keep watch, ain't we?"

Sprint like chimps. Drop, sweating, by a wall.

"Can't see a bloody thing."

What does he want? X-ray? "It's front yards. No cover."

"Thought we'd do more than this."

He's breathing on my cheek; don't want that. Don't want breath on my face. Not his and not in a quarantine road, in a dead end of the Province, waiting on two old men to find nothing while, nearby, some bastard loads my bullet.

Walsh and the Sergeant, cripple-slow, go house to house. Each time they emerge we snap alert, trying to cover them off from what we can't see. When they're inside, we're suspended terror: trigger-ready, numb, knowing—wherever we look—we'll see nothing.

Inbetween acting tough, I ask why he joined. He flinches, like when policemen ask where you were Thursday last. Says you've got to do something. Puts it back on me. I tell him the usual: laid off work—not down the pit: the office—no other tunes to a one-note town so I chanced the shilling. Got told Germany. Says he was too. Civilised, West Germany, says Hoskins. They don't shut off streets and put up walls. "Do you know life expectancy in West Germany is seventy-nine years?" he tells me.

"Long time to be miserable, eh?"

Get back, three hours gone and spine in bits. Captain's restless: where's the metal, the gelignite? There's gossip the spooks want out. Lads coming back are nervy: it's the quiet. Not even birdsong.

Take a smoke out back, surprised to see Sam. Not a regular smoker. Says he packed it in down Ceylon, when he got monsoon lungs. He calls me lad, forgetting his stripe is a bar between us.

"How'd you get on with Harry, lad?"

"He was with Walsh. I was keeping shop with Hoskins."

"He's a good lad. Keeps spirits up."

"He was hoping we'd see Hamburg."

"A lot were that, lad. What the missus don't know does her good, eh? But all this . . . happened."

"That business the Paras didn't do?"

"You know the way I come, lad: out from school, straight in. Never had no other life. Even met the missus on camp. Gold Coast. Some of them shows down Africa: devious bastards. Africans are made for it, fighting. Wherever you go, they like a fight. Built for it. But no matter where, there was contact, push-and-pull. Not like now. Look at them Viet lads—they're bloody good, mind. Japs couldn't take 'em, y'know. They was all holed up in Burma then, waiting out the Frogs. What's this lot about, lad? Petrol bombs and nails. Can't tell who's what, not down any street. What do they want? To say their prayers? We should've got out in '23 and stayed out. We saw this miles off and walked right in. And now what we doing? Searching sad ghosts of houses, shifting some concrete, then filing a dispatch to say we won. Two years, lad. Two years and handshake off the General, a cottage down Somerset way. And these," he tugs his ribbons, "won't bloody wear these come Sunday."

"I want to lead a search."

"You heard orders, lad. Experience leads searches. Recruits are static presence."

"Captain's puce: we need to find something."

He gives me a look from Burma days. "Keen, eh, Terry? Reckon army life does you right?"

Lads need a dad to look up to. You could look up to mine. I don't.

"This barricade—there's flats the other side. The boys aren't eager, y'know. That's the Paddy side. You could do the flats. Take

Roberts: he needs something to do."

"Who's on cover?"

"There's none spare. Captain wants static presence where we've cleared. You'll be right. Take Roberts."

The back door is rich with velvet; I stop but my heart goes faster. "Excuse me, sir."

He looks down off the back step, his authority vivid in my dirty bones. Slight as a lad again, waiting under foreign leaves for hands proved in coal dust. He must see what I've done.

"So which of this happy breed are you? Is it Wilson?"

His voice is mammy's Christmas sweets, warm and drowsy tingles through my belly. "Yes, sir. Wilson, sir."

"Famous name. Much heard."

"Yes, sir.

"So what d'you think to this outfit, Wilson? D'you think they're up to the job?"

His eyes strip, clean, return me, eager as a good gun. "We've a sound unit, sir. Very able."

"Your Captain's surely the action man. Is this your first time in Ireland, Wilson? In Ulster?"

"Yes, sir."

"No holidays as a wee laddie you might neglect to recall?"

"No, sir. We didn't have holidays, sir."

"They were hard times. It's different here. People come and go. You married, Wilson?"

"No, sir."

"Engaged? Spoken for? Walking out as our maiden aunties had it?"

"No, sir."

"You must keep busy. I'd step inside: your Captain's building steam for a pasting."

"We have been here since crack of dawn and what have we found?" He's mean as a tinker's dog. "Not tuppence-ha'penny of dynamite. Not a pistol. Not a catapult. Nothing. How many premises have we searched, Sergeant? Sergeant?"

Harry Steele looks tired; his backbone can't hold him to attention. "About five hundred and fifty, sir."

I watched him turn every house down three long, lousy

221

streets.

"About, Sergeant?"

"Five hundred and fifty . . . sir."

"So where are the guns? The explosives? The papers? The plans? Do I need to remind you we have very reliable information? Brigade expects something. I expect something. We have been here hours."

We jump. Did he stamp his foot?

"Every hooligan in every pub knows by now. We have to leave before nightfall. We must search faster and harder, do you understand? Do you understand?"

Chorus: Yes sir, like schoolboys. Mean it, like schoolboys. I search for a big man who can stop this fool talking. But he's outside with Brigade. I want him to know I'm a good solider. "Sir."

"Private Wilson if this wastes time, every latrine on base is yours to care for."

"There's the flats, sir. Far side of the barricade. They'll be quicker to search."

"So why haven't we? Sergeant? Corporal?"

Harry stares, hopeless. Sam looks lonely. I look away.

"Sergeant?"

"We are being . . . methodical . . . sir."

"Well it's not bloody working, is it? Form details, search the flats. And shift that bloody barricade."

I burn in Roberts' prissy look. "Gold star, Wilson. You can catch my bullet for me."

"Are you fucking coming Roberts?"

"Temper. You'll ruffle your hair."

The one thing to Private William Roberts is he's certain to kill anyone who gets in his way. Reckon that includes me. He's the look to his eyes I've seen before, in men who'd knock mammy's door late of an evening. Who'd call me laddie and give me a shilling to piss off out the way.

"Have you spoke with the Brigade types?"

Every question he asks is a copper's inflexion: why? When? Can you prove that, sir?

"No."

"No?"

222

"Not unless spoken to."

"I spoke with them. Very interesting men. Very interested in friend Broadford."

The street's giving up, fissures opening the asphalt. Doesn't take long, once men leave, till what they've made falls apart.

"I mentioned things he's said. Just in conversation. I don't like secrets, do you?"

"I don't like anything."

"Bit spiky, Terry. Bit precious."

"Has it dawned on you, Billy, there's snipers around us now, licking their lips at your big head?"

"Should've thought of that before you wet yourself for the Captain."

Never much of a scrapper. Done some, in the playground, in alleys, getting called names. But never the man: I always run before long. In the park, I'd pretend the big coal men would save me, hide my bare and skinny bones in their lignite shadow. But they watched their back not mine; they'd press cash in my hand like it got too grotesque for their pockets. I want to smash Roberts till all the wrong comes out, smash him a long time. But never much of a scrapper, I don't begin.

"What the . . . ?"

We stop: a border instinct that transgression's waiting. Barricades aren't sticks and stones: they're castle walls to defend, to die attacking. Their concrete silence howls who you are makes this where you can't go. They shout who made them, why, and what happens to those who shout back. A steep of man-made rock, no promised land the far side but wastes where hate and hygiene drive a fissure through the war. A Berlin, extinguishing life around it.

"What now, General?"

The wall's wedged tight across the road, tucked against fractured, sightless houses. "Climb?"

"Oh very good, Terry. And what about those snipers Paddy-side?"

"Can't blow it, can we?"

"We'll go round, stupid. Come on."

Follow his stocky, boxer's build in a broken door; no risk

from shots ahead: nothing would get through his skull. Limpet to a wall through still and dusty morning, I thought Walsh and the Sergeant went too slow. Now I get it. Mammy's house was sparse and clean, tidy with poverty. Aunties' houses reeked of eau de cologne and old times. Houses hung with memorial clocks, family shrines. Doors closed by strangers' soft voices. This isn't a house: it's an avalanche, earthquake brick and shingle. A collapse, every end and beginning, thrown ceilings beneath our feet, cellar lights blown above. An Icarus of small dreams, fallen in burned hate. This is liturgy. This is the war of God.

"Pigs," says Roberts, cheerfully certain. "See: they've had the wiring out. All the copper. That's subbed a few peashooters."

No chance to go stealthy: no jungle training could silence savaged rubble that crackles with each step. Crockery and glass crunch like seashells; walls creak: old trawler hulls when a northerly comes seeking damage. In the back, shreds of furniture soak sun and rain.

Roberts tests the yard wall with his steel-tip. "You first, Commander. If you're hit, bleed away from my jacket."

Never a physical man, the one hope I had of the army was build some spine. Maybe some other army. Take a couple of goes at the wall. Roberts gives me a shove.

"Won't bruise your arse, precious."

All my life I've known it's better to run. Jump down the other side, biting my lip as landing knocks me sideways. The next yard's full of kiddies' clothes and Bibles.

Scrabbles rat-like and he's over, gun at the ready. "Do the next one. Get clear."

Over the next yard wall, he leads through a house wrecked different the same. Leads with a bullet itching, into the cratered street. We look sharp at the barricade—this side there's a wooden hut: shed windows, a stove chimney giving a sore touch of home.

"All mod cons. Nice the bastards keep comfy."

Roberts fights every step. His fists twitch in his sleep.

At the corner, mansion blocks hang ruined over the street. We crouch in a door: I'm watchman, he radios in. I'm holding this gun for real, light-headed. All the cleaning, training; the Present

224

Arms on square-bashing Sundays; now I'm a gun for real. Breathless, dizzy right down in my legs. Hard in this solider-boy drag: I'm a gunman, in a world of gunmen.

"Bastard's dead." He throws the headphones back in the case.

"What?"

"There's no signal. Can't raise base."

"What?"

"Base don't know where we are you stupid poof."

Flick, cock the gun at him. "Don't call me names."

"Wilson." He's steady, eye-to-eye with extinction. "We're in Paddy-town, in Paddy-land, wrong side of the rainbow. We can't get a radio signal. Base don't know where we are. Our unit is scattered across the district. No one will hear us scream. For all you know, there's some white nigger in one of them flats with a shotgun barrel for both of us, laughing his balls off. You die here. Good for you. But I haven't finished yet. So get off your high horse and think what we're going to do."

I can't shoot: he knows it. Defeat is the huge, empty hole opening inside me. Set the catch, let go the trigger. Only a muscle reflex stops me dropping the gun. What does it matter? I was always told: truth hurts.

"Tell you what I think."

He will anyway. Roberts is here completely: he's ordered, detailed, armied. And Wilson? Who's Wilson?

"We got here. It's a black eye turning back. We've orders: we have to search. And what's it worth finding those guns, eh? And we've checked the barricade. We can tell the Captain fetch his ten-tonner. Come on."

Meek as a boy, I trail him through the shadows. Cross the corner with precise caution, enough to make Harry proud: check the road, the sky, the angles; scurry like men in a pipe. He's solid but nimble: alert and ready. Slim, I'm awkward, spasticky in his wake. He's in the lobby before I got his back. "Hold up."

"You hold up. There's work on."

The stone floor tell-tale with our boots; instinct and knuckles white to the trigger.

"Seen this."

I stare at the noticeboard, not seeing what he sees.

He jabs the torn scraps. "Come dancing. Learn a language. Historical and cultural society. Know what this is, don't you?"

"People with no tellies?"

"This is recruiting. Historical and cultural my arse. Knock three times, you're in. All of them, Wilson. Every last one. Come on."

"What?"

"Search the building, man. Must be thirty flats here. Lots of hidden treasure."

The flats have more or less walls, more or less ceilings. Some, there's walking space, a bare minimum of boards. Some, we tiptoe joists across ragged views of rooms below. Some, like this, have corners of floor. I sit, to rub the backs of my knees.

He walks in from the kitchen; looks disgusted. "Do you want to be easily reached by séance?"

"Got cramp. It's these boots."

"You queer."

Now I'm down, and he's got the gun. "Gets you, doesn't it Roberts? It's legal, if you've not noticed."

"Not in the army, Wilson. Not down my bloody street. And what gets me isn't that you're queer. Every squad has a queer. What gets me is you're a liar."

Back home, everyone knew before I opened my mouth. Before I walked in a room.

"Dishonesty corrodes: saps discipline. You be the squad poof, I don't care. Those lads may not be quick but they've been to Brighton. But there's more, isn't there Wilson? There's more about you. Cowardice betrays. I don't like getting betrayed."

I stare at the fizzing gob of spit at my feet. Now I should fight. Must be now. But I've only words and a smile no one's needed since 1969. I could tell the truth. Then he could shoot me. "What about you, Roberts? You honest?"

He looks up from rolling a smoke. "I'll be honest, Wilson. This is goodbye, old son."

Spread my arms in crucifixion. "Try not to make a mess. Should be close enough even for you."

He sparks up, his hard, clever eyes cutting the haze. "It's

chatter like that makes your kind worthless. Why would I waste the Queen's bullet? If I thought you'd go for your gun, you'd be worth killing. But you shoot dirty looks, don't you precious? I'll be honest. I volunteered for this circus. I've got business. That's why I came on your stupid mission. I'm missing in action, aren't I, Terry? While fools like your Captain chase their dicks in evermore dangerous circles, this land is moving at the speed of destiny. The Union's had it, take my word. The Unionists have had it. The UDR won't win this war. The British can't, the Paras saw to that. I'm not getting found face down in the uniform of failures. There's a new force, Terry. A Protestant force. Not London, Terry. Belfast. Not the power some piss-pant in Whitehall gives us. The power we take. A force for Ulster people. And not one inch for Popish scum. You'll see the fires, Terry: the light of a thousand idols when we burn them from our land. No surrender, eh, pretty lad? No surrender. That's where I'm going: to fight for this country. My country. We'll see you Brits on Poppy Day. If you live that long." He turns. "And you should watch for that Fenian MI5: he's on to you all ways."

If I was loyal to my country and Sunday teatime movies, I'd put one through his head just . . . now. I'd say: that's it, for traitors. But I hear his boots on the stairs echo through the block. His slick of spit stands guard on me as I struggle to my feet; as I dust down Wilson the squad queer. Wilson won't betray him.

Try the radio: a hiss could be distant speech or nasty weather.

Day's getting on. I'm trapped. Wilson and Roberts: lost on patrol. They'll look for the bodies, the army never forgets. But they won't look far. They won't find us like they won't find guns. They'll visit whatever painted tribe Roberts sprang from; another martyred red-hand son. Died serving his God. This scrap metal, this cheap ribbon: this is what he deserved. They'll visit the address I gave but find no Rita Wilson, widowed mother of the deceased. They'll find a bomb site, thirty years overgrown, tender brambles taken root in Nazi wreckage. Built by the same lads that got the Yanks to the moon.

I know more than the Captain's toy army. More than bastards like Roberts. Than the bastard who knocked mammy's door and gave me a shilling to piss off to Germany. Except the First Battalion Parachute Regiment made other arrangements. Got us all shipped to looking-glass land, to grow red poppies between the orange and green. I'd be safer in Vietnam. That's what I do: stay safe. There was that kid: Mikey Spiller. Big and thick: he could have shifted the Captain's barricade. Ton weight on my back, pushing my face in the mud. He told me poofs eat mud. Held me down to prove it. Held me down so I couldn't breathe for shite in my face. Said not to make him a liar: show that poofs eat mud. So I did. To make him stop. And when he said to say I liked it, I said I liked it and he pushed me down again. And when he left I rolled over in greasy filth, saw this big stone in a puddle, an island in the grey sea. In a second I could grab it, pitch it at his head. But I didn't. I watched him go. That time; every time. The coal men wanted the taste their wives wouldn't give when they bit my shoulders. When they made me worth it, just for a while. I'd get mammy things dad never got. She'd take the gift, look away, say not to vex daddy's friends who came of a night time: looking-glass men, not friends even to their own shadow.

Soon be dark. Good time to run from a fight. Missing in action I can be dead. Dead: I'm free. Run where? Streets are filthy with army. Imagine their joy to find a lost soldier, back from the dead. If I cleared their lines, how far would I get in this drag? Where Roberts has gone I guess it's a joke; I'm headed nowhere so loyal. Not much time to explain between shot and bullet.

Clothes. Somewhere in this block; jacket and trousers, civvy shoes, all I need. Quick: before dark. This place'll be death after dark. Flat by flat: work through. Got gun. Got grenades. Step careful. What's that? That noise . . . okay. Boards settle as air turns cold. Jungle warfare. Don't step on a twig of glass, watch hanging vines of wires. Search cupboards, wardrobes, for what's left behind. Keep going. Next floor. That noise . . . keep going. Getting hard to see, like dark grows inside the building, spreads under doors, through derelict halls, to seep from broken windows and smother day with night. Dark from empty places; like smoke from coal and lynchings, night rises from things ruined, tells us the light is ours only a short while. Can't see the stairs, the angles. Take a fall, I'm done for. Have to hide till morning. There's another block

228

and another. Must be clothes somewhere. They haven't lifted the barricade: I'd hear them. Maybe they'll come tomorrow. Maybe they're dead. Need a room with some floor. Got no kit, no bed roll. But maybe tomorrow.

Every sound echoes: my deafening steps; clink of gun and grenades. The building creaks and shivers, amplified by dark. Feel the helplessness that wants a man to find me, to hold and say it's all right. To make it all right. I'm the worst disappointment: I need to be a man. But I've been a man since the day I knew what I wanted. You can be a man and run away. Can't you?

This place is a maze: I've no thread; paralysed by dark, I can't go on. That noise.. What's that noise? A knock? A step? What? There's light. There's light under that door. Oh shit oh shit. Roberts? No, he wouldn't . . . Someone living here? A tramp? Got their own light. Oh shit. I'm hungry. Scared hungry. But I've a gun. I am a gun. They must have clothes, food. I'm hungry. Square to the door. Trained for this. Army trained. One kick. All it takes. One hard kick and . . .

A room. Intact. Hurricane lamps, a calor stove. A man in a black roll-neck, packing a kit bag.

Find the voice of a gun. "Who are you?"

He looks up.

Shit: he's got a revolver. "What are you doing here?"

He looks across my shoulder. "Shut the door, soldier-boy."

Fiona Ritchie Walker

Fiona Ritchie Walker is originally from Montrose, Scotland, now living in Blaydon, where she writes in a loft overlooking the Tyne. A former journalist, she works for the fair trade organisation, Traidcraft, visiting producer groups in developing countries and helping them to tell their own stories.

Travel and a whole range of working experiences—including chambermaid, waitress, shop assistant and a short stint gluing display boards in a factory in Amsterdam—help to provide settings for her writing.

Fiona's poetry has appeared in magazines and anthologies, including the *New Writing Scotland* series, with her last collection, *Garibaldi's Legs*, published by Iron Press. Several of her short stories have also been published.

fionaritchiewalker.com

He Tells Me

Dream yourself back before birth.
Reappear as a kite
reckless with harlequin colours
and a ribbon, slippy with unravelling.

Live in another language.
Translate the past
and arrange by syllables.

Even the smallest word
has its own hue,
a place within the rainbow.

Memories lie
like seeds in cold earth
with no set time or season.

Remember how you taught yourself
to love the taste of olives.

Also published in Rowing Home *anthology (Cruse Bereavement Care)*

The Second Week
of the Soap

I buy six bars before the season starts,
just like my dad used to do.
When I get to the trailer I stack them
in the cupboard with my shirts and boots.

Riding back each night, my hands sweating
on the reins, that's what keeps me going,
knowing I'll lather up that second skin,
slick away the work and dirt
so I'm ready for a beer, whatever
I feel like one-pot cooking.

Out here there's an empty pattern
to the days. I figure I like
those second weeks best.
First one, the bar's a virgin,
too big for my hand.

Seven days of soaping and the hard edges
are gone, it glides smoothly over my shoulders,
brings back memories of other bathtubs,
makes me so mellow that sometimes
I open a second bottle after supper,
drink it slowly as the sun goes down.

In the third week
there's a cussedness about it all.
Darn thing slips through my fingers,
flies into a corner and won't be caught.

By the last night it's thin as a ghost,
buckles under my toes
as I push it down the drain.

Today Joe told me
he unwraps a new bar ahead of time,
gets them both nice and wet
then squashes the fresh and the old together.

What use is that? How can you know
when the second week starts?

Through the Car Window

A boy steers his leashed monkey
up and down the dhaba tables.

A man drinking chai glances up,
the boy nods his head.

The monkey somersaults
to the top of the boy's stick.

The boy presses his fingers together
as in prayer.

The monkey presses its fingers together
as in prayer.

The man rises,
throws rupees on the table.

The monkey picks up the coins,
hands them to the boy.

Last I see they are at the counter,
the woman handing over two cigarettes.

This song

is red.
Flaps like a flag.
There's a hint
of exhaust fumes
around its edges,
a base of patchouli.

These notes sing silver,
dulling to pewter,
black.

Here I'm seeing
a turned field,
now it's barley
and above it August blue.

Something's flying.
That's the beat of a wing
or it could be pale
butter falling from a churn.

This chorus,
tart as apples,
high kicks
in red stilettos
across a marble floor.

Somewhere
I've lost the title.
I'll be humming
red all day.

Aftershock

What has happened to the bar in Cauquenes
where we ate salted pork
from a gnarled wood platter
and tasted wine
made with grapes you had grown.

And what has happened to the shuttered room
where cool linen covered the table
and we speared our conversation
with green olives.

The sweetness of papayas
as we watched fishing boats depart.

Somewhere I have that photograph
of the seaweed stalls.
Behind them, crested waves
and the deep blue you said
was the colour you longed to wear
around your head and shoulders.

KC Wilder

KC Wilder has called himself a poet trapped in a person's body, and in a metaphysical sense, he is. He is also the founder of fauxbrow, an aesthetic that conflates lowbrow with a dreamy sense of wonder.

Wilder's underdog-centric, freewheeling irony embraces non-attachment as a virtue.

A musician and composer as well as poet, lyricist, and journalist, widely published and written about, Wilder's recent recorded work includes swirling musical/poetic collaborations on two new CDs with the amazing Acme Rocket Quartet. Free clips are available at bewilderama.com and at spokengreen.com. Pushing the edges of poetry, music, performance art and video, Wilder's video gallery shows 8 free videos which combine his poetry with music and visuals, at frankmedia.com/video.

Wilder's talents and forays in (and out of) the arts cover a wide area—writer, artist, musician, webgeek, video producer, first amendment activist, photographer (photo gallery at frankmedia.com/wilderphoto), as well as eco-journalist and former U.S. national champion athlete. He has performed to packed houses with the 40-piece 'punk rock orchestra' as a baritone soloist, and has toured throughout America as a singer/songwriter. Publishing credits include *Polluto*, *The Seattle Review*, *Poetry New Zealand*, *Lichen*, *Poetry Canada*, *Contemporary Rhyme*, *Chronogram*, *Feathertale*.

Wilder's writing advances a pop-culture argot. Stylistically, his craft derives influences and inspiration from a variety of sources, including ee cummings, R. Crumb, Vincent Van Gogh, Frank Kafka, James Dean, Emily Dickinson, Dylan Thomas, Jackson Pollock, Vachel Lindsay, Ennio Morricone, Charles Bukowski, Terence McKenna, and John Berryman, to name a few.

#351: aspiration city

sally was a yuppy girl
   from aspiration city
     she got so high on ecstasy
   she sat on toppa staircase
at a party
   pulled off blouse

stroking both her tits
   she cackled
     "anybody want to feel my tits
       c'mon c'mon"

     focusing on fetish
   she fetishized completely
her tits her tits her tits her tits
   amazed she had
     two ample tits

     her nipples rigid
   pink & pert

she laughed
   throwing head back
     rolling eyes
   inviting everyone
to stroke her boobies

     two days later
   prim & proper
at a mindless office job
   sally was a denizen of
     aspiration city

#309: a damage control party

sorting the carnage
i cart dismembered bodies off
hands arms legs intestines
shaking uncoiled livers
into trash receptacles

stumps
with pained looks on faces
blown to bits by i.e.d.'s
a scowling courtroom judge imparts
"a punishment appropriate for
cruelties in you"

in the sad gray plume
that clings to battlefields
i am sent to find
piles of fresh flesh
placing into hefty bags
the sinewy & disconnected

chunks of pre-teen children
limbs torn off by rpg's
by high explosive bomb blasts
riddled by machine guns
babies with no heads
my job is to tag & toss them
into teensy wooden boxes

imprisoned by
a grandiose & efficient
western industrial state
i work
a damage control party

#292: peter pan aboard a c130 to afghanistan

peter pan
    aboard a c130
        to afghanistan

    boasting he can hardly wait
to find and kill some taliban
    entertaining navy seals
        he throws handstands
            and he squeals

            crackin' jokes about
        bin laden's butthole being tight
    peter pan itchin' for
a phrickin' desperate fight

peter pan's an inspiration
    for the young men of our nation
        one can see in his eyes
            he is not like other guys

        from the roughest toughest jobs
    he'll not shirk or flinch
fear is not an option
    he does not give an inch

        a special kind of special forces
    few folks understand
    his only plans to wade into
the fiery teeth of danger

though he might come back a fragment
    of his former self one day
        he believes that from the worst
            he'll simply sigh and fly away

peter pan
  aboard a c130
    to afghanistan

#237: my signature roots

a groundless philosophy
   underlies this poetry
      dada dada dada
   if you don't know what that is
what do you know

fauxbrow's the name
   poetry's the game

     fauxbrow culture i declare
   shifting gears like phred astaire
fauxbrow transcendentalist
   seductio ad absurdum

stalwart visions
   yes indeed
     what on earth else
       do u need

   my world tumblesaults
     & shimmies
       outwardly head fakes

thinking this is half-baked
   narrow minded ninnies
     frowning at my book they say
       "such work does not move me"

     ninnies who exalt
   a trendoid concept called
blank verse

"rhyme is for the birds" they say
   "anything that's musical
has humor wit or wordplay
   is not serious enough
      has no substance
         has no weight"

    that's the attitude of late
   milliscent
i'm tired of these

highbrow ninnies
   squelching belching
     they're too scared
   & overschooled & stuffy

    with no taste for tastefulness
   they distrust a rhyme scheme
that might involve laughter

a squishy musicality
   that rightly swings from rafters
     fauxbrow's bacchanalian flair
       ninnies can not master

#1.0: illustration

for julie doucet

rainbow colored
   spears of moonlight
      splinter off her pinky ring

      she's in touch with
    otherworldly forces
  these awakening
an emptiness inside her
   rearing like an angry horse

    she orchestrates
  then switching on
johnny cash
   grandmaster flash
     a kurt cobain cd

   her rancor rockets round and round
     she laughs a bit
       haphazardly
         beset by complexity
        taut beneath a glassine city
     office tower skyline

   so connected to her hands
     julie deeply understands
       winds that wind through
     fraying wires
  on the dashboards
of desire

peeling mystic perturbations
   from the flashpoints of her brow
      skillful artist julie draws
        as only she knows how

#22: sailing to
yup-star byzantium

merry prankster i decides
neptune's triton at my sides
to brave shallows deep inside
a yuppie cocktail party

mannekins wit face and hair
toxins splashing everywhere
thoughtful minds in here might think
stiffs & stuffed shirts like these stink

brassy waves of brazen bigmouths
tripe dispensers left & right
massing in this mess tonight
the empty getting tight

amongst a herd of blowhard whales
intransigent that's how i see
them sorriest of sorry
captains from the age of sail

long john silver's wooden peg
nightmarish all night long it raps
narrow-minded attitudes
wafting up from traps

seemingly a nimrod
in some thimble-headed fog
verigo vespucci spouts
his gullet full of grog

captains on the poopdeck
nelson crinkling maps
hudson and courageous parked
for hours trading flaps

hudson isn't joking
circling to the west
boasting he will conquer
apparently obsessed

rolly poly captain hook's
falling off his chair
shouting something garbled
hoisting mug into the air

dorky pirates bloviate
a crusty-looking guide appears
steering boatloads of guffaws
into sunken sallow ears

i resemble fletcher christian
here's my plan to row ashore
this soiree for me is done
in my scope i want no more

no more kreepy kaptains
no blustery conquistadors
heading off for parts unknown
heaving ho my rearward jibe

a ship of fools
these shifty-eyed
loaded in a bloated ark
sailing to yup-star
byzantium

#75: fashion roundup

down in downtown culturesville
   he dubs himself a cultured guy

     who he really is
   is really not up for discussion

trapped inside a crowded room
   with throbbing clumps of lust 4 eyes
      he stands and claps for supermodels
     on the runway flouncing by

"fabulous direct from france"
   extolling tight pink satin pants
unctuous male orangutan
   continuing to bray

"what could be more satisfying
   than a swath of girly butt
     socketed and zippered into
     tight pink satin pants

"oh to be so bracketed
   by back door pomp and circumstance
     praise each perfect pert round bottom
   squished in tight pink satin pants"

from the burnished monkey bar'd
   playgrounds of his mind
     genuflecting primate
      singing praise of
       curvy lines

#350: this is religion

next to johnny rotten barking
   rays of sunlite
      shine from pate
         of salvador dali lama

    hot below
   its mizzen masthead
hms bewilderama

Oz Hardwick: Afterwords

Well, here we all are, somehow, caught
in the deliberate accident of words and pages,
disparate strangers in the same cell, banged up
for looting lines, setting fire to syntax, breaking
rules and joyriding meaning down back alleys
with the headlights off.. And I remember
poems on basement café walls and Chicago bars
where everyone spoke German and apocalyptic rain
without the safety of punctuation. And it's damn good
to feel the pulse of new comrades-at-arms, fearlessly
ripping beauty from beneath upturned noses
and shoving it right back in faces: Take a sniff of this.

So thank-you, Mr Dog Horn, for the B&D
of true words, disciplined and transgressive,
the benevolent tyranny of 'competition'
where we're all exquisite losers, believing
in the transcendence of flesh and ink,
every one of us running, crawling, longing,
dreaming, screaming, racing, reaching
after words.

More Fiction from Dog Horn Publishing

Shark by Wes Brown
RRP: £9.99, 176pp, ISBN: 9781907133145

Yorkshire writer Wes Brown's debut novel, *Shark* is a story about the dispossessed and how they get by.

Ex-soldier and violent deadbeat John Usher returns to his boyhood home of Leeds to find things have changed. His community has been unravelled by gang culture, ethnic tensions and hopelessness. Unable to sleep, his only consolation is drinking late into the night and playing pool by himself. That is, until an encounter with a hard right activist leads him into a twisted relationship of deceit, cuckoldry and hatred.

The Bride Stripped Bare by Rachel Kendall
RRP: £9.99, 123pp, ISBN: 9781097133046

Finally bound into one collection, twenty three stories of creation and mutation. From twisted fairy tales and grubby nights to circus freaks and insect bites, these tales of depravity reveal the bride in her most scabrous form.

Hemorrhaging Slave of an Obese Eunuch by Tom Bradley
RRP: £9.99, 140pp, ISBN: 9781907133039

In the middle of the Adriatic Sea during Neronic times, in Hiroshima Cathedral's demon-infested basement, in the royal elephant stables of a Hindustani town three millennia ago, in a Tokyo AIDS hospice disguised as a derelict kindergarten, on a yacht anchored off a South

China leper isolation colony, and on top of a skull-shaped and -textured geothermal formation in the prune-colored midnight.

Celebrated author Tom Bradley's latest short story collection *Hemorrhaging Slave of an Obese Eunuch* will take you to all of these places.

A History of Sarcasm by Frank Burton
RRP: £9.99, 158pp, ISBN: 9781907133015

Sometimes stories that I've used to mythologize my childhood resurface in my mind as actual memories . . . Perhaps if you tell a story enough times, it will become the truth.

This admission by Mark Greensleeves, the compulsive liar in the story 'Some Facts About Me', sums up Frank Burton's sharp, surreal and subversive short story collection, *A History of Sarcasm*. The seventeen stories in this collection blur the boundaries between fact and fantasy through a series of obsessive characters and their skewed versions of reality. Among them are a man who insists on living every aspect of his life in alphabetical order, a girl who believes she is receiving secret messages through the TV, a paranoiac who is pursued by an army of giant lobsters, and an academic who turns into a cat.

Cabala, edited by Adam Lowe
RRP: £9.99, 158pp, ISBN: 9781907133169

The Milky Bar Kid is dead. He bit the Californ-I-A dust. Popped yon popsicle clogs. Met his candybar maker
—A.J. Kirby

From gothic fairytale to humorous pop-culture satire, five of the North's top writers showcase the diversity of British talent that exists outside the country's capital and put their strange, funny, mythical landscapes firmly on the literary map. Over the course of ten weeks, Adam Lowe worked with five budding writers as part of the Dog Horn Masterclass series. This anthology collects together the best work produced both as a result of the masterclasses and beyond.

Featuring: Jodie Daber, Richard Evans, Jaqueline Houghton, Rachel Kendall and A.J. Kirby.

Women Writing the Weird, edited by Deb Hoag
RRP: £14.99, 216pp, ISBN: 9781907133268

Stories that delight, surprise, that hang about the dusky edges of 'mainstream' fiction with characters, settings, plots that abandon the normal and mundane and explore new ideas, themes and ways of being. —Deb Hoag

Featuring: Nancy A. Collins, Eugie Foster, Janice Lee, Rachel Kendall, Candy Caradoc, Mysty Unger, Roberta Lawson, Sara Genge, Gina Ranalli, Deb Hoag, C. M. Vernon, Aliette de Bodard, Caroline M. Yoachim, Flavia Testa, Aimee C. Amodio, Ann Hagman Cardinal, Rachel Turner, Wendy Jane Muzlanova, Katie Coyle, Helen Burke, Janis Butler Holm, J.S. Breukelaar, Carol Novack, Tantra Bensko, Nancy DiMauro, Moira McPartlin.

UK Distribution: **Central Books**
99 Wallis Road, London, E9 5LN, United Kingdom
orders@centralbooks.com
Phone:+44 (0) 845 458 9911
Fax: +44 (0) 845 458 9912

Overseas (Non-UK) Distribution: **Lulu Press, Inc**
3101 Hillsborough Street
Raleigh, NC 27607
Phone # +1 919 459 5858
Fax # +1 919 459 5867
purchaseorder@lulu.com

ND - #0472 - 270225 - C0 - 234/156/21 - PB - 9781907133275 - Gloss Lamination